WEST OF THE TULAROSA

**Center Point
Large Print**

Other titles by Louis L'Amour and available from Center Point Large Print:

Trailing West: A Western Quartet
Big Medicine: A Western Quartet
Hanging Woman Creek

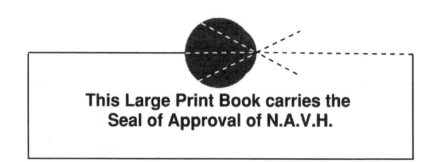

**This Large Print Book carries the
Seal of Approval of N.A.V.H.**

Louis L'Amour

WEST OF THE TULAROSA

CENTER POINT PUBLISHING
THORNDIKE, MAINE

This Circle Ⓥ Western is published by
Center Point Large Print in the year 2010
in cooperation with Golden West Literary Agency.

The text of this Large Print edition is unabridged.
In other aspects, this book may vary
from the original edition.
Printed in the United States of America
on permanent paper.
Set in 16-point Times New Roman type.

ISBN: 978-1-60285-672-1

Library of Congress Cataloging-in-Publication Data

L'Amour, Louis, 1908-1988.
  West of the Tularosa : a Western trio / Louis L'Amour.
    p. cm.
  ISBN 978-1-60285-672-1 (library binding : alk. paper)
  1. Western stories. 2. Large type books.
   I. L'Amour, Louis, 1908-1988. Showdown trail.
   II. L'Amour, Louis, 1908-1988. Sixth shotgun. III. Title.
  PS3523.A446W48 2010
   813'.52--dc22
  2009038297

TABLE OF CONTENTS

Foreword

by Jon Tuska

Louis Dearborn LaMoore (1908-1988) was born in Jamestown, North Dakota. He left home at fifteen and subsequently held a wide variety of jobs although he worked mostly as a merchant seaman. From his earliest youth, L'Amour had a love of verse. His first published work was a poem, "The Chap Worth While", appearing when he was eighteen years old in his former hometown's newspaper, the *Jamestown Sun*. It is the only poem from his early years that he left out of SMOKE FROM THIS ALTAR which appeared in 1939 from Lusk Publishers in Oklahoma City, a book which L'Amour published himself; however, this poem is reproduced in THE LOUIS L'AMOUR COMPANION (Andrews and McMeel, 1992) edited by Robert Weinberg. L'Amour wrote poems and articles for a number of small circulation arts magazines all through the early 1930s and, after hundreds of rejection slips, finally had his first story accepted, "Anything for a Pal" in *True Gang Life* (10/35). He returned in 1938 to live with his family where they had settled in Choctaw, Oklahoma, determined to make writing his career. He wrote a fight story bought by Standard Magazines that year and became acquainted with editor Leo

Margulies who was to play an important role later in L'Amour's life. "The Town No Guns Could Tame" in *New Western* (3/40) was his first published Western story.

During the Second World War L'Amour was drafted and ultimately served with the U.S. Army Transportation Corps in Europe. However, in the two years before he was shipped out, he managed to write a great many adventure stories for Standard Magazines. The first story he published in 1946, the year of his discharge, was a Western, "Law of the Desert Born" in *Dime Western* (4/46). A talk with Leo Margulies resulted in L'Amour's agreeing to write Western stories for the various Western pulp magazines published by Standard Magazines, a third of which appeared under the byline Jim Mayo, the name of a character in L'Amour's earlier adventure fiction. The proposal for L'Amour to write new Hopalong Cassidy novels came from Margulies who wanted to launch *Hopalong Cassidy's Western Magazine* to take advantage of the popularity William Boyd's old films and new television series were enjoying with a new generation. Doubleday & Company agreed to publish the pulp novelettes in hard cover books. L'Amour was paid $500 a story, no royalties, and he was assigned the house name Tex Burns. L'Amour read Clarence E. Mulford's books about the Bar-20 and based his Hopalong Cassidy on Mulford's original creation.

Only two issues of the magazine appeared before it ceased publication. Doubleday felt that the Hopalong character had to appear exactly as William Boyd did in the films and on television and thus the novels in book form had to be revamped to meet with this requirement prior to publication.

L'Amour's first Western novel under his own byline was WESTWARD THE TIDE (World's Work, 1950). It was rejected by every American publisher to which it was submitted. World's Work paid a flat £75 without royalties for British Empire rights in perpetuity. L'Amour sold his first Western short story to a slick magazine a year later, "The Gift of Cochise" in *Collier's* (7/5/52). Robert Fellows and John Wayne purchased screen rights to this story from L'Amour for $4,000 and James Edward Grant, one of Wayne's favorite screenwriters, developed a script from it, changing L'Amour's Ches Lane to Hondo Lane. L'Amour retained the right to novelize Grant's screenplay, which differs substantially from his short story, and he was able to get an endorsement from Wayne to be used as a blurb, stating that HONDO was the finest Western Wayne had ever read. HONDO (Fawcett Gold Medal, 1953) by Louis L'Amour was released on the same day as the film, HONDO (Warner, 1953), with a first printing of 320,000 copies.

With SHOWDOWN AT YELLOW BUTTE (Ace, 1953) by Jim Mayo, L'Amour began a series of short Western novels for Don Wollheim that could be doubled with other short novels by other authors in Ace Publishing's paperback twofers. Advances on these were $800 and usualiy the author never earned any royalties. HELLER WITH A GUN (Fawcett Gold Medal, 1955) was the first of a series of original Westerns L'Amour had agreed to write under his own name following the success for Fawcett of HONDO. L'Amour wanted even this early to have his Western novels published in hard cover editions. He expanded "Guns of the Timberland" by Jim Mayo in *West* (9/50) for GUNS OF THE TIMBERLANDS (Jason Press, 1955), a hard cover Western for which he was paid an advance of $250. Another novel for Jason Press followed and then SILVER CAÑON (Avalon Books, 1956) for Thomas Bouregy & Company.

The great turn in L'Amour's fortunes came about because of problems Saul David was having with his original paperback Westerns program at Bantam Books. Fred Glidden had been signed to a contract to produce two original paperback Luke Short Western novels a year for an advance of $15,000 each. It was a long-term contract but, in the first ten years of it, Fred only wrote six novels. Literary agent Marguerite Harper then persuaded Bantam that Fred's brother, Jon, could help fulfill the contract and Jon was signed for eight Peter Dawson Western novels. When Jon died suddenly before completing even one book for Bantam, Harper managed to engage a ghost writer at the Disney studios to write these eight "Peter Dawson" novels, beginning with THE SAVAGES (Bantam, 1959). They proved inferior to anything Jon had ever written and what sales they had seemed to be due only to the Peter Dawson name.

Saul David wanted to know from L'Amour if *he* could deliver two Western novels a year. L'Amour said he could, and he did. In fact, by 1962 this number was increased to three original paperback novels a year. The first L'Amour novel to appear under the Bantam contract was RADIGAN (Bantam, 1958).

Yet I feel that some of Louis L'Amour's finest work is to be found in his early magazine fiction. Several of those stories are collected here, reprinted as they first appeared, and possessing the characteristics in purest form that I suspect account in largest measure for the loyal following Louis L'Amour won from his readers: the young male hero who is in the process of growing into manhood and who is evaluating other human beings and his own experiences; a resourceful frontier woman who has beauty as well as fortitude; and the powerful, romantic, strangely compelling vision of the American West that invests

L'Amour's Western fiction and makes it such a delightful escape from the cares of a later time—in this author's words, that "big country needing big men and women to live in it" and where there was no place for "the frightened or the mean."

Showdown Trail

I

With slow, ponderously rhythmical steps, the oxen moved, each step a pause and an effort, each movement a deadening drag. Fine white dust hung in a sifting cloud above the wagon train, caking the nostrils of animals and men, blanketing the lean sides of oxen and horses, dusting with a thin film the clothing of men and women.

Red-rimmed and bloodshot eyes stared with dazed weariness into the limitless distance before them, seeing nothing, knowing nothing. Long since all had been forgotten but heat, dust, and aching muscles. Each succeeding step lifted a powdery dust, stifling and irritating. It lay a foot deep on the endless plain, drowning the sparse grass and sage.

Rock Bannon, riding away from the train and alone, drew in his steel-dust stallion and turned in the saddle, looking back over the covered wagons, sixteen of them in a long line with some lead horses and a few outriders, yet not one who rode so far out as himself.

From where he sat he could not see their faces, but in the days just past he had seen them many times, and the expression of each was engraved in his mind. Haggard, worn, hungry for rest and cool water, he knew that in the secret heart of each was a longing to stop.

The vision was in them yet, the golden promise of the distant hills, offering a land of milk and honey, the fair and flowering land sought by all wandering peoples of whatever time and whatever place. No hardship could seem too great, no trail too long, no mountains impassable when the vision was upon them.

It was always and forever the same when men saw the future opening beyond the hills where the sun slept. Yet this time the vision must hold meaning, this time the end of the trail must bring realization, for they had brought their women and children along.

All had done so but Rock Bannon. He had neither woman nor child, or anyone, anywhere. He had a horse and a saddle, a ready gun, and a mind filled with lore of the trail, and eyes ever fixed on something he wanted, something faint and indistinct in outline, ever distant, yet ever real.

Only of late, as he rode alone on the far flank of the wagon train, had that something begun to take shape and outline, and the shape was that of Sharon Crockett. His somber green eyes slanted back now to the last wagon but one, where the red-gold hair of Sharon on the driver's seat was a flame no dust could dim. In the back of that heavily loaded wagon was Tom Crockett, her father, stirring, restless with fever, and hurt, nursing a bullet wound in his thigh, a memento of the battle with Buffalo Hide's warriors.

From the head of the train came a long, melodious halloo, and Cap Mulholland swung his arm in a great circle, and the lead oxen turned ponderously to swing in the beginning of the circle. Rock touched the gray with his heels and rode slowly toward the wagon train. He was never sure these days as to his reception.

Cap's beard was white with dust as he looked up. Weariness and worry showed in his face. "Rock," he said, "we could sure use a little fresh meat. We're all a mite short on rations, and you seem to be the best hunter amongst us."

"All right," Rock said, "I'll see what I can do after I get Crockett's wagon in place."

Mulholland's head turned sharply. "Bannon, I'd let that girl alone if I were you. No offense intended, but she ain't your kind. I ain't denyin' you've been a sight of help to us. In fact, I don't know what we'd have done without you, and we're glad you came along, but Sharon Crockett's another story. Her pa's bedded down now, and in no shape to speak."

Bannon turned the steel-dust sharply. His face was grim and his jaw hard. "Did he ask you to speak to me? Or did she?"

"Well, no . . . not exactly," Mulholland said uncomfortably. "But I'm headin' this train."

"Then I'll thank you to mind your own business. Headin' this wagon train is job enough for any man. Any time the Crocketts ask me to stay away, I'll stay, but that's their affair."

17

Mulholland's face flushed and his eyes darkened with anger. "She ain't your kind," he persisted, "you bein' a killer and all."

Rock Bannon stared at him. "You didn't seem to mind my killing Indians," he said sarcastically. "In fact, you killed a few yourself."

"Don't get me wrong," Cap persisted. "I ain't gainsayin' you ain't helped us. Without you I don't know if we could have beat off those Indians or not, but killin' Indians and killin' our own kind is a lot different thing!"

"You're new to the West, Cap." Bannon's voice was rough. "In a short time you'll find there's men out here that need killin' a sight worse than Indians. In fact, I'm not so sure those Indians jumped us without help."

"What do you mean?" Mulholland demanded.

"I mean," Bannon said, "that Morton Harper told you there'd be no hostile Indians on this route. I warned you of Buffalo Hide then, but he told you he ranged farther north. You took his advice on this trail, not mine."

Pagones and Pike Purcell were coming up to join them. Pike heard the last remark, and his lean, lantern-jawed face flushed with anger.

"You ridin' Harper again?" he harshly demanded of Bannon. "He said this was a better trail, and it is. We ain't had no high passes, and we had six days of the best travel we've had since we left Council Bluffs, with plenty of water and plenty of grass. Now we get a few bad days and a brush with Indians, but that ain't much." He glared at Rock. "I'm sick of your whinin' about this trail and Harper! I figure he's a durned good man. He was sure a help to me when I needed it. Out of supplies, no medicine for the wife, and he staked me."

"I wasn't talking to you," Rock replied shortly, "and I don't like your tone. As far as your loan from Harper, remember that you haven't heard from him on it yet. I've a hunch he'll collect, and plenty."

"I don't need no killer to tell me my business!" Pike snapped, reining his horse around to face Rock. "And I ain't afeerd of no reputation for killin', neither. You don't bluff me none."

"Here, here!" Cap protested. "We can't afford to have trouble in camp. You'll have to admit, Pike, that we'd have been in bad shape a couple of times in that fight if it hadn't been for Bannon. He's been a help. I don't agree with him on Mort Harper, either, but every man to his own idea."

Rock swung the steel-dust and cantered off toward the hills. Inwardly he was seething. He was a fool to stay on with the wagon train—he understood that perfectly well. Not a man here liked him; not a man here talked to him except on business. He was not even a member of their train except by accident.

They had found him at the crossing of the

Platte. Riding, half dead, with two bullet wounds in his body, his horse ready to drop with fatigue, he had run up to the wagon train. Sharon Crockett had bedded him down in her wagon and cared for him, and he had ridden on in the same place where her father rode now.

He had offered no explanation of his wounds, had talked but little. A grim and lonely man, gentle words came hard, and he could only look up into Sharon's face and wonder at her beauty, tongue-tied and helpless. Yet his hard, tough, trail-battered body was too used to pain to remain helpless for long. He had recovered rapidly, and afterward he had ridden along with the wagons, hunting for fresh meat and helping when he could.

He was not a man who made friends easily, yet gradually the ice was melting, and the clannishness of the wagon train was breaking down. Twice he had even talked with Sharon, riding beside her wagon, speaking of the mountains and his own wild and lonely life. All that had ended abruptly that night beside the campfire at the fort.

They had been seated around the fire eating supper, listening to the bustle of life around the fort, when a tall, handsome man rode up on a beautiful black mare. Perfectly groomed, his wide, white hat topping coal-black hair that hung to his shoulders, a drooping black mustache and a black broadcloth suit, the trousers tucked into hand-tooled boots, Morton Harper had been a picture to take any eye.

Swinging down, he had walked up to the fire. "Howdy, folks!" His voice was genial, his manner warm and pleasant. In an instant his personality and voice had done what Rock Bannon's could not do in two weeks. He had broken down their reserve and become one of the group. "Headin' for California?"

"Reckon we are," Mulholland had agreed. "We ain't rightly decided whether to stay on the Humboldt Trail or to swing north and go to Oregon."

"Why go either way?" Harper asked. "There's a southern route I could recommend that would be much easier going for your womenfolks." His alert eyes had already found and appraised Sharon Crockett. "More water, plenty of grass, and no high mountain passes."

Cap Mulholland looked up interestedly. "We ain't heard of no such pass, nor no such trail," he admitted. "How does she go?"

"Man named Hastings scouted some of it, and I scouted the rest myself. It is a more southerly route, and within another few months all the travel will be going that way. Right now"—he winked—"the trains that go that way are going to have a mighty fine trip of it. Very little dust except in one stretch, fine grass, lots of water.

Also, the hostile Indians are all raiding far north of there along the traveled routes.

"But," he added, "I can see you're well led, and you'll no doubt learn about this trail yourselves. From the look of your teams I'd say you were lucky in your choice of a leader."

Leaning against the hub of a wagon wheel, Rock Bannon ate in silence. The even, smooth flow of the stranger's language had an enchanting quality, but his own hard-grained, cynical character was impervious to mere talk.

As the hours flowed by, Harper sat among them, pleasing the men with subtle flattery, the women with smiles. The reserve of the group thawed under his easy manner, and before long they began to discuss his trail and its possibilities, considering themselves fortunate to know of it first.

There was some talk of putting it to a vote, but it was morning before it came to that. Until then, Rock was silent. "You'd do better," he interposed suddenly, "to stick to the regular trail."

Harper's head came up sharply, and his eyes leveled at Bannon. "Have you ever been over the trail I suggest, my friend?"

"Part way," Rock replied. "Only part of it."

"And was that part easy going for oxen and horses? Was there a good trail? Grass? Water?"

"Yes, I reckon it has all that, but I wouldn't advise it."

"You say it is a better trail but you wouldn't advise it?" Harper glanced around at the others, smiling tolerantly. "That doesn't make much sense, does it? I've been over the entire trail and found it very good going. Moreover, I can give you a map of the trail showing the water holes, everything. Of course, it's nothing to me what route you take, but if you want to avoid Indians. . . ." He shrugged.

"What about Buffalo Hide?"

Morton Harper's face tightened, and his eyes strained to pry Rock Bannon's face from the shadows in which he sat. "He's a Blackfoot. He ranges farther north." Harper's eyes shifted to Mulholland. "Who is this man? I'm surprised he should ask about Buffalo Hide, as he isn't known to most white men other than renegades. I can't understand why he should try to persuade you to neglect an easier route for a more dangerous one. Is he one of your regular train?"

Pike Purcell was abrupt. From the first day he had disliked and been suspicious of Bannon. "No, he ain't none of our crowd, just a feller what tied up with us back yonder a ways. He ain't got no wagon, nothin' but the horse he's ridin'."

"I see." Morton Harper's face became grave with implied doubt. "No offense, friend, but would you mind telling me your name? I know most of the men along this trail, and Colonel

Warren was asking about some of them only tonight. You'll admit it is safer to be careful, for there are so many renegades who work with the Indians."

"My name's Rock Bannon."

Morton Harper's lips tightened and his eyes grew wary. For a moment he seemed taken aback. Then, as he perceived where his own interests lay, his eyes lighted with triumph.

"Ah? Bannon, eh? I've heard of you. Killed a man in Laramie a month or so back, didn't you?"

"He drew on me."

Rock was acutely conscious of the sudden chill in the atmosphere, and he could see Sharon's shocked gaze directed at him. The people of the wagon train were fresh from the East. Only Cap had been as far West as the Platte before, and he only once. They were peace-loving men, quiet and asking no trouble.

Morton Harper was quick to sense his advantage. "Sorry to have brought it up, Bannon," he said smoothly, "but, when a man advises a wagon train against their best interests, it is well to inquire into the source of the advice."

Bannon got up. He was a tall man, lean-hipped and broad-shouldered, his flat-brimmed hat shadowing his face, his eyes glowing with piercing light as he spoke.

"I still say that route's a darned fool way to go.

This ain't no country to go wanderin' around in, and that route lays through Hardy Bishop's country. You spoke of Hastings. He was the man who advised the Donner party."

As his footsteps died away in the darkness, the members of the wagon train sat very still, their enthusiasm suddenly dampened by that ill-fated name. They all knew the story. The horror of it still blanketed the trail with its bloody shadow of the party caught by snows in the high passes and starving until they resorted to cannibalism as a way out.

Morton Harper shrugged. "Of course. They started on Hastings's trail, but left it too soon, and the route I suggest avoids all the higher passes." His eyes swung around the group, gathering their attention like the reins of a six-horse team, and he led them on with promises and suggestions, an easy flow of calm, quiet talk, stilling their fears, quieting their doubts, offering them grass and water instead of dust and desert.

In the morning, when they moved out, they took the trail Harper had advised, turning off an hour after they left the fort. Harper glanced back, and smiled when he saw he was unobserved. Then he wished them luck and promised to overtake them when a message came for which he waited. Turning, he galloped back to the fort.

Rock Bannon was with them. He rode close to Sharon's wagon, and after a time she looked up.

He had watched her the night before, had seen her fascinated eyes on Harper's face.

"You don't approve, do you?"

He shook his head. Then he smiled, somewhat grimly. He was a dark, good-looking man with a tinge of recklessness in his green eyes.

"My views aren't important," he said. "I don't belong."

"Pike shouldn't have said that," she said. "He's a strange man. A good man, but very stubborn and suspicious."

"Not suspicious of the right folks, maybe."

Her eyes flashed. "You mean Mister Harper? Why should we be suspicious of him? He was only trying to help."

"I wonder."

"I think," Sharon said sharply, "you'd do better to be a little less suspicious yourself. You admitted this was a good trail."

"You haven't met Hardy Bishop yet. Nor Buffalo Hide."

"Mister Harper said that Indian was farther north." She looked at him. "Who is Hardy Bishop? You mentioned him before?"

"He's a man who is trying to run cattle at Indian Writing. They said he's insane to try it, but he's claimed seventy miles of range, and he has cattle there. We have to cross his range."

"What's wrong with that?"

"If you cross it, maybe nothing, but Bishop's a

funny man. He doesn't like strangers very much. He's going to wonder why you're so far south. He's going to be suspicious."

"Well, let him be suspicious then!" Sharon said, her eyes bright and her chin lifting. "We don't care, and we won't bother him any. Does he think he owns the whole country?"

"Uhn-huh," Rock said. "I'm afraid he does. With some reason as far as that valley goes. He made it what it is today."

"How could any man make a valley?" Sharon protested. "This is all free country. Anyway, we're just going through."

The conversation had dwindled and died, and after a while he rode off to the far flank of the wagon train. Sharon's manner was distinctly stiff and he could see she was remembering that story of the killing in Laramie. After a few rebuffs he avoided her. Nobody talked to him. He rode alone and camped alone.

II

It had remained like that for six days. They were six days during which Morton Harper's name became one to reckon with. The long green valley down which they moved was unrutted by wagon trains, the grass was green and waving, and water was plentiful. Harper's map showed an accurate knowledge of the country and was a great help.

On the sixth day after leaving the fort, the Indians hit them.

The attack came at daybreak. Rock Bannon, camping near a spring a half mile from the wagons, awoke with a start. It was scarcely light, yet he felt uneasy, and, getting to his knees, he saw the steel-dust staring, ears pricked, at a distant pile of rocks. Then he noticed the movement.

Swiftly and silently he saddled the stallion, bridled it, and stowed his gear in the saddlebags. Then, rifle in hand, he skirted the trees along the tiny stream and headed back for the wagons. He rode up to them, and the man on guard got up, stretching. It was the short, heavy-set Pagones. A good man and a sharp one. He smiled at Bannon.

"Guess Harper had it more right than you when he said there were no hostiles here," he said. "Ain't that right?"

"No," Bannon said sharply. "Get everybody up and ready. We'll be attacked within a few minutes!"

Pagones stared. "Are you crazy?"

"Get busy, man!" Bannon snapped at Pagones. He wheeled and, running from wagon to wagon, slapped the canvas and said: "On your feet! Indians!"

Men boiled from the wagons, crawling into their clothes and grabbing at rifles. "Get around the whole circle!" Bannon told them. "They are in those rocks and a draw that runs along south of us."

Mulholland rushed out and halted, glaring around. The sky was gray in the east, and everything lay in a vague, indistinct light. Not a movement showed in all the dark width of the prairie. He started for Bannon to protest, when he heard a startled exclamation. Wheeling, he saw a long line of Indian horsemen not over 200 yards away and coming at a dead run!

Even as his eyes touched them, the nearest Indian broke into a wild, shrill whoop. Then the whole charging line broke into yells.

Rock Bannon, leaning against the Crockett wagon, lifted his Henry rifle and fired. A horse stumbled and went down. He fired again, and an Indian threw up his arms and vanished in the turmoil of oncoming horses and men, and then the other men of the wagon train opened up.

Firing steadily, Bannon emptied his rifle before the Indians reached the edge of the circle. One brave, his wild-eyed horse at a dead run, leaned low and shot a blazing arrow into the canvas of the Crockett wagon. Rock fired his right-hand pistol and the Indian hit the dirt in a tumbling heap, just as a second arrow knocked off Rock's hat. Reaching up with his left hand, Rock jerked the burning arrow from the canvas. The fire had not yet caught. Then he opened up, firing his pistol, shifting guns, and firing again. The attack broke as suddenly as it had begun.

Tom Crockett was kneeling behind a water

barrel, his face gray. A good shot, he was not accustomed to killing. He glanced up at Rock, a sickened expression on his face.

"I never killed nothing human before," he said weakly.

"You'll get used to it out here," Rock said coldly. His eyes lifted to Sharon.

"You saved our wagon," she said.

"It might have been anybody's wagon," he said brutally, and turned away. He counted seven dead Indians on the prairie. There were probably one or two more hidden in the tall grass. He could see several dead ponies. The Indian who had shot the flaming arrow lay not more than a dozen feet away. The bullet had gone through his stomach and broken his spine.

Rock walked around. He had eyes only for the men. Cap looked frightened, but determined. Pagones had fired steadily and with skill. Bannon nodded at the short man.

"You'll do," he said grimly.

Pagones started to speak, started after him, and scowled a little. He was ashamed of himself when he realized he was pleased at the compliment.

They were good men, Rock decided. Purcell was reloading his rifle, and he looked up as Bannon passed, but said nothing. Rock walked back to the Crockett wagon. Cap was standing there, his rifle in the hollow of his arm.

"Will they come again?" he asked.

Bannon nodded. "Probably several times. This is Buffalo Hide. Those were his warriors."

"But Morton said . . . ," Crockett started to protest.

Bannon looked around, and then he pointed at the dead Indian. "You goin' to believe Morton Harper or that?" he demanded. "That Indian's a Blackfoot. I know by the moccasins."

This time they came in a circle, going around and around the wagon train. A volley of flaming arrows set two wagon tops afire. Rock stood at the end of the Crockett wagon and fired steadily, carefully, making every shot count.

Dawn came with a red, weird light flaming in the east and turned the wagon colors to flame. Guns crashed, and the air was filled with wild Indian yells and the acrid smell of gunpowder and burned canvas. Three times more they attacked, and Bannon was everywhere. Firing, firing, firing. Crockett went down with a bullet through his thigh. Bjornsen was shot through the head, and a warrior leaped from a horse into Greaves's wagon and the two men fought there until the Indian thrust a knife into Greaves's side. Bannon shot the brave with a snapped pistol shot, almost from the hip.

The last attack broke, and the sun lifted into the sky. As if by magic the Indians were gone. Rock Bannon wiped the sweat from his forehead and stared out over the plain. Buffalo Hide had lost men in this fight. At least twenty of his braves were dead, and there would be wailing and the death chant in the Blackfoot villages tonight.

Two horses and an ox had been killed. They gathered around, buried the two dead men, and butchered the ox. Rock sat on a wagon tongue alone. Cap walked over to him. The man's face was round and uncomfortable.

"Reckon you saved us, Rock," he said. "Don't rightly know how to thank you."

Bannon got up. He had been cleaning his rifle and reloading it while the men were being buried. "Don't try," he said.

Bob Sprague walked over and held out his hand. "Guess we haven't been very friendly," he said, "but you were right about the Indians."

Suddenly, boyishly Bannon grinned. "Forget it, Bob. You did a right good job with that rifle of yours."

They were the only two who mentioned it. Rock helped lift Crockett into the back of the wagon, and then harnessed the oxen. He was gone, riding out on the flank on the steel-dust when Sharon came to thank him. She looked after him, and her heart felt suddenly lost and alone.

It was late that day when they reached the dry country. The settlers did not realize the change until the dust began to rise, for in the distance it had looked much the same, only the grass was darker and there was less of it. Within a mile they were suffused in a cloud of powdery, sifting dust, stifling and irritating in the heat.

This was no desert. Merely long miles of plain where the hills receded and there was no subirrigation to keep the grass green and rich. All the following day the dust cloud hung over the wagon train, and from Mulholland's place in the van the last wagons could not even be distinguished.

Mulholland looked up at Bannon, who was riding beside him. "Harper said there was one bad stretch," he said almost apologetically.

Bannon did not reply. He alone of all the party knew what lay ahead. He alone knew how brutal the passage would be. Let them find out.

Days later, when Cap asked him to go for game, they all knew. They were still in that desert of dust and dirty brown brush. They had camped in it five days now. Their water barrels were empty, the wagons so hard to pull in the thick dust that they made only a few miles each day. It was the worst kind of tough going.

When he had killed two antelope in the hills, Rock rode back to join the party. Pagones, hunting on the other side, had killed one. Rock turned toward Sharon's wagon and swung down from the saddle. She looked up at him from over a fire of greasewood.

"Hello," she said. "We haven't seen much of you."

He took off his black, flat-brimmed hat. His dark, curly hair was plastered to his brow with sweat.

"There are some here who don't want me talking to you," he said dryly. "Figure I'm a bad influence, I guess."

"I haven't said that!" she protested. She brushed a strand of hair from her eyes. "I like to have you riding close. It . . . it makes me feel safer."

He looked at her an instant, and then looked away. "How's your dad?"

"Better, I think. But this heat! It's so awful! How long before we get out of this dust?"

"Tomorrow night, at this rate. This bad stretch is over."

"Then we're free of that. Morton said there was only one."

He noticed that she had called Harper "Morton."

"He was wrong. You'll strike another near Salt Lake that's much worse than this. You'll never get across unless you swing back and take the old trail for Pilot Peak."

"But he said . . . ," Sharon protested.

Rock Bannon looked up at her from where he squatted on his haunches. "I know he did. I heard everything he said, and I'm still wondering what he has to gain by it. Nobody takes this route. Crossing the Salt Lake Desert by this route is suicide . . . with wagons, at least. You've all placed a lot of faith in a stranger."

"He was right, Rock. Those first six days were heaven, and from now on it should be good."

"From now on it will be good until you hit the desert," he admitted, "unless you stop."

"Unless we stop?" Sharon dished up a plate and handed it to him, and then poured the coffee. "Why?"

"Tomorrow we get into Hardy Bishop's country." Rock Bannon's face was somber.

"You always refer to him as if he were an outlaw or something awful."

"No," he said. "Bishop isn't any of those things. If you are his friend or a guest, he's one of the finest men alive. If you are an enemy or try to take something that's his, he is absolutely ruthless."

When she returned from feeding her father, she sat down beside him on the wagon tongue. The sun was down, and the dust had settled. Near a fire on the far side of the circle, Dud Kitchen was singing softly over his mandolin.

The air was cool now, and the soft music mingled in the air with the scent of wood smoke, the low champing of the horses, and the mumbling of the oxen. In the distance they could see the hills, purple with the last shadows before darkness, and shadowed with a promise of coolness after the long days of heat and dust and bitterness.

35

He stared away at the hills, remembering so much, worried, uncertain, wondering again about Morton Harper. What did the man have in mind? Who was he? Purcell said Harper had lent him money. Perhaps he had lent others in the wagon train money. It was not like a man to loan money and not follow it up to get back what was his. Behind all of this was a reason, and in the back of his mind Rock was afraid he knew that reason.

Sharon spoke suddenly. "What are you thinking of, Rock? You are always so silent. You seem so bitter sometimes, and I can never understand what you have in your mind."

"It isn't anything." He had no desire to mention Harper again. "I was just thinking about this country."

"You like it, don't you?"

"Like it?" He looked up suddenly, and his eyes changed. He smiled suddenly and with warmth. "Like it? I love it. This is a man's country. And that ahead? Wait until you see Bishop's Valley. Miles upon miles of tumbling streams, waving green grass dotted with cattle.

"You should see Bishop's Valley. You go down through a deep gorge along a roaring mountain stream, and you can look up at cliffs that rise for three thousand feet, and then suddenly the gorge widens and you look down a long valley that is six or seven miles wide and all of fifty miles long.

"On each side, high mountain ridges shut it in,

and here and there deep gorges and ravines cut back into those ridges and there are green meadows and tumbling waterfalls. And all the hills around are timbered to their crests. It's a beautiful country."

Sharon stared at him, enchanted. Rock had never talked like this before, and, as she listened to him tell of the hills and the wild game, of deer, elk, bear, and mountain goats, of the catbirds calling in the willows and the hillsides white with groves of silver-columned birch, she suddenly forgot where she was and who was talking.

"You seem to love it so much," she said. "Why did you ever leave?"

"It belongs to one man, to Hardy Bishop," Rock said. "He's carving a little empire there. He went there long before any other white man dreamed of anything but going on to California, before they thought of anything but getting rich from gold mines. They came through the country like a pack of vultures or wolves, taking everything, building nothing. They want only to get rich and get out.

"He was different. Once, when only a boy, he went into that valley on a trapping venture, and he was never content until he came back. He drove a herd of cattle west when there were no cattle in this country, and he got them into that valley and turned them loose. He fought Indians and outlaws, he built a dam, built a home, built irrigation ditches where he wanted them, and planted trees.

"He made the valley, and you can't blame him if he wants to keep it his way now."

Long after Sharon lay in her blankets, she thought of that and of Rock Bannon. How tall he was! And how strange! He had risen suddenly and with scarcely a word had walked into the night, and then she heard him mount his horse and ride away. Yet even as she heard the dwindling hoof beats, she heard something else, the sound of other horses drawing near. Still wondering who the riders could be, she fell asleep.

Scarcely were they moving in the morning before a black mare wheeled alongside the Crockett wagon. Flushing suddenly, Sharon saw Morton Harper, hat in hand, bowing to her.

"Good morning!" he said. "I hoped to catch up with you before this, but by tomorrow you'll be in green country again."

"Yes, I know."

He looked at her quickly. "You know? Who told you?"

"Rock Bannon."

His face sharpened, and she could sense the irritation in the man. "Oh? Then he's still with you? I was hoping he had left you alone. I'm afraid he's not a good man."

"Why do you say that? He's been very helpful."

Harper shrugged. "I'd rather not say. You know of that killing in Laramie, and, if that were the only one, it would not matter. There are others. He has killed five or six men. He's a trouble-maker wherever he goes. I'm glad Purcell and your men understand that, for it will save a lot of trouble."

He smiled at her. "You look so lovely this morning that it is unbelievable that you have come so far across the prairies. It is a pity you have so far to go. I've been thinking some of set-tling in this country here." He waved ahead. "It is such a beautiful land, and there is nothing in California so desirable."

Rock Bannon had heard the horses the night before, and he had reined in long enough to see them come up to the fire. Harper he recognized at once. There were two men with him, one a lean, sharp-faced man with a long nose. The other man was short, chuckleheaded, and blunt-featured. Bannon's lips tightened when he recognized Pete Zapata. The half-breed killer was notorious, a gunfighter and desperado of the worst stripe, but none of the wagon train would know that.

All that day he stayed away from the train, riding on ahead. He drank at the spring, killed an antelope and a couple of teal, and then rode back under a clump of poplars and waited for the wagon train to come up. They were already on

Hardy Bishop's V Bar. Only a short distance behind the poplars, the long cañon known as Poplar Cañon ran down into Bishop's Valley.

He got up when he saw the first of the long caravan of wagons. Better than the others, he knew what this would mean and knew on how bad a trail they had started. He was standing there, close to the steel-dust stallion, when the wagons moved in.

The fresh water and green grass made everyone happy. Brown-legged children rushed downstream from where the drinking water was obtained, and there was laughter and merrymaking in the camp. Fires sprang up, and in a short time the camp was made and meals were being cooked.

Watchfully Rock saw Morton Harper seated on a saddle at Cap Mulholland's fire. With them were the sharp-featured stranger, Satterfield, Lamport, and Pagones. They were deep in a conference. In a few minutes Tom Crockett walked over to join them.

Dud Kitchen was tuning his mandolin when he saw Bannon sitting under the willows.

"All alone?" Kitchen said with a grin, and dropped on the grass beside Bannon. "Saw how you handled those guns in that Indian fight. Never saw the like. Make more tune with 'em than me with a mandolin!"

Rock chuckled. "But not so nice to hear." He

nodded at the group of men around the fire. "Wonder what's up?"

Dud shrugged. "Harper's got some plan he's talkin' about. Sayin' they are foolish to go on when there's good country right here."

Rock Bannon sprang to his feet, his eyes afire with apprehension. "So that's it," he said. "I might have known it."

Kitchen was startled. "What's the matter? I think it would be a good idea myself. This is beautiful country. I don't know that I've ever seen better. Harper says that down this draw behind us there's a long, beautiful valley, all open for settlement."

But Rock Bannon was no longer listening. Stepping across the branch of the creek, he started for the fire. Morton Harper was talking when Rock walked up.

"Why not?" Harper was saying. "You all want homes. Can you find a more beautiful country than this? That dry plain is behind you. Ahead lies the Salt Lake Desert, but, in here, this is a little bit of paradise. Beyond this range of hills . . . you can reach it through Poplar Cañon . . . is the most beautiful valley you ever saw. It's just crying for people to come in and settle down. There's game in the hills and the best grazing land in the world, all for the taking."

"What about Hardy Bishop?" Bannon demanded harshly.

41

Harper looked up, angered. "You, again? Every time these people try to do anything, you interfere! Is it your business where they stop? Is it your business if they remain here or go on to California? Are you trying to dictate to these people?"

Pike Purcell was on his feet, and Rock could see all the old dislike in the big Missourian's face. The other men looked at him with disapproval, too. Yet he went on recklessly, heedlessly.

"Hardy Bishop settled that valley. He's running two thousand head of cattle in there. You try to settle in that valley and you're asking for trouble. He won't stand for it."

"An' we won't stand for you buttin' in!" Purcell said suddenly. He dropped a hand to the big Dragoon pistol in his holster. "I've had enough of your buttin' around, interferin' in our affairs. I'm tellin' you now, you shut up an' get out."

"Wait just a minute!" Bob Sprague stepped closer. "This man warned us about that Indian attack, or we'd all be dead, includin' you, Pike Purcell. He did more fightin' in that attack than any one of us, or two of us, for that matter. His advice has been good, and I think we should listen to him!"

Dud Kitchen nodded. "Speak up, Rock. I'll listen."

"There's little to be said," Bannon told them quietly. "Only the land this man is suggesting you settle on was settled on over ten years ago by a man who fought Indians to get it. He fought Indians and outlaws to keep it. He won't see it taken from him now in his old age. He'll fight to keep it. I know Hardy Bishop. I know him well enough to be sure that, if you move into that valley, many of the women in this wagon train will be widows before the year is out.

"What I don't know is Morton Harper's reason for urging you into this. I don't know why he urged you to take this trail, but I think he has a reason, and I think that reason lies in Bishop's Valley. You are coming West to win homes. You have no right to do it by taking what another man fought to win and to keep. There is plenty for all farther West."

"That makes sense to me," Sprague said quietly. "I for one am moving West."

"Well, I'm not," Purcell said stubbornly. "I like this country, and me and the wife have seen enough dust and sun and Indians. We aim to stay."

"That valley is fifty miles long, gentlemen," Harper said.

"I think there is room enough for us all in Bishop's Valley."

"That seems right to me," Cap said. He looked around at Tom Crockett, limping near the fire. "How about you, Tom?"

"I'm staying," Crockett said. "I like it here."

Satterfield nodded. "Reckon I'll find me a place to set up a blacksmith shop," he said. "But there's a sight of things we all need. There ain't no stores, no place to get some things we figured to get in California."

"That will be where I come in." The man with the sharp features smiled pleasantly. "I'm John Kies, and I have six wagonloads of goods coming over the trail to open a store in our new town!"

III

Silently Rock Bannon turned away. There was no further use in talking. He caught Sharon's eye, but she looked away, her gaze drawn to Mort Harper where he sat now, talking easily, smoothly, planning the new home, the new town.

Bannon walked back to his blankets and turned in, listening to the whispering of the poplar leaves and the soft murmur of the water in the branch. It was a long time before he fell asleep, long after the last talking had died away in the wagon train and when the fires had burned low.

When daylight came, he bathed and saddled the stallion. Then, carefully, he checked his guns. At a sound, he glanced up to see Sharon Crockett dipping water from the stream.

"Good morning," he said. "Did you finally decide to stay?"

"Yes." She stepped toward him. "Rock, why are

you always against everything we do? Why don't you stay, too? I'm sure Morton would be glad to have you. He's planned all this so well, and he says we'll need good men. Why don't you join us?"

"No, not this time. I stayed with the wagon train because I knew what you were going into. I wanted to help you . . . and I mean *you*. In what is to come, no one can help you. Besides, my heart wouldn't be in it."

"You're afraid of this crabby old man?" she asked scornfully. "Morton says as soon as Bishop sees we intend to stay, he won't oppose us at all. He's just crabby and difficult because he's old, and he has more land than he needs. Are you afraid of him?"

Rock smiled. "You sure set a lot of store by this Harper fellow, don't you? Did he tell you that Bishop's riders were all crabby old men, too? Did Harper tell you why he carries Pete Zapata along with him?"

"Who is he?" Sharon looked up, her eyes curious, yet resentful.

"You've called me a killer," Bannon replied. "I have killed men. I may kill more, although I hope not, but Pete Zapata, that flat-faced man who rides with Harper, is a murderer. He's a killer of the most vicious type and the kind no decent man would have near him."

Her eyes flared. "You don't think Morton

Harper is decent? How dare you say such a thing behind his back?"

"I'll face him with it," Bannon said dryly. "I expect I'll face him with it more than once. But before you get in too deep, ask yourself again what he is getting out of all this? He goes in for talk of brotherly love, but he carries a gunman at his elbow."

He turned and swung into the saddle as she picked up her bucket. He reined in the horse at a call. It was Bob Sprague.

"Hey, Rock! Want to come on West with us?"

He halted. "You're going on?"

"Uhn-huh. Six wagons are going. We decided we liked the sound of what you said. We're pullin' on for California, and we'd sure admire to have you with us!"

Bannon hesitated. Sharon was walking away, her head held proudly. Did she seem to hesitate for his reply? He shrugged.

"No," he said. "I've got other plans."

Sharon Crockett, making frying-pan bread over the fire beside her wagon, stood up to watch Bob Sprague lead off six wagons, the owners of which had decided not to stay. All farewells had been said the night before, yet now that the time for leave-taking had come, she watched uneasily.

For years she had known Bob Sprague, ever since she was a tiny girl. He had been her father's friend, a steady, reliable man, and now he was going. With him went five other families, among them some of the steadiest, soberest men in the lot.

Were they wrong to take Morton Harper's advice? Her father, limping with the aid of a cane cut from the willows, walked back, and stood beside her, his face somber. He was a tall man, almost as tall as Harper and Bannon, his hair silvery around the temples, his face gray with a slight stubble of beard. He was a fearless, independent man, given to going his own way and thinking his own thoughts.

Pagones walked over to them. "Did Bannon go along? I ain't seen him."

"I don't think he went," Crockett replied. "Sprague wanted him to go."

"No, he didn't go," said Satterfield, who had walked up to join them. Satterfield had been a frontier lawyer back in Illinois. "I saw him riding off down the cañon, maybe an hour ago."

"You think there will be trouble?" Pagones asked.

Satterfield shrugged. "Probably not. I know how some of these old frontiersmen are. They hate to see civilization catch up with them, but, given time, they come around. Where's Harper?"

"He went off somewhere with that dark-lookin' feller who trails with him," Pagones said. "Say,

I'm glad Dud Kitchen didn't go. I'd sure miss that music he makes. He was goin', then at the last minute changed his mind. He's goin' down with Harper and Cap to survey that town site."

"It'll seem good to have a town again," Crockett said. "Where's it to be?"

"Down where Poplar Cañon runs into Bishop's Valley. Wide, beautiful spot, they say, with plenty of water and grass. John Kies is puttin' in a store, I'm goin' to open an office, and Collins is already figurin' on a blacksmith shop."

"Father, did you ever hear of a man named Zapata?" Sharon asked thoughtfully. "Pete Zapata?"

Crockett looked at her curiously. "Why, no. Not that I recall. Why?"

"I was just wondering, that's all."

The next morning they hitched up the oxen and moved their ten wagons down Poplar Cañon to the town site. The high, rocky walls of the cañon widened slowly, and the oxen walked on, knee deep in rich green grass. Along the stream were willow and poplar, and higher along the cañon sides she saw alder, birch, and mountain mahogany, with here and there a fine stand of lodgepole pine.

Tom Crockett was driving, so she ranged alongside, riding her sorrel mare.

As they rounded the last bend in the cañon, it

spread widely before them, and she saw Morton Harper sitting his black mare some distance off. Putting the sorrel to a gallop, she rode down swiftly, hair blowing in the wind. Dud Kitchen was there with Zapata and Cap. They were driving stakes and lining up a street.

Before them the valley dropped into the great open space of Bishop's Valley, and she rode on. Suddenly, rounding a knoll, she stopped and caught her breath.

The long, magnificent sweep of the valley lay before her, green and splendid in the early morning sun. Here and there over the grassland, cattle grazed, belly deep in the tall grass. It was overpowering; it was breathtaking. It was something beyond the grasp of the imagination. High on either side lifted the soaring walls of the cañon, mounting into high ridges, snow-capped peaks, and majestic walls of gray rock.

This was the cattle empire of Hardy Bishop. This was the place Rock Bannon had spoken of with such amazing eloquence.

She turned in her saddle at the sound of a horse's hoofs. Mort Harper rode up beside her, his face glowing.

"Look!" he cried. "Magnificent, isn't it? The most splendid view in the world. Surely that's an empire worth taking."

Sharon's head turned quickly, sharply. At something in Harper's eyes she caught her breath, and, when she looked again at the valley, she was uneasy.

"What . . . what did you say?" she asked. "An empire worth taking?"

He glanced at her quickly, and then laughed. "Don't pay any mind. I was thinking of Bishop, the man who claims all this. He took it. Took it from the Indians by main force." Then he added: "He's an old brute. He'd stop at nothing."

"Do you think he will make trouble for us?" she inquired anxiously.

He shrugged. "Probably not. He might, but, if he does, we can handle that part of it. Let's go back, shall we?"

She was silent during the return ride, and she kept turning over in her mind her memory of Bannon's question: *What's he going to get out of this?* Somehow, half hypnotized by Harper's eloquence, she had not really thought of that. That she thought of it now gave her a twinge of doubt. It seemed, somehow, disloyal.

For three days, life in the new town went on briskly. They named the town Poplar. Kies's store was the first building up, and the shelves were heavy with needed goods. Kies was smiling and affable. "Don't worry about payment," he assured them. "We're all in this together. Just get what you need, and I'll put it on the books. Then, when you get money from furs or crops, you can pay me."

It was easy. It was almost too easy. Tom Crockett built a house in a bend of the creek among the trees, and he bought dress goods for Sharon, trousers for himself, and bacon and flour. Then he bought some new tools.

Those first three days were hard, unrelenting labor, yet joyful labor, too. They were building homes, and there is always something warming and pleasant in that. At the end of those first three days, Kies's store was up, and so were Collins's blacksmith shop, Satterfield's office, and Harper's Saloon and Theater. All of them pitched in and worked.

Then one day, as she was leaving Kies's store, she looked up to see three strange horsemen coming down the street. They were walking their horses, and they were looking around in ill-concealed amazement.

Mulholland had come out behind her, and at the sight of him one of the horsemen, a big, stern-looking man with a drooping red mustache, reined his horse around.

"You!" he said. "What do you all think you're doin' here?"

"Buildin' us a town," Cap said aggressively. "Any objections?"

Red laughed sardonically. "Well, sir," he said, "I reckon I haven't, but I'm afraid the boss is sure goin' to raise hob."

"Who's the boss?" Cap asked. "And what difference does it make? This is all free land, isn't it?"

"The boss is Hardy Bishop," Red drawled, glancing around. He looked approvingly at Sharon, and there seemed a glint of humor in his eyes. "And you say this is free land. It is and it ain't. You see, out here a man takes what he can hold. Hardy, he done come in here when all you folks was livin' fat and comfortable back in the States. He settled here, and he worked hard. He trapped and hunted and washed him some color, and then he went back to the States and bought cattle. Drivin' them cattle out here ten years ago was sure a chore, folks, but he done it. Now they've bred into some of the biggest herds in the country. I don't think Hardy's goin' to like you folks movin' in here like this."

"Is he so selfish?" Sharon demanded. "Why, there's land here enough for thousands of people!"

Red looked at her. "That's how you see it, ma'am. I reckon to your way of thinkin' back East, that might be true. Here, it ain't true. A man's needs run accordin' to the country he's in and the job he has to do. Hardy Bishop is runnin' cows. He expects to supply beef for thousands of people. To do that he needs a lot of land. You see, ma'am, if thousands of people can't raise their own beef, somebody's got to have land enough to raise beef for all those thousands of people. And Hardy, he come by it honest."

"By murdering Indians, I suppose!"

Red looked at her thoughtfully. "Ma'am, somebody's been tellin' you wrong. Plumb wrong. Hardy never murdered no Indians."

"What's going on here?" Morton Harper stepped into the street. To his right was Pete Zapata, to his left Pike Purcell. Lamport lounged in the door of the store.

"Why, nothin', mister," Red said thoughtfully. His gaze had sharpened, and Sharon saw his eyes go from Harper to Zapata. "We was just talkin' about land and the ownership of it. We're ridin' for Bishop, and. . . ."

"And you can ride right out of here!" Harper snapped. "Now!"

Sharon was closer to the Bishop riders, and suddenly she heard the second man say softly: "Watch it, Red. That's Zapata."

Red seemed to stiffen in his saddle, and his hand, which had started to slip off the pommel of the saddle with no aggressive intention, froze in position. Without a word, they turned their horses and rode away.

"That's the beginning," Harper stated positively. "I'm afraid they mean to drive us from our homes."

"They didn't sound much like trouble," Cap ventured hesitantly. "Talked mighty nice."

"Don't be fooled by them," Harper warned. "Bishop is an outlaw, or the next thing to it."

Tom Crockett was a man who loved the land. No sooner had he put a plow into the deep, rich soil of the cañon bottom than he felt he had indeed come home. The soil was deep and black, heavy with richness, land that had never known a plow. Working early and late, he had in the next day managed to plow several acres. Seed he bought from Kies, who seemed to have everything they needed.

There were several hours a day he gave to working on the buildings the others were throwing up, but logs were handy, and all but Zapata and Kies worked on the felling and notching of them. Kies stayed in his store, and Zapata lounged close by.

Morton Harper helped with the work, but Sharon noticed that he was never without a gun, and his rifle was always close by. At night in his saloon he played cards with Purcell and Lamport and anyone else who came around. Yet several times a day he managed to stop by, if only for a minute, to talk to her.

He stopped by one day when she was planting a vine near the door. He watched her for a few minutes, and then he stepped closer.

"Sharon," he said gently, "you shouldn't be doing this sort of thing. You're too beautiful. Why don't you let me take care of you?"

She looked at him, suddenly serious. "Is this a proposal?"

His eyes flashed, and then he smiled. "What else? I suppose I'm pretty clumsy at it."

"No," she returned thoughtfully, "you're not clumsy at it, but let's wait. Let's not talk about it until everyone has a home and is settled in a place of their own."

"All right," he agreed reluctantly. "But that won't be very long, you know."

It was not until they were eating supper that night that her thoughts suddenly offered her a question. What about Morton's home? He had not even started to build. He was sleeping in a room behind the saloon, such in name only as yet, for there was little liquor to be had.

The thought had not occurred to her before, but it puzzled and disturbed her. Tom Crockett was full of plans, talking of crops and the rich soil.

The next day Morton Harper was gone. Where he had gone Sharon did not know, but suddenly in the middle of the morning she realized he was not among them. The black mare was gone, too. Shortly after noon she saw him riding into town, and behind him came six wagons, loaded with boxes and barrels. They drew up before the store and the saloon.

He saw her watching and loped the mare over to her door.

"See?" he said, waving a hand. "The supplies! Everything we need for the coming year, but if we need more, I can send a rider back to the fort after more."

"Then you had them coming from the fort?" she asked. "You were far-sighted."

He laughed, glancing at her quickly. "Well, I thought these things would sell in the mining camps out in California, but this is much, much better."

In spite of herself, Sharon was disturbed. All day as she went about her work, the thought kept recurring that those supplies offered a clue to something, yet she could find nothing on which to fasten her suspicions. Why should their arrival disturb her so much? Was it unusual that the man should start several wagonloads of supplies to California?

Pagones stopped by the spring to get a drink. He smiled at her, pushing back his hat from a sweating brow.

"Lots of work, ma'am. Your pa's sure getting in his plowing in a hurry. He'll have his seed in before the rest of us have started."

"Pag, how do the supplies reach the gold fields in California?" Sharon said suddenly.

He looked up over his second dipper of water. "Why, by sea, of course. Much cheaper that way. Why do you ask? Something botherin' you?"

"Not exactly. Only ever since those wagons came in this morning, I've been wondering about them. Morton said he had started them for

56

California, but thought they would sell better here. Why would he send them to California to sell when they can get supplies by sea?"

"Might mean a little ready money," Pagones suggested. He hung the dipper on a shrub. "Now that you mention it, it does seem kind of strange."

The expected trouble from Hardy Bishop did not materialize as soon as she expected. No other riders came near, although several times she noticed men, far out in the valley. All of Morton Harper's promises seemed to be coming true. He had said Bishop would not bother them.

Yet all was not going too smoothly. The last wagons had brought a load of liquor, and several of the men hung around the saloon most of the time. Purcell was there every evening, although by day he worked on his place. Pete Zapata was always there when not off on one of his lonely rides, and the teamsters who had brought the wagons to Kies's store had remained, loitering about, doing nothing at all, but always armed. One of them had become the bartender.

During all this time, her work had kept Sharon close to the house and there had been no time for riding. Time and again she found herself going to the door and looking down toward the cluster of buildings that was fast becoming a thriving little village. And just as often she looked back up the trail they had followed when first coming into Poplar Cañon.

Not even to herself would she admit what she was looking for. She refused to admit that she longed to see the steel-dust stallion and its somber, lonely rider. She had overheard him say he would not leave, yet where was he?

The sound of a horse's hoofs in the trail outside brought her to the cabin door. It was Mary Pagones, daughter of George Pagones, who had long since proved himself one of the most stable men in the wagon train.

"Come on, Sharon . . . let's ride! I'm beginning to feel cramped with staying down here all the time."

Sharon needed no urging, and in a few minutes they were riding out of the settlement toward the upper reaches of the cañon.

"Have you seen that Pete Zapata staring at the women the way he does?" Mary asked. "He fairly gives me the creeps."

"Somebody said he was a gunman," Sharon ventured.

"I wouldn't doubt it!" Mary was an attractive girl, always gay and full of laughter. The freckles over her nose were an added attraction rather than otherwise. "Dud doesn't like him at all. Says he can't see why Harper keeps him around."

As they rode out of Poplar Cañon, an idea suddenly occurred to Sharon, and without voicing it she turned her mare toward their old encampment, but as they burst through the last line of trees, disappointment flooded over her. There was no sign of Rock Bannon.

They had gone almost a mile farther, when suddenly Mary reined in sharply.

"Why, look at that!" She pointed. "Wagon tracks coming out of that cañon! Who in the world would ever take a wagon in there?"

Sharon looked at them and then at the cañon. It was narrow-mouthed, the only entrance into a wild, rugged region of crags and ravines, heavily forested and forbidding. Riding closer, she looked down. The wagon tracks were coming from the cañon, not going into it. She studied the mountains thoughtfully. Then, wheeling her horse, with Mary following, she rode out on their own trail. All the tracks she had observed were old.

She looked at Mary, and Mary returned the glance, a puzzled frown gathering around her eyes. "What's the matter?" Mary asked. "Is something wrong?"

"I don't know," Sharon said. "There are no tracks here since we came over the trail, but there are tracks coming out of that cañon."

Mary's eyes widened. "You mean those wagons of Harper's? Then they must have come over a different trail."

That wasn't what Sharon was thinking, but she just shook her head. "Don't say anything about it," she said.

They rode on. That wall of mountains would not offer a trail through, and, if it did, where would it go? If it joined the Overland Trail to the north, it would still be almost twice as far as by the trail they had come, and through one of the most rugged sections she had ever seen. Suddenly she knew. Those wagons had been here before. They had been back there, in some remote cañon, waiting.

Waiting for what? For a town to begin? But that was absurd. No one had known the town would begin until a few hours before. No one, unless it had been Morton Harper.

IV

On, through hills of immeasurable beauty, the two girls rode. Great, rocky escarpments that towered to the skies and mighty crags, breasting their saw-toothed edges against the wind. Long, steep hillsides clad with alder and birch or rising to great, dark-feathered crests of lodgepole pine mingled here and there with an occasional fir.

Along the lower hillsides and along the mountain draws were quaking aspen, mountain mahogany, and hawthorn. They had come to the edge of a grove of poplar when they saw the horseman. They both saw him at once, and something in his surreptitious manner brought them to a halt. They both recognized him at the same instant.

"Sharon," Mary said, "it's that Zapata!"

"*Ssh!* He'll hear us." Sharon held her breath. Suddenly she was frightened at the idea of being found out here, even with Mary along, by Zapata. But Zapata seemed to have no eyes for them or even their direction. He was riding by very slowly, not over fifty yards away, carrying his rifle in his hands and watching something in the valley below that was beyond their vision.

Yet, even as they watched, he slid suddenly from the saddle and crouched upon some rocks on the rim. Then he lifted his rifle and fired!

"What's he shooting at?" Mary asked in a whisper.

"I don't know. A deer, probably. Let's get home." Turning their horses, they rode back through the trees and hit the trail back to the settlement.

All the next day Sharon thought about that wagon trail out of the mountains. Several times she started to speak to her father, but he was preoccupied, lost in plans for his new home, and thinking of nothing but it. Later in the day she saw Dud Kitchen riding over. He reined in and slid from the saddle.

"Howdy, Sharon! Sure glad to see you all! We been talkin' some, Mary and I, about us gettin' up a sort of party. Seems like Satterfield plays a

61

fiddle, and we thought we might have a dance, sort of. Liven things up a mite."

"That's a good idea, Dud," Sharon agreed. She looked up at him suddenly. "Dud, did Mary tell you anything about that wagon trail we saw?"

His blue eyes sharpened and he ran his fingers back through his corn-colored hair. "Yeah," he said, "she did."

"Dud, it looks to me like those wagons were out here before we were, just waiting. It begins to look like somebody planned to have us stop here."

"You mean Mort? But what would he do that for? What could he gain? And even if he did, you've got to admit it's a good place."

"Yes, it is, but just the same I don't like it."

Her father was walking toward them with George Pagones and Cap Mulholland.

"What's this you young folks figurin' to do?" Cap said, grinning. "Hear we're havin' us a party."

Her answer was drowned by a sudden rattle of horses' hoofs, and she saw three men swing down the cañon trail. When they saw the group before the house, they reined in. One of them was Red, the man who had called on them the first day. Another was—her breath caught—Rock Bannon!

"Howdy!" Red said. He looked down at the men, and then recognized Cap. "Seen anything of a young feller, 'bout twenty or so, ridin' a bay pony?"

"Why, no," Cap said. "Can't say as I have. What's the trouble?"

"He's Wes Freeman, who rides for us. He was huntin' strays over this way yesterday and he never came back. We figured maybe he was hurt somehow."

"No, we haven't seen him," Crockett said.

Dud Kitchen was grinning at Rock. "Shucks, man! We figured you had left the country. What you doin'?"

Bannon grinned. "I'm ridin' for Hardy Bishop," he said. "Went over there right after I left you folks."

"What made you think your man might have come over here?" Pagones asked. "Was he ridin' thisaway?"

"As a matter of fact," Red said, "he was ridin' back northeast of here. Pretty rough country, except for one cañon that's got some good grass in it."

The third man was short, thick-set, and tough. "Hurry up, Red," he said. "Why beat around the brush. Tell 'em."

"All right," Red said. "I'll just do that, Bat." He looked down at the little group before the house. "Fact of the matter is, Wes's horse come in about sundown yesterday, come in with blood on the saddle. We back-trailed the horse and we found Wes. We found him in the open valley we spoke

63

of. He was dead. He'd been shot through the back and knocked off his horse. Then whoever shot him had followed him up and killed him with a hunting knife."

Zapata! Sharon's eyes widened, and she looked around to see Dud staring at her, gray-faced. She had seen Zapata shoot!

In stunned silence the men stared up at the three riders. Rock broke the silence.

"You can see what this means?" he said sternly. "Wes was a mighty nice boy. I hadn't known him as long as these men, but he seemed to be a right fine feller. Now he's been murdered . . . dry-gulched. That's going to mean trouble."

"But why come to us?" Cap protested. "Sure, you don't believe we. . . ."

"We don't believe!" Bat broke in harshly. "We know! We trailed three riders down out of those hills! Three from here! Wes was my ridin' partner. He was a durned good boy. I'm goin' to see the man who done that."

"Turn around."

The voice was cold and deadly. As one person, they turned. Pete Zapata, his guns low slung on his hips, was staring at the three riders. Flanking him were two men with shotguns, both of them from the teamsters' crowd. The other two were Lamport and Purcell of the wagon train.

Behind them, and a little to one side, was Morton Harper. He was wearing two guns.

"Get out of here!" Harper snapped harshly. "Don't come around here again, aimin' to make trouble. That's all you came for, and you know it! You've been looking for an excuse to start something so you could get us out of here, take our homes away from us. Now turn your horses and get out!"

His eyes riveted on Rock Bannon. "As for you, Bannon," he said sharply, "you're a traitor! You rode with us, and now you've gone over to them. I think you're the cause of all this trouble. If a man of yours is dead, I think it would be a good idea if these friends of yours back-trailed you. Now get moving, all of you!"

"This is a bad mistake, Harper," Rock said evenly. "I'm speaking of it before all these people." He nodded at the group in front of the house. "Bishop was inclined to let 'em stay, despite the fact that he was afraid they'd bring more after them. He listened to me and didn't run you off. Now you're asking for it."

"He listened to *you!*" Harper's voice was alive with contempt. "You? A trail runner?"

Red looked quickly at Rock and started to speak. Bannon silenced him with a gesture.

"We'll ride, Harper, but we want the man . . . or men . . . who killed Wes. And we want him delivered to us by sundown tomorrow. If not, we'll come and get him."

Turning abruptly, they started away. Wheeling,

Zapata grabbed a shotgun from one of the teamsters. "I'll fix him, the bluffer!"

"Hold it!" Pagones had a six-shooter and was staring across it at Zapata. "We don't shoot men in the back."

For an instant, they glared at each other. Then Harper interposed. "Put it down, Pete. Let them go." He looked around. "There'll be a meeting at the saloon tonight. All of you be there."

When they had all gone, Tom Crockett shook his head sadly. "More trouble, and all because of that Bannon. I almost wish we'd let him die on the trail."

"It wasn't Bannon, Father," Sharon said. "Those men were right, I think. Mary and I saw Zapata yesterday. Two of the horses they trailed back here were ours. The other one was his. We were not fifty yards away from him when he fired that shot. We didn't see what he shot at, but it must have been that man."

Crockett's face was gray. "Are you sure, Sharon? Are you positive?"

"Yes, I am."

"Then we must give him up," he said sadly. "If he killed, he should suffer for it. Especially if he killed that way." He got up and reached for his hat. "I must go and tell Morton. He'll want to know."

She put a hand on his arm. "Father, you mustn't. Don't say anything to him until you've told the others. Pagones, I mean, and Cap. I'm afraid."

"Afraid of what? Morton Harper is a fine man. When he knows what happened, he'll want something done himself."

Putting on his hat, he started across the road for the cluster of buildings. Only for an instant did she hesitate. Then she swung around and ran to her horse, standing saddled and bridled as she had planned to ride over to Mary's. Dud Kitchen would be there, and Pagones.

They were sitting at the table when she burst into the room.

"Please come!" she said when she had explained. "I'm afraid!"

Without a word, they got up and buckled on their guns. It was only a few hundred yards to the saloon, and they arrived just a few moments after Tom Crockett had walked up to Harper.

"Morton, my daughter and Mary Pagones saw Zapata fire that shot yesterday," Crockett was saying. "I think we should surrender him to Bishop. We don't want to have any part in any killings."

Harper's face hardened and he started to speak. Zapata, overhearing his name, stepped to the door, his hand on a gun. Then Harper's face softened a little, and he shrugged.

"I'm afraid they were mistaken," he said carelessly. "You're being needlessly excited.

Probably Pete was up that way, for he rides around a good deal, the same as the girls do. But shoot a man in the back? He wouldn't do it."

"Oh, but he did," Dud Kitchen interrupted. "What the girls say is true."

"You call me a liar?" Harper turned on him, his face suddenly flushed with anger.

"No," Kitchen replied stiffly, his face paling. "I ain't callin' no man a liar, 'specially no man who come over the trail with me, but I know what I seen with my own eyes. Mary, she done told me about that, and I'll admit I figured there was something wrong with what she said, so I went up and back-trailed 'em. I didn't have no idea about no killin' then, but I trailed the girls, and then I trailed Pete. Pete Zapata stalked that cowhand for two miles before he got the shot he wanted. I went over every inch of his trail. He was fixin' to kill him. Then I trailed him down to the body. I seen where he wiped his knife on the grass, and I seen some of them brown sort of cigarettes he smokes. Pete Zapata killed that man, sure as I'm alive."

Zapata had walked, cat-footed, to the edge of the wide plank porch in front of the saloon. He stood there now, staring at Dud.

"Trailed me, huh?" His hand swept down in a streaking movement before Dud could as much as move. His gun bellowed, and Dud Kitchen turned halfway around and dropped into the dust.

"Why, Mort!" Crockett's face was gray. "What does this mean? I. . . ."

"You'd better all go back to your homes," Harper said sternly. "If Pete Zapata shot that man, and I don't admit for a minute that he did, he had a reason for it. As for this shooting here, Kitchen was wearing a gun, and he accused Zapata of murder."

Pagones's face was hard as stone. Two of the teamsters stood on the porch with shotguns. To have lifted a hand would have been to die.

"That settles it," Pagones said. "You can have your town! I'm leaving!"

"I reckon that goes for me, too," Crockett said sadly.

"I'm afraid you can't go," Harper said smoothly. There was a glint of triumph in his eyes. "My friend, John Kies, has lent you all money and supplies. Unless you can repay him what you owe, you'll have to stay until you have made a crop. California is a long ways away, and he couldn't be sure of collecting, there.

"Besides," he added, "Indians have rustled some of our stock. I have been meaning to tell you. Most of your oxen are gone." He shrugged. "But why worry? Stay here. This land is good, and these little difficulties will iron themselves out. There are always troubles when a new community begins. In a few years all this will be over and there will be children born here, a church built, and many homes."

Dud Kitchen was not dead. In the Pagones' house, Mary sat beside his bed. Satterfield had removed the bullet, and he sat at the kitchen table, drinking coffee.

"He's got him a chance," Satterfield said. "A good chance. I'm no doctor, just picked up a mite when I was in that Mexican War, but I think he'll come through."

Pagones, his heavy head thrust forward on his thick neck, stared into the fire, somber, brooding. He turned and looked at Satterfield and Crockett.

"Well," he said, "it looks bad. Looks like we're in a fight whether we want it or not. Hardy Bishop hasn't bothered us none, even after all of Mort Harper's preaching about him. Now Zapata has killed one of his men."

"That Red feller," Satterfield muttered, half to himself, "he don't look like no man to have trouble with. Nor Bat, neither."

"Where does Rock stand?" Pagones demanded. "That's what I'm wonderin'."

"Said he was ridin' for Bishop," Satterfield replied. "That's plain enough."

"If we'd listened to him, this wouldn't have happened," Mary said.

There was no reply to that. The three men stood quietly, listening to Dud Kitchen's heavy breathing. The rap at the door startled them, and they looked up to see Rock Bannon standing there.

Sharon drew in her breath, and she watched him, wide-eyed, as he stepped into the room and closed the door after him. Hat in hand, his eyes strayed from them to the wounded man lying in the bed.

How tall he was! And his shoulders had seemed to fill the door when he entered. He wore buckskin trousers tucked into hand-tooled star boots and a checked shirt with a buckskin jacket, Mexican fashion, over it. On his hips were two big Dragoon Colts in tied-down holsters.

"He hurt bad?" he asked softly.

"Yes, but Jim Satterfield says he's got a chance," Mary replied.

Rock Bannon turned to look at them. "Well," he said, "you saw me ride in here today. You know I'm riding for Bishop. From what's happened, I reckon you know that war's been declared. You've got to make up your mind whose side you are on. I talked Hardy Bishop into lettin' you stay on against his better judgment. He was all for runnin' you off *pronto*, not because he had anything against you, but because he could see settlers gettin' a toehold in his domain.

"Now one of our boys has been killed. Even Bishop might have trouble holdin' the boys back after that. I've talked to 'em, and they want the guilty man. They don't care about nobody else. What happens now is up to you."

"Not necessarily," Pagones objected. "We'll call a vote on it."

"You know how that'll go," Bannon objected. "Ten of you came in here with Mort Harper. Then he brought in Kies and Zapata. Now he's got other men. Supposin' you three vote to turn over the guilty man. How many others will vote that way? Cap may think right, but Cap will vote pretty much as Harper says. So will Purcell and Lamport. Anyway you look at it, the vote is going to be to fight rather than turn Zapata over."

"No way to be sure of that," Satterfield objected. "Harper may decide to turn him over."

Bannon turned, his temper flaring. "Haven't you learned anything on this trip? Harper's using you. He brought you down here for his own reasons. He's out to steal Bishop's Valley from Hardy . . . that's what he wants. You're just a bunch of dupes!"

"You got any proof of that?" Crockett demanded.

"Only my eyes," Rock admitted, "but that's enough. He owns every one of you, lock, stock, and barrel. I heard about that matter of you being in debt to Kies. Don't you suppose he planned all that?"

The door opened and Mulholland came in. With

him was Collins. Cap's face flushed when he saw Rock.

"You'd better light out. If Pete Zapata sees you, he'll kill you."

"That might not be so easy," Bannon said sharply. "All men don't die easy. Nor do they knuckle under to the first smooth talker who sells them a bill of goods."

Mulholland glared at him. "He promised us places, and we got 'em. Who's this Bishop to run us off? If it comes to war, then we'll fight."

"And die for Morton Harper? Do you think he'll let you keep what you have if he gets control of this valley? He'll run you out of here without a penny. You're his excuse, that's all. If the law ever comes into this, he can always say that Bishop used violence to stop free American citizens from settling on the land."

"That's just what he's doin'," Cap said. "If he wants war, he can have it!"

"Then I'd better go," Rock said. "I came here hopin' to make some peace talk. It looks like Zapata declared war for you. Now you've got to fight Mort Harper's war for him."

"You were one of us once," Pagones said. "You helped us on the trail. Why can't you help us now?"

Rock Bannon looked up. His eyes hesitated on Sharon's face, and then swept on. "Because you're on the wrong side," he said simply.

Sharon looked up and her eyes flashed.

"But you were one of us," she protested. "You should be with us now. Don't you understand loyalty?"

"I was never one of you after Mort Harper came," he said. Sharon flushed under his gaze. "Whatever I might have been, Harper took away from me. I ain't a smooth-talkin' man. Guess I never rightly learned to say all I feel, but sometimes them that says little feels a sight more." He put one hand on the latch. "As for loyalty, my first loyalty's to Hardy Bishop," he said.

"But how could that be?" Sharon protested.

"He's my father," Rock said quietly, and then he stepped quickly and silently out the door.

"His father!" Pagones stared after him. "Well, I'll be danged!"

"That don't cut any ice with me," Mulholland said. "Nor his talk. I got the place I want, and I aim to keep it. Harper says there ain't any way they can drive us off. He says we've got guns enough to hold our own, and this cañon ain't so easy to attack. I'm glad it's comin' to a showdown. We might as well get it over."

"All I want is to get to work," Collins said stubbornly. "I got a sight of it ahead, so if that Bishop aims to drive me off, I wish he'd come and get it over with."

"All that talk about him usin' us," Satterfield said uneasily. "That didn't make sense!"

"Of course not!" Cap said hotly. "Bannon was against everything we tried to do, right from the start. He just never had no use for Mort Harper, that was all."

"Maybe there is something to what he says," Sharon interposed.

Cap glanced around irritably. "Beggin' your pardon, Sharon. This is man's talk."

"I'm not so sure," she flashed. "We women came across the plains with you! If we fight, my father may die. That makes it important to me, and, if you think I'm going to stand by and let my home be turned into a shambles, you're wrong."

Her father started to speak, but she stepped forward. "Bannon said Harper was using you. Well, maybe he is and maybe he isn't, but there are a few things I'd like you to think about, because I've been thinking about them.

"Did Mort Harper look for this town site? No, he rode right to it, and to me that means he had planned it before. What affair was it of his which trail we took? Yet he persuaded us, and we came down here. Who got us to stay? It was him! I'll admit, I wanted to stay, and most of us did, but I'm wondering if he didn't count on that. And what about those wagons of supplies that turned up just at the right time?"

"Why, they just follered him on from the fort," Mulholland protested.

"Did they?" Sharon asked. "Go up and look at the trail. Mary and I looked at it, and no wagons have come over it since we did. Anyway, would he let those wagons come across that Indian country without more protection than they had? Those wagons were already here, waiting for us. They were back up in a cañon northeast of the trail."

"I don't believe that!" Collins said.

"Go look for yourselves then," Sharon said.

"You sound like you are against us," Cap said. "Whose side are you on, anyway?"

"I'm on the side of the wagon train people, and you know it," she said. "But a lot of this doesn't look too good to me. The first day we were here I rode down in the valley with Mort, and he said something that had me wondering, something about taking it for himself."

"Don't make sense," Cap said stubbornly. "Anyway, womenfolks don't know about things like this."

Sharon was angry. In spite of herself, and knowing her anger only made Cap more stubborn, she said: "You didn't think there were any Indians, either. You took Mort's word for that. If it hadn't been for Bannon, we'd all have been killed."

She turned quickly and went out of the cabin. Swinging into the saddle, she started across toward her own cabin. It was dark, and she could see the light in the saloon and the lights in Collins's blacksmith shop, where his wife and little Davy would be waiting for him to return.

Angry, she paid little attention where she was going until suddenly a horseman loomed in the dark near her. "Howdy!" he said, swinging alongside.

From his voice and bulk she knew him at once as Hy Miller, a big teamster who sometimes served as relief bartender. He had been drinking and his breath was thick.

She tried to push on, but he reached out and grabbed her wrist. "Don't be in no such hurry," he said, leering at her in the dimness. "I want to have a bit of palaver with you."

"Well, I don't want to talk to you!" she said angrily. She tried to jerk her wrist away, but he only tightened his grip. Then he pulled her to him and slid his other arm around her waist. She struggled, and her mare side-stepped, pulling her from the saddle.

Miller dropped her, and then slid from his own horse and grabbed her before she could escape. "I'll learn you a thing or two!" he said hoarsely. "It's about time you settlers were learnin' who's runnin' this shebang!"

What happened next, Sharon scarcely knew. She was suddenly wrenched from Miller's arms. She heard the crack of a blow, and Miller went down into the grass underfoot.

"Run for the house!" It was Bannon's voice. "Quick!"

Miller came up with an oath, and she saw him charge. Bannon smashed his left into the big teamster's mouth and staggered him, but the man leaped in, swinging with both hands. There was no chance for science or skill. In the dimness the two men fought like animals, tooth and nail, yet Bannon kept slamming his right to the bigger man's stomach. The teamster coughed and gasped, and then Rock swung a right to his chin that staggered him, and followed it up with a right and a left. Miller went down, and Bannon stooped and grasped his shirt collar in his left hand.

Holding the man at arm's length in a throttling grip, Bannon smashed him in the face again and again. Then he struck him in the body, and hurled him to the ground.

Sharon, wide-eyed and panting, still stood there. "Get to your house," Bannon snapped. "Tell your father to go armed, always. This is only the beginning."

As she fled, swiftly mounting her horse, somebody said: "Hey, what's goin' on here?"

Behind her, there was a pound of horse's hoofs, and she knew Rock was gone. Swiftly, when she reached the house, she stripped the saddle from the mare and turned her in the corral. Then she went into the house and lighted the lamp. A few minutes later, her father came in. She told him all that had happened.

He stood there, resting his fists on the table. Then he straightened.

"Honey," he said, "I'm afraid I did wrong to stop here. I wish now I'd gone on with Bob Sprague and the others. They'd be 'most to California by now. I'm afraid . . . I'm afraid!"

V

Rock Bannon stopped that night in a line cabin six miles west of Poplar and across the valley. When morning came, he was just saddling up when Bat Chavez rode in. With him were Johnny Stark and Lew Murray. All three were armed.

Bat grinned at him. Then his eyes fell on the skinned knuckles, and he chuckled.

"Looks like you had some action."

"A little," Rock said, and then explained briefly. "You watch yourselves," he said, "and stick together. That outfit's out for trouble."

"All I want's a shot at Zapata," Bat said harshly. "I'll kill him if I get it."

Rock mounted and rode north toward the ranch house. No act of his could avert trouble now. He had hoped to convince the settlers who came with the wagon train that they should break away from Mort Harper.

That would draw the lines plainly—the ranch

against the land-grabbers. That Mulholland was an honest if stupid man, he knew. The others of the train, to a man, were honest, but some of them, such as Purcell and Lamport, were firm adherents of Harper's and believed in him. This belief they combined with a dislike of Rock Bannon.

It had been a hard task to persuade Hardy Bishop to let them stay. The old man was a fire-eater, and he knew what it would mean to let settlers get a toehold in his rich valley. Once in, they would encroach more and more on his best range until he was crowded back to nothing. Only his affection for Rock had convinced him, and the fact that he had gleaned from Rock's talk that among the settlers was a girl.

Rock Bannon knew what the old man was thinking. Lonely, hard-bitten, and tough, Bishop was as affectionate as many big bear-like men are. His heart was as big and warm as himself, and from the day he had taken Rock Bannon in when the boy had been orphaned at six, when Kaw Indians had killed his parents, Bishop had lived as much for Bannon as for his ranch. Now, more than anything, he wanted Rock settled, married, and living on the broad acres of Bishop's Valley.

It had been that as much as anything that had brought him around to Rock's way of thinking when Rock had planned to go east to Council

Bluffs. Secretly he had hoped the boy would come back with a wife; certainly, there were no women around Bishop's Valley but an occasional squaw. He had never seen this girl with the wagon train, but he had gleaned more than a little from Rock's casual comments, and what he heard pleased him.

Hardy Bishop was a big man, weighing nearly 300 pounds now that he was heavy around the middle. Yet in the days of his raw youth he had tipped the beam at no less than 250 pounds. On his hip even the big Dragoon Colts looked insignificant, and he was scarcely less fast than Rock.

Seated deep in a cowhide-covered chair, he looked up when Rock came in, and grinned. He was just filling his pipe. There was a skinned place on Bannon's cheek bone, and his knuckles were raw.

"Trouble, you've had," Bishop said, his deep voice filling the room. "Been over to look at them settlers again? Think they killed Wes?"

"Not the settlers," Rock said. "One of the men with them."

He sat down on the butt of a log and quietly out-lined the whole situation, explaining about Harper, Zapata, and the teamsters.

"They had that stuff cached in the hills," Rock went on. "Red Lunney spotted it some time back. There were about a dozen men holed up back there with a lot of supplies, too many for themselves. He kept an eye on them, but they didn't wander around and made no trouble, so he left them alone.

"Evidently Mort Harper had them planted there. The wagon train, as near as I can figure, he planned to use as a blind in case the government got into this. He could always say they were honest settlers looking for homes, and the government would be inclined to favor them. What he really wants is Bishop's Valley."

"He'll have a time gettin' it," Bishop said grimly. "I'll bank on that. I fought Indians all over these hills, but this here valley I bought fair and square from old War Cloud. We never had no Indian trouble until lately, when the wagon trains started comin' through. Those Mormons, they had the right idea. Treat Indians good, pay for what you get, and no shootin' Indians for the fun of it, like some folks do. Why, Rock, I trapped all over these here mountains. Lived with Indians, trapped with them, hunted with them, slept in their teepees. I never had trouble with them. I was through this country with Wilson Price Hunt's Astorians when I was no more'n sixteen, but a man growed. I was with John Day in this country after that, and he saw more of it than any other man.

"Took me two years to drive these cattle in here. First ever seen in this country! I drove them up from Santa Fé in six or seven of the roughest drives any man ever saw, with Indians doin' most of my drivin' for me. They said I was crazy then, but now my cattle run these hills and they eat this valley grass until their sides are fit to bust. One of these days you'll start drivin' these cattle east. Mark my words, there'll come a day they'll make you rich. And then some whippersnapper like this Harper . . . why . . . !" He rubbed his jaw irritably, and then looked up at Rock. "You see that girl? That Crockett girl?"

"Uhn-huh," Rock admitted. "I did."

"Why not stop this here cayusin' around and bring her home, Son? Time you took a wife. Ain't no sense in a man runnin' loose too long. I did, and then hadn't my wife very long before she died. Fine girl, too."

"Hardy," Rock said suddenly, calling him by his first name as he had since Bishop first took him in hand as a child, "I don't want war with those people. They are askin' for it, and that Mulholland is simple enough to be led by the nose by Harper. Why don't you let me go get Zapata? I'll take him on myself. In fact," he added grimly, "I'd like to! Then we can take some of the boys, get Harper and his teamsters, and start them out of here."

"Separate the sheep from the goats, eh?" Bishop looked at him quizzically. "All right, Son. I've gone along with you this long. You take the boys, you get that Harper out of there, and start him back for Laramie.

"As for Zapata, do what you like. I've seen some men with guns, and you're the fastest thing I ever did see, and the best shot. But don't leave him alive. If I had my way, we'd string every one of 'em to a poplar tree, and right quick."

The old man grinned briefly at Bannon, leaned back, and lighted his pipe. So far as he was concerned, the subject was closed.

Bat Chavez was a man who made his own plans and went his own way. Loyal to the greatest degree, he obeyed Rock Bannon and Hardy Bishop without question. They were his bosses, and he liked and respected them both. However, he had another loyalty, and that was to the memory of Wes Freeman.

He and Wes had ridden together, hunted together, fought Indians together. Wes was younger, and Bat Chavez had always considered himself the other's sponsor, as well as his friend. Now Wes was dead, and to Bat Chavez that opened a feud that could only be settled by blood.

Johnny Stark and Lew Murray were like-minded. Both were young, hardy, and accustomed to live by the gun. They understood men like Zapata. Of the three, perhaps the only one who rated anything like an even break with Zapata was the half-Mexican, half-Irish Chavez. However, no one of them would have hesitated to draw on sight.

They weren't looking for trouble, but they were ready. In that frame of mind they started down the valley to move some of the cattle away from the mouth of Poplar Cañon. No one of them knew what he was riding into, and had they known, no one of them would have turned back. . . .

Mort Harper, seated in his own living quarters in the back of the saloon, was disturbed. Things had not gone as he had planned. Secure in his familiarity with men of Hardy Bishop's type, he had been positive that the arrival of the wagon train and the beginning of their settlement would precipitate trouble. He had counted on a sudden attack by Bishop and perhaps the killing of one or more of the settlers. Nothing more, he knew, would have been required to unite them against the common enemy. Peace-loving they might be, but they were men of courage and men who believed in independence and equal rights for all. Typically American, they wouldn't take any pushing around.

On his knowledge of their character and that of Bishop he had built his plans. Over a year before he had seen Bishop's Valley, and the sight had aroused a lust for possession that he had never known could live within him. Since that day he had lived for but one thing—to possess Bishop's Valley, regardless of cost.

It was beyond the reach of law. Few people in the country had any idea the valley existed or that it had been settled. His first thought was to ride in with a strong band of outlaws recruited from the off scourings of the border towns and take the place by main force, but times, he knew, were changing.

Morton Harper was shrewd enough to understand that the fight might arouse government inquiry. Frémont and Carson knew this country, and it was possible the Army might soon move into it. It would behoove him to have justice on his side.

The wagon trains offered that chance. From the first he had seen what a good chance it was. At the fort he watched them go through, and he saw the weariness of the women and children, the haggard lines of the men's faces. The novelty of the trip was over, and miles upon miles remained before they could reach Oregon. Now, if he could but get some of them into the valley country, he believed he could persuade them, by some method, to stay on. With that end in view, he watched until he saw the wagon train he wanted.

Those who were led by able and positive men he avoided. He talked to a number, but when he encountered Cap Mulholland, he was quick to perceive his opportunity.

In his visit to the camp he noted that Tom Crockett was a mild, tolerant man, friendly, and interested mainly in finding a new home and getting a plow into the ground. Pagones was a strong, able man, but not outspoken, or likely to push himself into a position of leadership.

Pike Purcell and Lamport were honest, able men, but ignorant and alike in their dislike of Rock Bannon. Lamport, who was unmarried and thoroughly undesirable, had fancied himself for an inside track with Sharon Crockett until Bannon joined the train.

As Rock Bannon was constantly with her, first as a wounded man needing care and later as a rider, Lamport grew jealous. Purcell, married to a nagging wife, had looked after Sharon with desire. His own dislike of Bannon stemmed from the same source, but grew even more bitter because Pike sensed Bannon was the better man. Pike hated him for it.

Mort Harper was quick to curry the favor of these two. He talked with them, flattered them in subtle fashion, and bought them drinks. He learned that Purcell was desperately hard up and lent him some money. He gave Lamport a gun he had admired.

The only flaw in the picture had been Rock Bannon, and, in Rock, Harper was quick to recognize a formidable and dangerous antagonist. He also realized he had an excellent weapon in the veiled enmity of Purcell and Lamport.

His plans had gone ahead very well until an attack by Bishop failed to materialize. Despite himself, he was disturbed. Would the old man really let them settle there? He caused a few cattle to be killed for meat and left evidence about. That Rock Bannon had found the remains of the slaughtered cattle and buried them, he could not know. The expected attack failed to come and he sensed a falling away from him on the part of the settlers.

The only way he could hope to get the valley was by precipitating open warfare, killing all of the Bishop forces, and taking possession. Then in due time he could eliminate the settlers themselves and reign supreme, possessor of one of the largest cattle empires in the country.

Pete Zapata was under no orders to kill, but the fact that he had killed Wes Freeman fell in line with Harper's plans. Yet he could sense the disaffection among the settlers. Crockett and Pagones could be a strong force against him if they became stubborn. Something was needed to align them firmly on his side.

That chance came, as he had hoped it would come. With Pete Zapata, Hy Miller, Pike Purcell, Lamport, and Collins, he was riding down into the valley when they saw Bat Chavez and the two Bishop riders approaching. Had Harper continued with his party along the trail on which they had started, the paths of the two groups would not have intersected, but Harper reined in and waited.

Chavez wasn't the man to ride around trouble. In Lew Murray and Johnny Stark he had two companions who had never ridden around anything that even resembled trouble. With guns loosened in holsters they rode on.

"Howdy!" Bat Chavez said. His eyes swung and fastened on Pete Zapata. "Where you ridin'?"

"Who's askin'?" Purcell demanded truculently. "We go where we want."

"Not on this range, you don't! You stick to your valley. This here's Bishop range."

"He own everything?" Miller demanded. "We ride where we please!"

"Looks like you been ridin' where somebody else pleased," Johnny Stark said, grinning. "In fact, that face looks like somebody rid all over you with spikes in his boots."

Miller's face flamed. "There was three of 'em!" he snapped. "You couldn't do it. I think it's time we taught you Bishop riders a lesson, anyways."

"You mean," Chavez demanded insolently, "like that murderin' Zapata killed Wes Freeman . . . in the back?"

Zapata's hand flashed for his gun, and Chavez was scarcely slower. Only the jerk of Zapata's horse's head saved him, as the horse took the bullet right through the head. It leaped straight up into the air, jerking Zapata's gun and spoiling his aim.

There was a sudden flurry of gunshots, and Mort Harper was quick to sense his chance. He drew his six-shooter and calmly shot Collins through the back.

The attack broke as quickly as it had begun. Zapata's horse had leaped and then hit the ground, stone dead. Thrown from the horse, Zapata lost his gun and sprawled in the grass, showing no desire to get up and join the fight or even hunt for his gun.

Outnumbered, and with Murray shot through the leg, the Bishop riders drew off. Purcell had been burned along the cheek, and Miller's horse was killed, so the battle ended after only a few seconds with two horses and one man dead. In the excitement, only Mort Harper had seen the flare of pained astonishment and accusation in Collins's eyes.

The blacksmith's mouth refused to shape words, and he died there in the grass. Harper looked down at him, a faint smile on his face. Collins had been a popular man, quiet and well-liked. This would do what all Harper's other plans had failed to do.

"Collins got it." Pike stood over him, his hard face saddened. "He was a good man." Collins was the only man in the wagon train Pike Purcell had known before the trip began. They had come through the war together.

"Might as well bury him, I guess," Mort said.

Pike looked up. "No, we'll tote him back home. His widow will be wantin' to see him. Reckon it'll go hard with her."

Mort Harper's lips thinned, but there was nothing more he could say without arousing suspicion. Silently the little cavalcade started back. Collins's body was tied to Pike's horse, and Pike walked alongside, trailed by Zapata and Miller.

For two days ominous quiet hung over the town of Poplar. Collins had been buried, and the faces of the settlers as they gathered about to see his body lowered into the grave proved to Harper how right he had been. No longer was there any doubt or hesitation. Now they were in the fight. He had walked back from that grave filled with triumph. Only a few days longer, and then he would begin the war in earnest.

Tom Crockett was a quiet man, but his face was stern and hard as he walked back home beside Sharon.

"Well, we tried to avoid it, but now it's war," he said. "I think the sooner we have some action the better."

Sharon said nothing, but her heart was heavy within her. She no longer thought of Mort Harper. His glamour had faded, and, always now, there was but one man in her thoughts, the tall, shy, hesitant Rock Bannon.

She always marveled that a man so hard, so sure of himself when with men, horses, or guns, could be so quiet and diffident with women. As a matter of fact, Rock Bannon had never seen any woman but an Indian squaw until he was eighteen years old, in Santa Fé.

Rock Bannon had never talked to a woman until he was twenty. In his life until now, and he was twenty-seven, he had probably talked to no more than six or seven women or girls.

With deepening sadness and pain, she realized that the killing of Collins had done all they had hoped to avoid. There would be war now, and, knowing her father as she did, she knew the unrelenting stubbornness in him once he was resolved upon a course.

She had seen him like this before. He always sought to avoid trouble, always saw the best in people, yet when the battle line was laid down, no man would stay there longer than Tom Crockett.

Only one man was silent on the walk back from the grave. Dud Kitchen, weak and pale from his own narrow escape, was out for the first time. He was very tired, and he was glad when he was back in the Pagones' house and could lie down and rest. He was up too soon, he knew that, but Collins had been his friend. Now, lying alone in the gathering darkness and hearing the low mutter of men's voices in the other room, he was sorry he had gone.

He had been over to the Collins house to see his old friend once before he was buried, and he was there when the widow and Satterfield had dressed him in his Sunday-go-to-meeting clothes. He saw something then that filled the whole inside of him with horror. He saw not only that Collins had been shot in the back, but something more than that, and it was that thing that disturbed him.

Dud Kitchen was a friendly, cheerful young man who liked nothing better than to sing and play the mandolin. Yet in his life from Missouri to Texas, he had had more than a little experience with guns. Once, too, he had gone down the river to New Orleans, and he had learned things on that trip.

Among other things, he knew that the Dragoon Colt had the impact of an axe and would blow a hole in a man big enough to run a buffalo through, or so it was phrased on the frontier. The hole in Collins had been small at the point of entry, but it had been wide and ugly at the point of exit.

Opening the door between the living room and the kitchen of the Pagones' house, Pike walked in to look down at Dud. "Better get yourself well, Dud," Pike said. "We'll need all hands for this fuss."

"Was it bad, Pike?" Kitchen asked. His voice was faint, and in the dim light Pike could not see what lay in the younger man's eyes.

"No, I figger it wasn't so bad," Pike said. "Only a few shots fired. It was over so quick I scarce got my gun out. That Bat Chavez, him and Zapata were fastest, but Pete's horse swung around and spoiled his aim for him. Guess it saved his life, though, 'cause Bat's bullet hit the horse right in the head. Between the eyes.

"The horse reared up and throwed Pete, and I jumped my horse away to keep from gettin' in a tangle. Lamport, he scored a shot on one of them other fellers. We seen him jerk and seen the blood on him as they were ridin' off."

Dud Kitchen waited for a long moment, and then he said carefully: "Who killed Collins?"

Purcell seemed to scowl. "Don't rightly know. There was a sight of shootin' goin' on. Might have been any one of them three. Don't you worry about that. We'll get all three of them, so we won't miss gettin' the right one."

"Have they got good guns?" Dud asked. "I'll bet they have!"

"Same as us. Dragoon Colts. One of 'em had an old Walker, though. Big gun, too. Shoots like a rifle."

After Pike Pursell was gone, Dud Kitchen lay alone in the dark room, thinking. His thoughts frightened him, and yet he was himself down from a shot by Zapata, who was on their own side. Collins had been shot in the back.

Whatever he had been shot by, Dud Kitchen was willing to take an oath it had not been by either a Walker or a Dragoon Colt. The hole was much too small, although the chest of the man had been frightfully torn. Sometimes men cut their bullets off flat across the nose to make them kill better. Dud had seen that done. It usually tore a man up pretty bad.

VI

Johnny Stark brought the news of the fight to Rock Bannon. He was with Bishop at the time, and the old man's face hardened.

"Well, there it is, Rock. We can't give them any more time now. They've had their chance, and from now on she'll be open warfare." Bishop looked up at Stark. "Take six men back with you. Have Monty go with the buckboard and bring Lew here to the ranch house where he can have proper care. You tell Red I want to see him, but he'll be in charge when he goes back."

Rock got up and paced the floor. He ran his fingers through his shock of black, curly hair. His face was stern and hard. He knew what this meant. One man had gone down, Johnny said. From his description of the man it would be Collins, one of the good men. That would serve to unite the settlers in a compact lot. Despite all his desires to avoid trouble, they were in for it now, and it would be a case of dog eat dog. What would Sharon think of all this?

Hastily he computed the numbers at the town site. Their numbers were still slightly inferior to those on the Bishop Ranch, but, because of expected Indian trouble and the stock, many of the Bishop hands must remain on the far ranges.

"I'm going out," he said at last. "I'm going down to Poplar. Also, I'm going to have a look in that cañon where Harper's stuff was cached."

"You watch yourself, boy," Bishop said. He heaved himself up in his chair. "You take care! I'm figurin' on you havin' this ranch, and I ain't wantin' to will it to no corpse."

Rock hurried down to the corral and saw Johnny Stark leading out the steel-dust, all saddled and ready.

"I figured you'd be ridin', Rock," he said grimly. He handed the reins to him and started to turn away, but then he stepped back.

"Rock," he said, "somethin' I been goin' to tell somebody. I forgot to mention it back there. Rock, I don't think any of us killed Collins!"

Bannon wheeled and grabbed the cowhand by the arm. His eyes were like steel.

"What do you mean? Give it to me quick!"

"Hey!" Johnny said. "Ease up on that arm!" He grinned. "You got a grip like a bear trap." He rubbed his arm. "Why, I been thinkin' about that ever since. Bat, he was thinkin' only of Zapata. I shot at that Miller, the guy you whupped. I got his horse. Lew, he burned that long, lean mountain man along the cheek, tryin' for a head shot. Actually this here Collins *hombre* was off to our left. None of us shot that way."

"You're sure about that?" Bannon demanded.

His mind was working swiftly. If one thing would arouse anger against Bishop among the settlers, it would be the killing of one of their own number, and particularly one so well liked as Collins had been.

Bannon stared at the rider. "Did you see anybody near him? Who was over at that side?"

"This here Collins *hombre* who got shot, he was in the front rank," Johnny said. "Then there was a heavy-set, sandy sort of guy with a beard and a tall *hombre* with a white hat with a dark coat."

The bearded man would be Lamport. The man in the white hat was Mort Harper.

Rock Bannon swung a leg over the saddle. "Johnny, you tell Red to sit tight," he said. "I'm riding to Poplar."

"Want me along?" Stark asked eagerly. "You better take some help. Those *hombres* are killin' now. They are in a sweat, all of them."

Rock shook his head. "No, I'll go it alone," he said. "Tell Red to wait at the cabin."

Rock wheeled the steel-dust and cut across the

valley. There was still a chance to avoid a battle if he could get to Poplar in time, yet he had a feeling that Harper would not wait. Hostilities had begun, and that was what he had been playing for all the time. Now he had his excuse to wipe out the Bishop forces, and he would be quick to take advantage of it.

Before he was halfway down the valley, he reined in on the slope of a low hill. Miles to the south he could see a group of horsemen cutting across toward the line cabin. Bat Chavez was there alone with the wounded Murray.

Red would be starting soon, but would get there too late to help Bat or Murray. Within a matter of a half hour they would be attacking. From where he was, it would take him all of that time and probably more to reach them. There was no time to go back. Wheeling the steel-dust, he started down the valley, angling away from the group of riders.

In the distance around the peaks towering against the sky, dark clouds were banking. A jagged streak of lightning ripped the horizon to shreds of flame and then vanished, and there was a distant roll of thunder, muttering among the dark and distant ravines like the echoes of a far-away battle.

The gray horse ran through the tall grass, sweeping around groves of aspen and alder, keeping to the low ground. He splashed through a swale, crested a long low hill that cut athwart the valley, and turned at right angles down the draw toward the cover of the far-off trees. The cool wind whipped against his face, and he felt a breath of moist wind as it shifted, feeling for the course of the storm.

The big horse was running smoothly, liking the feel of running as he always did, letting his powerful muscles out and stretching them. Leaning forward to break the wind and let the weight of his body help the running horse, Rock Bannon talked to him, speaking softly to the stallion. He knew the stallion loved his voice, for between horse and man there was that companionship and understanding that come only when they have known many trails together, shared the water of the same creeks, and run over long swells of prairie as they were running now.

Then he heard the distant sound of a rifle, followed by a roll of shots.

"Bat, I hope to heaven you're under cover," he muttered. "I hope they didn't surprise you."

He eased the horse's running now because he might rush upon some of them sooner than he expected. He slid his rifle from the scabbard and raced into the trees. The sound of firing was nearer now. He slowed the horse to a walk, letting him take a blow, his eyes searching the brush. There was still some distance to go, but there was firing, and that meant that Bat was under cover. They had not caught him flat-footed at least.

He swung the horse up into the rocks and slid from the saddle, easing forward to the rim of the shelf overhanging the line cabin. Lying face down among the rocks, he could see puffs of smoke from the brush around the cabin. Waiting until he saw a gleam of light on a rifle, he fired.

Almost instantly a man some distance away leaped up and started to run for a boulder. Swinging his rifle, he snapped a shot at him, and the man went to his knees, and then started to crawl for shelter.

A rifle bellowed down below, and a shot glanced off a rock, kicking splinters into Bannon's face. He eased back and worked down the slope a bit, studying the situation below. One man was wounded, at least.

Suddenly a horseman leaped a horse from behind some trees and, dragging a flaming mass of brush, raced toward the cabin. It was a fool-hardy thing to do, but instantly Bannon saw his purpose. The rifle fire had attracted Bat Chavez to the other side of the cabin. Rock lifted his own rifle and steadied it. A flashing instant of aim, and then he fired.

The horseman threw up his arms and toppled back off the horse, right into the mass of flaming brush. He screamed once, horribly, and then rolled clear, fighting the fire in his garments and dragging himself in the dust. Another man rushed from the brush to aid him, and Rock held his fire.

Suddenly there was a heavy roll of thunder. Looking around, he saw the clouds had come nearer, and now there was a sprinkle of rain. At the same instant he heard the pounding of horses' hoofs. Snapping a quick shot at the brush, he heard a startled yell. Then the attackers broke from the brush and, scrambling to their saddles, charged away across the valley. At that moment, the rain broke with a thundering roar, a veritable cloudburst.

Rushing to the steel-dust, he swung into the saddle. He put the animal around to a steep slide of shale and rode down to the barn near the corral. Johnny rushed up to him.

"You all right?"

"Yeah. How's Bat?"

"Don't know. Red went in. You go ahead. I'll fix your horse up."

Rock sprinted for the house and got in, slamming the door after him. Bat looked around, grinning widely.

"Man, was I glad to hear that rifle of yours," he said. "They had me surrounded. Lew wanted to get into it, but I was afraid his wound would open and start bleedin' again. Well, we drove 'em off."

"You get anybody?"

"Scratched a couple. Maybe got one. You got one that first shot. I seen him fall. That'll be one down and two bad hurt, maybe four. Looks like we come out of that on top."

"I was headed for Poplar and saw them comin'. I was afraid you'd be outside and they'd split up on you."

Chavez spat. "They mighty near did. I'd just been to the spring for water."

Rock stared into the fire. This would mean nothing one way or another. They had been turned back from the first attack, but they would not be convinced. He had killed a man. Who was it? That would matter a great deal, he knew. Certainly, if it was another of the settlers, he would have small chance of selling them on quitting.

Yet he was just as resolved now as before the attack. This thing must be stopped. It was never too late to try. The rain was roaring upon the roof. They would never expect him in a flood like that. They would be inside and expecting everyone else to be there, too. If he circled around and came down the cañon, it would be the best chance. If they were keeping watch at all, it would be from this direction. He would start in a few minutes. They were making coffee now. . . .

Sharon was outside when she saw the rain coming, and she waited for it, liking the cool air. Over the distant mountains across the valley, there were vivid streaks of lightning. It was already storming there, a frightful storm by all appearances.

She was alone and glad of it. Mary had wanted her to come to the Collins house, where several of the women had gathered, but she knew she could not stand to be cooped up now. She was restless, worried. Her father was out there, and, for all his courage and willingness to go, Tom Crockett was no fighting man. He was not like Bannon. Strangely now, she was but little worried about him. He was hard, seemingly impervious to harm.

Even now he might be over there across the valley. He might be killing her father, or her father might be shooting him. Twelve men had ridden away. Eight of them were settlers. Collins was dead and Dud Kitchen still too weak to ride, but the others had gone to a man. Mulholland, Satterfield, Pagones, Lamport, Purcell, Olsen, and Greene. And, of course, her father.

Then the rain came, a scattering of big drops, and then the rolling wall of it. She turned and went inside. There were a few places where the roof was not too tight. She put pans under them and lighted a light, which she put on the table near the window. Her father's leg was still not overly strong, and it worried her to think he was out there in all this.

She caught a glimpse of herself in the mirror, a tall, lovely girl with a great mass of red-gold hair done in two thick braids about her head, her face too pale, her eyes overly large.

She heard them coming before she saw them, and saw a horseman break away from the others and cross the grass, now worn thin from much travel. When the horse was stabled, he came in, stamping his feet and slipping out of his slicker. His gray hat was black with rain, and she took it close to the fire. The coffee was ready, and she poured a cup, and then went for a bowl to get some thick soup for him.

He sat down at the table, sat down suddenly, as if his legs had been cut off, and she noticed with a sudden qualm that he looked old, tired. His eyes lifted to hers and he smiled wanly.

"Guess I'm no fighting man, Sharon," he said. "I just wasn't cut out for it. When that man fell into the flames today, I nearly wilted."

"Who was it?" she asked quickly. "One of our men?"

"No, it was a teamster. One of the bunch that hangs around the saloon. His name was Osburn. We rushed the house, and one of the men inside opened fire. Wounded one of the men, first shot. We had the house surrounded, though, and would have had them in a few minutes. Then someone opened up on us from the cliff.

"It was Bannon, I'm sure of that. He killed Hy Miller. Got him with his first shot, although how he saw him I can't imagine. Then he wounded

Satterfield. Shot him through the leg, about like I was. This Osburn got on a horse, and. . . ." His voice rambled on, and all she could think about was that her father was home, that her father was safe.

After it all, when his voice had died away and he was eating the hot soup, she said: "And Bannon? Was he hurt?"

"No, he wasn't hurt. He never seems to get hurt. He's a hard man, Sharon."

"But a good man, Father!" she said suddenly. "He's a good man. Oh, I wish things were different."

"Don't think it, Sharon," her father said, shaking his head. "He's not for you. He's a wild, ruthless man, a man who lives by the gun. Collins is dead, and by one of this man's friends, and they'll never let up now, nor will we. It's a war to the end."

"But why, Father? Why?" Sharon's voice broke. "Oh, when I think that we might have gone by the other trail! We might have been in Oregon now. Sometimes I believe that everything Bannon ever said about Mort Harper is true. All we've done is to come on here into this trap, and now our oxen are gone, all but the two you use to plow, and we're in debt."

"I know." Crockett stirred restlessly. "But it might have been as bad wherever we went. You must understand that. We may be mistaken in

Mort. He's done what he could, and he's standing by us in this fight."

The fire flickered and hissed with the falling drops of rain in the chimney, and Sharon crossed and knelt beside the fire, liking the warm feel of it on her knees. She sat there, staring into the flames, hearing the unrelenting thunder of the rain, and wondering where Rock Bannon was.

Where would it all end? That boy, Wes Freeman, slain in the hills. Then Collins, and now Miller. Dud Kitchen recovering from a wound. Jim Satterfield down, and the whole affair only beginning and no end in sight. The door opened suddenly and without warning, and she whirled, coming to her feet with her eyes wide.

Disappointment swept over her, and then fear. Pete Zapata was closing the door after him. He was smiling at her, his queer, flat face wet with rain, his narrow rattler's eyes searching the corners of the room.

"Not here?" he whispered hoarsely. "Pretty soon, maybe."

"Who . . . who do you mean?" she gasped.

Her father was sitting up very straight, his eyes on the man. Zapata glanced at him with thinly veiled contempt, and then shrugged.

"Who? That Rock Bannon. A few minutes ago he came down the cañon on his horse. Now he is here somewhere. Who knows? But soon he will come here, and when. . . ." He smiled, showing his yellow teeth between thick lips. His eyes shifted from her to her father. "If one speaks to warn him, I'll kill the other one, you see?"

Fear left her lips stiff, her eyes wide. Slowly she turned back to the fire. Bannon would come here. Zapata was right. She knew he would come here. If Rock had come again to Poplar, he would not leave without seeing her. He might come at any minute. She must think, she must somehow contrive to warn him—somehow!

The steel-dust liked the dim, shallow cave in which Rock stopped him, but he didn't like being left alone. He whimpered a little and made believe to snort with fear as Bannon started to move away, but when Rock spoke, the stallion quieted, resigned to what was to come.

Rock Bannon moved out swiftly, keeping under the trees but working his way closer and closer to the house of Pagones. He didn't know what he was getting into, but Pagones was the most reliable of them all, and the strongest one. If resistance to Harper was to come, it must come from him. Crockett lacked the force of character, even though he might have the will. Besides, Pagones knew that one of Harper's men had shot down Dud Kitchen.

Pagones hadn't chosen his potential son-in-law. Mary had done that for herself, but Pagones couldn't have found anyone he liked better. Dud was energetic, tireless, capable, and full of good humor. George Pagones, in his heart, had never felt sure of Mort Harper. He had listened with one part of his mind to Bannon's protests, even while the smooth words of Harper beguiled him.

Pagones had returned wet and tired. Like Crockett, he had no love of killing. He had seen Osburn tumble into the flames, and he had seen Miller killed. Knowing the trouble Miller had caused and how he had attacked Sharon while drunk, Pagones was not sorry to see him die. If it had to be someone, it might as well have been Miller. Yet seeing any man die is a shock, and he had been close to the man.

Many men are aggressive and willing enough to fight, but when they see death strike suddenly and horribly, their courage oozes away. Pagones had the courage to defend himself, but his heart was not in this fight, and the action of the day had served to make him very thoughtful.

Something was worrying Dud Kitchen. He had been noticing that for several days, yet there had been no chance to talk to him when the women-folk were not around. He felt the need of talking to him now and got up and went into the room. He was there, beside the bed, when a breath of cold air struck him and he heard a startled gasp from his wife.

Gun in hand, he stepped back to the door. Rock

Bannon was closing it after him. He turned now and looked at the gun in Pagones's hand. Bannon smiled grimly.

"Well, you've got the drop on me, Pag. What happens now?"

"What do you want here?" Pagones demanded sternly. "Don't you know if you keep coming back, they'll kill you?"

"Just so it isn't you, Pag," Bannon said. "I always reckoned you a friend."

Pagones holstered his gun. "Come in," he said. "I take it you've come to talk."

Mary and his wife stood facing him, their eyes shining with apprehension. There was a scuffling of feet from the other room, and Dud Kitchen was in the door.

"Howdy," he said. "They'll kill you, Rock. I heard Zapata say he was after you. He said he was going to get you next."

"All right." Rock dropped into a chair, his right-hand holster in his lap, the ivory gun butt near his right hand. His dark blue shirt was open at the neck, his leather jacket unbuttoned. The candle- and firelight flickered on the bright butts of the cartridges in his twin belts.

Dud's face was very pale, but somehow Rock sensed that Dud was glad to see him, and it made him feel better and made the talk come easier. Pagones's cheek bones glistened in the firelight, and his eyes were steady on Bannon's face as he waited for him to begin. It was very still in the room. A drop of water fell into the fire and hissed itself into extinction.

Mary Pagones stooped, her freckles dark against the pallor of her face, and dropped a handful of small sticks on the fire.

"Pag," Bannon began slowly, "I've never wanted this fight. I don't think you have. I don't think Crockett did, either, or Dud here. There's no use me tryin' to talk to Tom. He's a good man and he knows what he wants, but he hasn't force enough to make it stick. He couldn't stand against Harper. There's only one man here can do that, Pagones, and that's you."

"Harper's my friend," Pagones said evenly. "He led us here. This is his fight and ours."

"You don't believe that," Rock said. "Not down inside, you don't. Collins's death brought you into it. That made it your fight and Crockett's fight. The truth is, all you men want is homes. That's what your wife wants, and Mary. That's what Sharon wants, too. That's what Cap wants, and the rest of them.

"What Mort Harper wants is land and power. He intends to have them, no matter who dies or when. I've been here before to try to stop this trouble. I'm here again now.

"One of our men died first, and he was a good boy. He was murdered, Pagones, murdered like no man in the wagon train would kill any man.

110

Purcell didn't like me. Neither did Lamport. Cap was your leader, but he listened too quick to that glib tongue of Harper's."

"We all did," Dud said. "I listened, too. I listened for a while, anyway." Mary moved up behind his chair and put her hand on his shoulder. He looked up quickly, and she smiled.

"Get to the point!" Pagones said. All that Bannon said was true. He knew it as well as Rock. He had listened to Harper, but secretly he had always been afraid that Bannon was right. He had been afraid of this trail. They had no oxen now, and they had no money. They were here, and they could not escape.

Rock leaned a hand on his knee. "Pagones, my boys say they didn't kill Collins."

VII

Dud Kitchen drew in his breath, and Mary looked at him in sudden apprehension.

"What's that you say?" Pagones demanded.

"I repeat. I talked to my boys, and they say they didn't kill Collins. Bat Chavez couldn't see anything, but Zapata, Stark, and Murray weren't even facing toward Collins then. They say they didn't kill him."

"There was a lot of shooting," Pagones said. "Anything might've happened."

"That's right," Bannon agreed. "But my boys

don't think they shot Collins, and that leaves a big question."

"It don't leave no question for me!" Dud flared suddenly. "I saw that wound of Collins's! And he was shot in the back!"

Pagones's face hardened. He stared down at the floor, his jaw muscles working. Was nothing ever simple any more? Was there nothing on which a man could depend? How had he got into this mess, anyway? What should he do?

"Who do you think?" he asked. "You mean Zapata?"

Their eyes were all on Rock Bannon, waiting, tense. "No," he said. "I mean Mort Harper."

"But, man, that's crazy!" Pagones leaped to his feet. "What would be the object? Is there any reason why he would kill a man on his own side?"

"You know the answer to that as well as I," Bannon said. He got up, too. "He wanted you in this fight, and that was the only way he could get you. Purcell and Lamport were fire-eaters. They were in, but they weren't enough. He wanted the rest of you, the good, sober, industrious citizens, the men whose reputations at home were good, the men who would look honest to the military if they ever came West."

"I saw that wound," Kitchen repeated. "Collins was killed with a small gun, a small gun with flat-nose or split-ended bullets."

"Who has such a gun?" Pagones said. "You all know that Harper carries a Dragoon, like the rest of us."

"In sight, he does," Bannon agreed. "Mort Harper may pack another one." He stopped, feet wide apart. "I've got to get out of here, Pag. I've got to get going and fast. There's not much chance of anybody being out tonight, but I can't gamble on that. I've got to get away from here, and this is the last time I'll come. I've tried to tell you about Mort Harper for a long time. You've got your last chance to break away, because I'm telling you flat. If you don't break away, there won't be a building standing on this ground within forty-eight hours."

Pagones's head jerked up. "Is that an ultimatum?"

"You bet it is!" Bannon snapped. "If I'd let Bishop have his head, you'd have all been out of here long ago. Wes would be alive now, and Collins, and Murray wouldn't be packin' that slug in his leg, and Dud would be on his feet. If I'd not kept Bishop off you, he would have faced you with forty armed men and ordered you off before you had a stake down or a foundation laid.

"Those boys of ours are spoilin' for a fight. They hate Harper's innards, and they want Zapata. He's a murderin' outlaw, and they all know it."

"I don't know that I can do anything," Pagones protested. "We have to think of Zapata as it is. Harper's the only thing that keeps him and those teamsters off our places and away from our women, anyway!"

Rock Bannon started for the door. With his hand on the latch, he turned, sliding into his slicker.

"You step aside and there won't be any Zapata or his friends," he declared. "We'll wipe them out so fast they'll only be a memory. We just don't want to kill good people. You can keep your places. We let you come in, and we'll let you stay."

He turned and slipped out the door into the rain. For an instant, he hesitated, letting his eyes grow accustomed to the dark. Rain fell in slanting sheets, striking his face like hail stones and rattling against his oilskin slicker like on a tin roof. Water stood in puddles on the ground, and, when he stepped down, a large drop fell from a tree down the back of his neck.

He hesitated, close against the wet tree trunk, and stared into the night. There was a glow of light from the window of the Crockett place. Somebody was still up. He hesitated, knowing it was dangerous to remain longer, yet longing for a sight of Sharon, for the chance to take her in his arms.

He never had. He had never kissed her, never

held her hand. It was all a matter of their eyes, and yet he felt she understood and, perhaps, responded a little to his feeling.

There were lights from the saloon. They would all be down there now, playing cards, drinking. It was a pity he had none of the boys here. They could go in and wipe them out in one final, desperate battle. Lightning flashed and revealed the stark wet outlines of the buildings, the green of the grass, worn down now, between him and the Crockett cabin.

He stepped out from the tree and started across the open, hearing the far-off thunder muttering among the peaks of the mountains beyond the valley, muttering among the cliffs and boulders like a disgruntled man in his sleep.

He did not fasten his slicker, but held it together with his left hand and kept his right in his pocket, slopping across the wet ground with the rain battering the brim of his hat, beating with angry, skeleton fingers against the slicker.

Under the trees, he hesitated, watching the house. There was no horse around. Suddenly a column of sparks went up from the chimney, as if someone had thrown some sticks on the fire. He started to move, and another cluster of sparks went up. He hesitated. A signal? But who would know he was near?

A third time. Three times was a warning, three smokes, three rifle shots—what could it be? Who could know he was here? It was nonsense, of course, but the sparks made him feel uneasy.

Then, again, three times, once very weakly, sparks mounted from the chimney. Somebody was playing with the fire, tapping with a stick on the burning wood or stirring the fire.

No matter. He was going in. He felt cold, and the warmth of the room would be good again before he began his long ride to the line cabin. A long ride, because it would be foolhardy to go down the cañon toward the valley.

He stepped out from under the tree and walked up to the house. His boots made sucking noises in the mud before the door. Lightning flashed and water glistened on the smooth boards of the door. He should knock, but he stepped up and, keeping to the left of the door, reached across with his left hand and drew the door wide.

A gun blasted, and he saw the sudden dart of fire from the darkness by the fireplace. The bullet smashed into the door, and then he went in with a rush.

He caught a glimpse of Sharon, her eyes wide with fright, scrambling away from the fire. Zapata lunged from the shadows, his face set in a snarl of bared teeth and gleaming eyes. His gun blasted again, and a bullet snatched at Rock's jacket. Bannon thumbed his gun.

Zapata staggered, as though struck by a blow in the stomach. As Rock started for him, he leaped for an inner door. Rock lunged after him, firing again. There was a *crash* as Zapata went through a sack-covered window.

Wheeling, Rock leaped for the door and went out. Zapata's gun barked, and something laid a white-hot iron across his leg. Rock brought his gun up, turned his right side to the crouching man, and fired again, fired as though on a target range.

Zapata coughed, and his pistol dropped into the mud. He clawed with agonized fingers at his other gun, and Rock Bannon could see the front of his shirt darkening with the pounding rain and with blood. Then Bannon fired again, and Zapata went down, clawing at the mud.

A door slammed, and there was a yell. Rock wheeled and saw Sharon in the doorway. "I can't stop," he said. "Talk to Pagones." And even as he spoke, he was running across the worn grass toward the trees.

A rifle barked and then another, then there were intermittent shots. Crying with fear for him, Sharon Crockett stood in the door, staring into the darkness. Lightning flared, and through the slanting rain she caught a brief glimpse of him. A rifle flared, and then he was gone into the trees. A moment later, they heard the pounding of hoofs.

"They'll never catch him on that horse," Tom Crockett said. "He got away!"

Sharon turned, and her father was smiling.

"Yes, Daughter, I'm glad he got away. I'm glad he killed that murderer."

"Oh, Father!" Then his arms were around her, and, as running feet slapped in the mud outside, he pushed the door shut. "He'll get away!" she cried. "He must get away."

The door slammed open, and Mort Harper shoved into the room. Behind him were four men, their faces hard, their guns ready.

"What was he doing here?" Harper demanded. "That man's a killer! He's our enemy. Why should he come here?"

"I don't know why he came," Crockett said coldly. "He never had a chance to say. Zapata had been waiting for him all evening. He seemed to believe he would be here. When Bannon came in, he fired and missed. He won't miss again."

Harper stared at him, his face livid and angry under the glistening dampness of the rain.

"You seem glad!" he cried.

"I am!" Crockett said. "Yes, I'm glad! That Zapata was a killer, and he deserved killing."

"And I'm glad," Sharon said, her chin lifted. "I'm glad Bannon killed him, glad that Bannon got away."

There was an angry mutter from the men behind Harper, but Mort put up a restraining hand. "So? This sounds like rebellion. Well, we'll have none of that in this camp. I've been patient with you people, and especially patient with you, Sharon, but my patience is wearing thin."

"Who cares about your patience?" Anger rose in Sharon's eyes. "Your soft talk and lies won't convince us any longer. We want our oxen back tomorrow. We've had enough of this. We'll get out of here tomorrow if we have to walk."

"Let's teach 'em a lesson, boss," one man said angrily. "To blazes with this palaver!"

"Not now," Harper said. His nostrils were flared with anger, and his face was hard. "Later!"

When the door closed after them, Tom Crockett's face was white. "Well, Sharon," he said quietly, "for better or worse, there it is. Tomorrow we may have to fight. Your mother helped me fight Indians once, long ago. Could you?"

Sharon turned, and suddenly she smiled. "Do you need to ask?"

"No." He smiled back, and she could see a new light in his eyes, almost as if the killing of Zapata and the statement to Harper had made him younger, stronger. "No, I don't," he repeated. "You'd better get some sleep. I'm going to clean my rifle."

Rock Bannon's steel-dust took the trail up the cañon at a rapid clip. They might follow him, Bannon knew, and he needed all the lead he could get. Some of those men had been in these hills for quite some time, yet if he could get away into the wilderness around Day's River, they would never find him.

Shooting it out with six or seven desperate killers was no part of his plan, and he knew the teamsters who had come to Poplar were just that, a band of renegades recruited from the scourings of the wagon trains passing through the fort. After the immediate dash, however, he slowed down to give the steel-dust better footing.

He turned northeast when he came out of Poplar Cañon and rode down into a deep draw that ended in a meadow. The bottom of the draw was roaring with water that had run off the mountains, but as yet it was no more than a foot deep. Far below, he could hear the thunder of Day's River, roaring at full flood now.

The cañon through the narrows would be a ghastly sight with its weight of thundering white water. Always a turmoil, now it would be doubled and tripled by the cloudburst. Rain slanted down, pouring unceasingly on the hills.

The trail by which he had come would be useless on his return. By now the water would be too deep in the narrow cañon up which he had ridden. He must find a new trail, a way to cut back from the primitive wilderness into which he was riding and down through the valley where Freeman had been killed, and then through the mountains.

Briefly he halted the big stallion in the lee of a

jutting shoulder of granite where wind and rain were cast off into the flat of the valley. Knowing his horse would need every ounce of strength, he swung down. His shoulder against the rock, he studied the situation in his mind's eye.

His first desperate flight had taken him northeast into the wild country. Had he headed south he must soon have come out on the plains beyond the entrance to Bishop's Valley, where he would have nothing but the speed of his own horse to assist his escape.

He was needed here, now. Any flight was temporary, so in turning north he had kept himself within striking distance of the enemy. His problem now was to find a way through the rugged mountain barrier, towering thousands of feet above him, into Bishop's Valley, and across the valley to home.

No man knew these mountains well, but Hardy Bishop best of all. Next to him, Rock himself knew them best, but with all his knowledge they presented a weird tangle of ridges, cañons, jagged crests, peaks, and chasms. At the upper end of the valley, the stream roared down a gorge often 3,000 feet deep and with only the thinnest of trails along the cliffs of the narrows.

The isolated valley might have been walled for the express purpose of keeping him out, for as he ran over the possible routes into the valley, one by one he had to reject them. Bailey's Creek would be a thundering torrent now, water roaring eight to ten feet deep in the narrow cañon. Trapper's Gulch would be no better, and the only other two routes would be equally impassable.

Rock stared at the dark bulk of the mountain through the slanting rain. He stared at it, but could see nothing but Stygian darkness. Every branch, every rivulet, and every stream would be a roaring cataract now. If there was a route into the valley now, it must be over the ridge. The very thought made him swallow and turn chill. He knew what those ridges and peaks were in quiet hours. They could be traveled, and he had traveled them, but only when he could see and feel his way along. Now, with lightning crashing, with thunder butting against the cliffs, and with clouds gathered around them, it would be an awful inferno of lightning and granite, a place for no living thing.

Yet, the thought in the back of his mind kept returning. Hardy Bishop was alone, or practically so. He had sent Red to the line cabin nearest Harper with most of the fighting men. Others were in a cabin near the narrows, miles away. Only two men would be at home aside from the cook.

Rock Bannon did not make the mistake of underestimating his enemy. Mort Harper had planned this foray with care. He would not have begun without a careful study of the forces to be arrayed against him. He would know how many men were at the line cabin, and the result of his figuring must certainly be to convince him that the ranch house was unprotected, and Hardy Bishop, the heart, soul, and brain of the Bishop empire, was there.

There was a route over the mountain. Once, by day, Bannon had traveled it. He must skirt a cañon hundreds of feet deep along a path that clung like an eyebrow to the sheer face of the cliff. He must ride across the long swelling slope of the mountain among trees and boulders, and then between two peaks, and angle through the forest down the opposite side.

At best, it was a twelve-mile ride, and might stretch that a bit. Even by day it was dangerous and slow going. And he needed only his own eyes to convince him that lightning was making a playground of the hillside now.

"All right, boy," he said gently to the horse. "You aren't going to like this, but neither am I." He swung into the saddle and moved out into the wind.

As he breasted the shoulder of granite, the wind struck him like a solid wall, and the rain lashed at his garments, plucking at the fastenings of his oilskin. He turned the horse down the cañon that would take them to the cliff face across which he must ride. He preferred not to think of that.

As he drew near, the cañon walls began to close

in upon him, until it became a giant chute down which the water thundered in a mighty Niagara of sound. Great masses of water churned in an enormous maëlstrom below and the steel-dust snorted and shied from its roaring.

Rock spoke to the horse and touched him on the shoulder. Reassured, he felt gingerly for the path and moved out. A spout of water gushing from some crack in the rock struck Rock like a blow, drenching him anew and making the stallion jump. He steadied the horse with a tight rein, and then relaxed and let the horse have his head. He could see absolutely nothing ahead of him.

Thunder and the rolling of gigantic boulders reverberated down the rock-walled cañon, and occasional lightning-lit flares showed him glimpses of a weird nightmare of glistening rock and tumbling white water that caught the flame and hurled it in millions of tiny shafts on down the cañon.

The steel-dust walked steadily, facing the wind but with bowed head, hesitating only occasionally to feel its way around some great rock or sudden, unexpected heap of débris.

The hoarse wind howled down the channel of rock, turning its shouting to a weird scream on corners where the pines feathered down into the passage of the wind. Battered by rain and wind, Rock Bannon bent his head and rode on, beaten, soaked, bedraggled, with no eyes to see, only trusting to the sure-footed mountain horse and its blind instinct.

Once, when the lightning lifted the whole scene into stark relief, he glimpsed a sight that would not leave him if he lived to be 100. For one brief, all-encompassing moment he saw the cañon as he never wanted to see it again.

The stallion had reached a bend and for a moment hesitated to relax its straining, careful muscles. In that instant, the lightning flared.

Before them, the cañon dropped steeply away, like the walls of a gigantic stairway, black, glistening walls slanted by the steel of driving rain, cut by volleys of hail, and accompanied by the roar of the cataract below.

The white water roared 200 feet down, and banked in a *cul-de-sac* in the rock was a piled-up mass of foam, fifteen or twenty feet high, bulging and glistening. At each instant, wind or water ripped some of it away and shot it, churning, down the fury of raging water below. Thunder roared a salvo, and the echoes responded, and a wild cliff-clinging cedar threshed madly in the wind, as if to tear free its roots and blow away to some place of relief from the storm.

Lightning crackled, and thunder drummed against the cliffs, and the scene blacked out suddenly into abysmal darkness. The steel-dust moved on, rounding the point of the rock and starting to climb. Then, as if by a miracle, they were out of the cañon, but turning up a narrow crevice in the rock with water rushing, inches deep, beneath the stallion's hoofs. A misstep here and they would tumble down the crevice and pitch off into the awful blackness above the water. But the stallion was sure-footed, and suddenly they came out on the swell of the mountain slope.

The lightning below was nothing to this. Here darkness was a series of fleeting intervals shot through with thunderbolts, and each jagged streak lighted the night like a blaze from Hades. Gaunt shoulders of the mountain butted against the bulging weight of cloud, and the skeleton fingers of long-dead pines felt stiffly of the wind.

Stunned by the storm, the stallion plodded on, and Rock swayed in the saddle, buffeted and hammered, as they walked across that bare, dead slope among the boulders, pushing relentlessly, tirelessly, against the massive wall of the wind. A flash of lightning, and a tree ahead detonated like a shell, and bits of it flew off into space with the wild complaining of a ricocheted bullet. The stub of the tree smoked, sputtered with flame, and went out, leaving a vague smell of charred wood and brimstone.

A long time later, dawn felt its way over the mountains beyond and behind him, and the darkness turned gray, and then rose and flame climbed the peaks. Rock rode on, sullen, beaten, overburdened with weariness. The high cliffs behind him turned their rust-colored heights to jagged bursts of frozen flame, but he did not notice. Weary, the stallion plodded down the last mile of slope and into the rain-flattened grass of the plain.

The valley was empty. Rock lifted his red-rimmed eyes and stared south. He saw no horsemen, no movement. He had beaten them. He would be home before they came. And once he was home, he could stand beside the big old man who called him son, and they would face the world together, if need be.

Let Harper come. He would learn what fighting meant. These men were not of the same flesh or the same blood, but the response within them was the same, and the fire that shaped the steel of their natures was the same. They were men bred to the Colt. Bred to the law of strength. Men who knew justice, but could fight to defend what was theirs and what they believed.

He was not thinking that. He was thinking nothing. He was only moving. The steel-dust plodded on into the ranch yard, and he fell rather than stepped from the saddle. Springer rushed out to get his horse.

"My stars, man! How'd you get here?"

"Over the mountain," Bannon said, and walked toward the house.

Awed, Springer turned and looked toward the towering, 6,000-foot ridge. "Over the mountain," he said. "Over the mountain!" He stripped the saddle from the big horse and turned it into the corral, and then almost ran to the bunkhouse to tell Turner. "Over the mountain!"

Hardy Bishop looked up from his great chair, and his eyes sharpened. Rock raised a hand, and then walked on through the room, stripping his sodden clothing as he went. When he reached the bed, he pulled off one boot and then rolled over and stretched out, his left spur digging into the blanket.

Bishop followed him to the room and stared down at him grimly, then he walked back and dropped into the chair. Well, he reflected, for that he could be thankful. He had a man for a son.

It was a long time ago that he first came into this valley with old John Day. They had come down through the narrows and looked out over the wide, beautiful length of it, and he had seen what he knew he was looking for. He had seen paradise.

There were men in the West then, men who roamed the streams for beaver or the plains for buffalo. They lived and traded and fought with the Indians, learning their ways and going them one better. They pushed on into new country, country no white man had seen.

There were men like John Coulter, who first looked into the Yellowstone region, old Jim Bridger, who knew the West as few men. There were John Day, Smith, Hoback, Wilson Price Hunt, Kit Carson, and Robert Stuart. Most of them came for fur or game, and later they came for gold, but there were a few even then who looked for homes, and of the first was Hardy Bishop.

He had settled here, buying the land from the Indians and trading with them long before any other white man dwelled in the region. Once a whole year had passed when he saw not even a trapper.

The Kaws were usually his friends, but the Crows were not, and occasionally raiding parties of Blackfeet came down from the north. When they were friendly, he talked or traded, and, when they wanted to fight, he fought. After a while, even the Crows left him alone, learning friendship was more profitable than death, and many had died.

Bad days were coming. From the seat in the great hide-bound chair, Hardy Bishop could see that. The trouble with Indians would be nothing to the trouble with white men, and he was glad that Rock was a man who put peace first, but who handled a gun fast.

He raised his great head, his eyes twinkling. They were keen eyes that could see far and well. Even the Indians respected them. He could, they said, trail a snake across a flat rock, or a duck downstream through rough water. What he saw now was a horseman, riding toward the ranch. One lone horseman, and there was something odd in the way he rode.

It was not a man. It was a woman. A white woman. Hardy Bishop heaved himself ponderously from the chair. It had been almost ten years since he had seen a white woman! He walked slowly to the door, hitching his guns around just in case.

The sun caught her hair and turned it to living flame. His dark eyes kindled. She rode up to the steps, and he saw Springer and Turner in the bunkhouse door, gaping. She swung down from her black mare and walked over to him. She was wearing trousers and a man's shirt. Her throat was bare in the open neck. He smiled. Here was a woman!

VIII

Sharon looked up at Bishop, astonished. Somehow, she had always known he would be big, but not such a monster of a man. Six feet four he stood, in his socks, and weighing 300 pounds. His head was covered with a shock of iron-gray hair, in tight curls. His eyes twinkled, and massive forearms and hands jutted from his sleeves.

"Come in! Come in!" he boomed. "You'll be Sharon Crockett, then. I've heard of you. Heard a sight of you!" He looked around as she hesitated on the steps. "What's the matter? Not afraid of an old man, are you? Come in."

"It isn't that. Only we've come here like this . . . and it was your land, and. . . ."

"Don't explain." He shook his head. "Come in and sit down. You're the first white woman who ever walked into this house. First one ever saw it, I reckon. Rock, he's asleep. Dead to the world."

"He's safe then?" she asked. "I was afraid. I saw them go after him."

"There was trouble?" He looked at her keenly. "What happened?"

She told him about the killing of Pete Zapata and what had happened afterward. "That's why I'm here," she said. "In a way, I'm asking for peace. We didn't know. We were foolish not to have listened to Rock in the beginning, when he told us about Mort. My father and the settlers want peace. I don't know about Pike Purcell and Lamport, but I can speak for the rest of us."

Bishop nodded his head. "Rock told me what he was goin' for. So he killed Zapata? That'll please the boys." He turned his head. "Dave!" he bellowed.

A face covered with a shock of mussed hair and beard shoved into the door.

"Bring us some coffee! And some of that cake! We've got a lady here, by. . . ." He flushed. "Excuse me, ma'am. Reckon my manners need a goin' over. We cuss a sight around here. A sight too much, I reckon. 'Course, I ain't never figured on gettin' into heaven, anyways. I been pretty much of a sinner and not much of a repenter. Reckon they'd have to widen the gate some. I'd be a sight of weight to get into heaven. Most likely, they'd have to put some cribbin' under the cloud I set on, too." He chuckled, looking at her. "So you're the girl what's goin' to marry Rock?"

She jumped and flushed. "Why! Why, I. . . ."

"Don't let it get you down, ma'am. Reckon I'm a blunt old codger. It's true enough, the boy ain't said a word to me about it, but I can see what's in his eyes. I ain't raised the lad for nothin'. When he took off on this rampage, I was hopin' he'd find himself a gal. You like him, ma'am?" He looked at her sharply, his eyes filled with humor. "You goin' to marry him?"

"Why, I don't know," she protested. "I don't know that he wants me."

"Now, listen here. Don't you go givin' me any of that demure, folded-hands palaver. That may go for those young bucks, but not for me. You know as well as I do, if a woman sets her cap for a man, he ain't got a chance. Only if he runs. That's all. Either give up and marry the gal or get clean out of the country and don't leave no address behind. Nor no trail sign, neither.

"You might fool some young sprout with that 'he hasn't asked me' business, but not me. I seen many a young buck Indian give twenty head of ponies for some squaw when he could have had better ones for ten. Just because she wanted him like and caused him to figure the price was cheap.

"No, sir. I'd rather try to get away from a bear trap on each foot and each hand than a woman with her head set on marriage."

Flushed with embarrassment, she ignored what he had said.

"Then . . . then, you'll let us have peace, sir? You won't be fighting us if we draw off from Harper?"

"Of course not, ma'am. I reckon it'd be a right nice thing to have a few folks around once in a while." His eyes flashed. "But no more, you understand. Only this bunch of yours. No more!"

"And we can have our land, then?" she persisted.

"Sure, you can have it. You can have what them other fellers got, too, when they get out. Sure, you can have it. I can't set my hand to paper on it, though, because I never did learn to write. That's true, ma'am. Never learned to write, nor to read. But I can put my name on the side of a house with a six-shooter. I can do that. But them pens. They always figured to be a sight too small for my hands. No, I can't read printin', but I can read sign. I trailed a Blackfoot what stole a horse from me clean to Montana one time. Trailed him six hundred miles, believe me or not. Yes, ma'am,

I come back with the horse and his scalp. Took it right in his own village."

A startled yell rang out, and Springer burst through the door.

"Boss! Boss! Here they come! Oh, quick, man! Here they . . . !"

His voice died in the report of a gun, and Hardy Bishop lunged from his chair to see men charging the porch.

Turner had started from the bunkhouse, but the rush of the horses rode him down. They heard his wild, agonized screams as he went down under the pounding hoofs. Sharon never saw the old man reach for his guns, but suddenly they were spouting flame. She saw a man stagger back from the door clutching at his breast, blood pouring over his hand.

Then a wild figure wearing one boot appeared from the other room, swinging gun belts about his hips. Then Rock Bannon, too, was firing.

A sound came at a rear window, and he turned and fired from the hip. A dark form looming there vanished. The attack broke, and Rock Bannon rushed to the rifle rack and jerked down two Henry rifles. Then he ran back, thrusting one at Bishop.

The old man dropped to his knees beside a window.

"Come up on us fast," he said. "I was talkin' to this gal." Rock's eyes swung to her, and then amazement faded to sudden grimness. With horror, she saw suspicion mount in his eyes.

A wild chorus of yells sounded from outside, and then a volley of shots smashed through the windows. The lamp scattered in a thousand pieces, and from the kitchen they heard a cursing, and then the *crash* of a buffalo gun.

"How many did you see?" Rock demanded.

"Most like a dozen," Bishop said. "We got two or three that first rush."

"A dozen?" He wheeled to the girl. "Did the settlers come? Did they? Are they fighting us now?"

"Can't be that," Bishop said, staring out at the ranch yard, his eyes probing the corral. "No chance of that. This girl come with peace talk."

"And while she was talking, they rode in on us!" Rock raged.

Sharon came up, her eyes wide. "Oh, you can't believe that! You can't! I. . . ."

The *thud* of bullets into the logs of the house drowned her voice, along with the *crashing* of guns. Rock Bannon was slipping from window to window, moving on his feet like an Indian. He had yanked off his other boot now. A shot smashed the water *olla* that hung near the door. Bannon fired, and a man toppled from behind the corner of the corral and sprawled on the hard-packed ground near the body of Turner.

"They're goin' to rush us," Bannon said suddenly. He began loading his Colts. "Get set, Hardy. They are goin' to rush."

"Let 'em come! The sneak-thievin', pelt-robbin', trap-lootin' scum! Let 'em come! More'll come than'll go back!" As the outlaws rushed suddenly, charging in a scattered line, the old man burst through the door, his Colt smoking. A man screamed and grabbed his middle and took three staggering steps, and then sprawled his full length on the ground. Another man went down, and then a gun bellowed and the old man winced, took another step, and then toppled back into the room.

Sharon stared at him in horror, and then ran to him. He looked shocked.

"Hit me! They hit me! Give me my gun, ma'am. I'll kill the scum like the trap-robbin' wolverines they are!"

"*Ssh*, be still," she whispered. She began tearing the shirt away from the massive chest to search for the wound.

Steadily, using now one gun and then the other, Rock Bannon fired. He could sense uncertainty among the attackers. They had shot the old man, but four of their own number were down, and probably others were wounded. They were beginning to lose all desire for battle.

Watching closely, Rock saw a flicker of movement behind a corral trough. He watched, lifted his rifle, and took careful aim, and, when the movement came again, he fired, just under the trough.

A yell rang out, and he saw a man lift up to his full height, and then topple over.

"All right!" Bannon shouted. "Come on and get me! You wanted me! But you'd better come before the boys get in from north camp, or they'll spoil my fun."

They wouldn't believe him, but it might make them doubtful. He heard voices raised in argument. Then there was silence. He reloaded all the guns, his own, Bishop's Henry, and the old man's six-guns. It was mid-afternoon, and the sun was hot. If they waited until night, he was going to have a bad time of it.

There was a chance, however, that they would believe his story or fear that someone from the line cabin might ride far enough this way to hear the shots. If both groups came, they would be caught between two fires and wiped out. An hour passed, and there was no sound.

"Rock." Sharon was standing behind him. "We'd better get him on a bed."

He avoided her eyes, but got up and put down his rifle. It was a struggle, but they lifted Bishop off the floor and put him on his homemade four-poster. While Sharon bent over him, bathing the wound and treating it as best she could, Rock walked back to the windows.

Like a caged panther, he prowled from window

to window. Outside, all was still. Only the bodies of the dead lay on the hard-packed ground of the ranch yard. A dust devil started somewhere on the plain and twisted in the grass of the meadow, and then skipped across the ranch yard, stirring around the body of Turner and blowing in his hair.

Turner was dead. The old man had been with them almost as long as Rock himself. He had been like one of the family. And Bob Springer was gone, blasted from life suddenly and all the young man's enthusiastic plans for a ranch of his own. Well, they would pay. They would pay to the last man.

The steel-dust had come back from the end of the corral near the creek. He seemed curious and approached the body lying near the trough with delicate hoofs, ready to shy. He snuffed at the body, caught the scent of blood, and jerked away, eyes distended and nostrils wide.

There was no one in sight. Apparently the attackers had drawn off. They had anticipated no such defense as this. They had had no idea that Rock Bannon was home, nor had they realized what a fighter the old man could be. They had to learn what the Crows had learned long since.

Rock waited another hour, continuing his slow prowl. Within the house he was comparatively safe, and he knew that to go out before he was sure was to tempt fate. From time to time he went into the bedroom where Bishop lay on the four-poster. He was unconscious or asleep, Sharon sitting beside him.

He avoided her eyes, yet the thought kept returning, filling him with bitterness, that she had ridden here with peace talk and that under cover of her talk Harper's men had made their approach. Knowing Bishop, he knew that unless his attention had been diverted, no rider or group of riders could have reached the ranch without being seen.

Had she planned with Mort Harper to do this thing? Everything he knew about the girl compelled him to believe she would do nothing of the kind, yet the thought persisted; it was almost too much of a coincidence.

After all, what reason had he to believe otherwise? Hadn't she admired Harper? Hadn't Pete Zapata been waiting in her cabin for him? Perhaps she had tried to warn him by throwing sticks on the fire, or it could have been an accident. The fact remained that, while visiting her, he had almost been killed in a trap laid by Zapata, and, while she had been making peace talk with Bishop, the raiding party had struck. It was not her fault they were not dead, both of them.

He knew she came to the door from time to time, and once she started to speak, but then turned away as he avoided her eyes.

Rock was crouching by a window when the

sound of horse's hoofs brought him to his feet. It was Bat Chavez astride a slim, fast buckskin. The horse shied violently at Turner's body, and Bat had a hard time getting him to the door.

Bannon rushed out. "Everything all right at the line cabin?"

"Shucks, man!" Bat exploded. "That's what I was goin' to ask you. What happened here?"

"They hit us. Dave opened up from the kitchen. Hardy and I shot it out up here. Bishop's down, hit pretty bad. They got Springer and Turner, as you can see."

"Saw them cuttin' across the valley for Poplar a few minutes ago. The boys are gettin' restless, Rock. They want to ride over and wind this up."

"No more than I do," Bannon said shortly. "Yes, we're goin'. We'll ride over and wipe that place out."

"Oh, no, you mustn't." Sharon had come into the door behind Rock. "Please, Rock. You mustn't. The settlers don't want to fight any more. It's just Harper's crowd."

"Maybe that's true," Bannon said, "but I've seen no sign of them quittin' yet. There were at least twelve men in this bunch. Did Harper have twelve men of his own? Not that I saw, he didn't. And Zapata's dead. So's Miller. Where would he get twelve men?"

He turned back to Chavez. "Get some food into you, Bat, and then ride back. I'll be down before long, and, when I am, we'll cross that valley. If the settlers get in the way, they'll get what the rest of them got . . . what they gave Turner and Springer here! We've dallied long enough."

Rock Bannon turned and walked back into the house. Sharon stared at him, her face white.

"Then you won't believe me?" she protested. "You'll go over there and kill innocent people?"

"Who killed Springer and Turner?" Rock demanded harshly. "In what way had they offended? I don't know that your settlers are innocent. I tried to tell them what they were going into, and they wouldn't believe me. Well, they came, and, if they get their tails in a crack, they've only themselves to blame.

"I argued with them. I argued with Bishop to give them a break, and now this happens. There were twelve men in that attack on us. At least twelve! Well, some of them died out there, but you and I both know that Harper didn't have twelve men. Perhaps eight, at best. They came in here and killed two of our boys and wounded Bishop. That old man in there has been a father to me. He's been more than most fathers. He's been a guide and a teacher, and all I know I learned from him. He may die, and, if he does, the fault was mine for ever letting this bunch of squatters in here."

The girl clasped her hands in distress. "Please, Rock!" she protested. "You can't do this. Most of your men don't know one from the other. The settlers would be killed whether they fought or not. Their homes will be burned."

"If they don't fight, they won't be hurt," he insisted stubbornly. "Next time that Harper attacks, he might get us all. Anyway, it looks to me like they were plenty willing to ride in on Harper's coattails and get all they could while the getting was easy."

"That's not true," she protested hotly. "They wanted to do the right thing. They thought they were doing the right thing. They believed Harper was honest."

Rock slid into his buckskin coat and picked up his hat. His face was grim and hard. He could not look at Sharon. He knew if their eyes ever met it would tear the heart out of him. Yet he also knew he had waited too long now, that if he had resorted to guns long ago, so many things might not have happened. Springer might be living, and Turner, and Collins, the settler. He started for the door, picking up his rifle from where he had left it.

"Rock," Sharon said, "if you go back, I will, too. The first one of your men who puts a hand on a settler's home, I'll kill with my own rifle."

For the first time he looked at her, and her eyes were flashing with pain and anger. "Go, then!" he said brutally. "But if you're half as smart as I think you are, you'll take your friends and head for the hills. Go! I'll give you a start. Warn Harper, too, if you want. Let him know we're coming. But if you want to save that precious pack of settlers, get them out of Poplar. Take to the hills until this is over . . . but be out of town before my boys ride in."

He walked to the door and went out. She saw him stop by the corral and pick up a rope, and then go to the corral for the steel-dust. Running from the house, she threw herself into the saddle of her own black mare, which had been tied at the corner of the house. Spurring her to top speed, she sprang out on the long ride across the valley.

Rock Bannon did not look up or turn his head, but in his heart and mind the hard hoofs pounded like the pulse in his veins, pounded harder and harder, and then vanished with the dying sound of the running horse.

He saddled the steel-dust, and, as Bat Chavez walked from the house, Rock swung into the saddle. "Dave!" he yelled at the cook. "You watch over Hardy. We won't be long gone."

Abruptly he swung the stallion south. Chavez rode beside him, glancing from time to time at Rock. Finally he burst out. "Bannon, I think that gal's on the level. I sure do!"

"Yes?" Rock did not turn his head. "You let me worry about that."

IX

Pike Purcell was a grim and lonely man. He had been loitering all day around the saloon. Only that morning before riding away to the attack on the Bishop ranch house, in which he and Lamport had taken part, Dud Kitchen had told him about the bullet that killed Collins.

Pike was disturbed. His heart had not been in the fight at the ranch, and he had fired few shots. In fact, he and Lamport had been among the first to turn away from the fight. Purcell was thoroughly disillusioned with Mort Harper. The attack on the ranch had been poorly conceived and carried out even more poorly. Purcell didn't fancy himself as a leader, but he knew he could have done better.

Men had died back there—too many of them. Pike Purcell had a one-track mind, and that one track was busy with cogitation over the story told him by Dud. He could verify the truth of the supposition. Mort Harper had been behind Collins. It worried him, and his loyalty, already shaken by inadequate leadership, found itself on uncertain ground.

On the ride back there had been little talk. The party was sullen and angry. Their attack had failed under the straight shooting of Bishop and Bannon. They were leaving six men behind, six men who were stone dead. Maybe they had killed two, but that didn't compensate for six. Bishop was down, but how badly none of them knew.

Cap Mulholland had ridden in the attack as well. Never strongly inclined toward fighting, he had had no heart in this fight. He had even less now. Suddenly he was realizing with bitterness that he didn't care if he ever saw Mort Harper again.

"They'll be comin' for us now," Cap said.

"Shut up!" Lamport snapped. He was angry and filled with bitterness. He was the only one of the settlers who had thrown in completely with Harper's crowd, and the foolishness of it was now apparent. Defeat and their own doubts were carrying on the rapid disintegration of the Harper forces. "You see what I saw?" he demanded. "That Crockett girl was there. She was the one dragged Bishop's body back. I seen her!"

Harper's head jerked up. "You lie!" he snapped viciously.

Lamport looked across at Harper. "Mort," he said evenly, "don't you tell me I lie."

Harper shrugged. "All right, maybe she was there, but I've got to see it to believe it. How could she have beaten us to it?"

"How did Bannon beat us back?" Lamport demanded furiously. "He was supposed to be lost in the hills."

"He must have come back over the mountain,"

Gettes put in. He was one of the original Harper crowd. "He must have found a way through."

"Bosh!" Harper spat. "Nothing human could have crossed that mountain last night. A man would be insane to try it."

"Well," Pike said grimly, "Bannon got there. I know good and well he never rode none of those cañons last night, so he must've come over the mountain. If any man could, he could."

Harper's eyes were hard. "You seem to think a lot of him," he sneered.

"I hate him," Pike snapped harshly. "I hate every step he takes, but he's all man!"

Mort Harper's face was cruel as he stared at Pike. Purcell had ridden on, unnoticing.

Pike did not return to his cabin after they reached Poplar. Pike Purcell was as just as he was ignorant and opinionated. His one quality was loyalty, that and more than his share of courage. Dud Kitchen's story kept cropping up. Did Harper own a small gun?

Suddenly he remembered. Shortly after they arrived at Poplar he had seen such a gun. It was a .34 Patterson, and Mort Harper had left it lying on his bed.

Harper was gone somewhere. The saloon was empty. Purcell stepped in, glanced around, and then walked back to Harper's quarters. The room was neat, and things were carefully arranged. He crossed to a rough wooden box on the far side of the room and lifted the lid. There were several boxes of .44s, and a smaller box. Opening it, he saw a series of neat rows of .34-caliber cartridges, and across the lead nose of each shell was a deep notch!

He picked up one of the shells and stepped back. His face was gray as he turned toward the door. He was just stepping through when Mort Harper came into the saloon.

Quick suspicion came into Mort's eyes. "What are you doin' in there?" he demanded.

"Huntin' for polecat tracks," Purcell said viciously. "I found 'em!" He tossed the shell on the table. It was the wrong move, for it left his right hand outstretched and far from his gun.

At such a time things happen instantaneously. Mort Harper's hand flashed for his gun, and Purcell was late, far too late. He had his hand on the butt when the bullet struck him. He staggered back, hate blazing in his eyes, and sat down hard. He tugged at his gun, and Harper shot him again.

Staring down at the body of the tall, old mountaineer, Mort Harper saw the end of everything. So this was how things finished? An end to dreams, an end to ambition. He would never own Bishop's Valley now. He would never own the greatest cattle empire in the West, a place where he would be a king on his own range, with nothing to control his actions but his own will.

He had despised Purcell for his foolishness in following him. He had led the settlers like sheep, but now they would survive and he would die. In a matter of hours, perhaps even minutes, Bannon would be coming, and then nothing would be left here but a ruin.

At that moment he heard a pounding of horse's hoofs and looked up to see Sharon go flying past on her black mare.

There was something left. There was Sharon. Rock Bannon wanted her. Sudden resolution flooded him. She was one thing Bannon wouldn't get! Mort Harper ran to his quarters, threw a few things together, and then walked out. Hastily, under cover of the pole barn, he saddled a fresh horse, loaded his gear aboard, swung into the saddle, and started up the cañon toward the Crockett home.

Cap Mulholland watched him go, unaware of what was happening. Dud Kitchen had heard the shots and had returned for his own guns. He watched Harper stop at the Crockett place, unaware of the stuffed saddlebags. When he saw the man swing down, he was not surprised.

Sharon had caught Jim Satterfield in the open and told him they should flee the village at once. At this moment Satterfield was headed for the Pagones' house as fast as he could move. Sharon ran into her house, looking for her father, but as usual he was in the fields. There was not a moment to lose. She ran out and was about to swing into the saddle when Mort Harper dismounted at the front steps. He heard her speak to the horse and stepped around the house.

"Sharon," he said, "you're just in time."

She halted. "What do you mean?" she demanded coolly.

He rushed to her excitedly. "We're leaving! We must get away now. Just you and me! The Bishop crowd will be coming soon, and they'll leave nothing here. We still have time to get away."

"I'm going to get my father now," she said. "Then we'll go to the hills."

"There's no time for that . . . he'll get along. You come with me!" Harper was excited, and he did not see the danger lights in Sharon's eyes.

"Go where?" she inquired.

Mort Harper stared at her impatiently. "Away! Anywhere for the time being. Later we can go on to California together, and. . . ."

"Aren't you taking too much for granted?" She reached for the black mare's bridle. "I'm not going with you, Mort. I'm not going anywhere with you."

It was a real shock. He stared at her, unbelieving and impatient. "Don't be foolish!" he snapped. "There's nothing here for you. You were practically promised to me. If it's marriage you want, don't worry about that. We can go on to California and be married there."

"It is marriage I want, Mort, but not to you. Never to you. For a little while I was as bad as the others, and I believed in you. Then I saw the kind of men you had around you, how you'd deliberately led us here to use us for your own ends. No, Mort. I'm not marrying you and I'm not going away with you." She made no attempt to veil the contempt in her voice. "If you're afraid, you'd better get started. I'm going for my father."

Suddenly he was calm, dangerously calm. "So? It's that Rock Bannon, is it? I never thought you'd take that ignorant cowhand seriously. Or," he sneered, "is it your way of getting Bishop's Valley?"

"Get out!" she said. "Get out now! Dad and Pagones will be here in a moment, and, when I tell them what you've said, they'll kill you."

"Kill me? Those two?" He laughed. Then his face stiffened. "All right, I'll get out, but you're coming with me!"

He moved so swiftly she had no chance to defend herself. He stepped toward her suddenly and she saw his fist start. The shock of the blow was scarcely greater than the shock of the fact that he had struck her. Dimly she realized he had thrown her into the saddle and was lashing her there. She thought she struggled, but she lived those moments only in a half world of consciousness, a half world soon pounded into oblivion by the drum of racing horses. . . .

It was Satterfield who finally got Crockett from the fields. The Bishop riders were already in sight when Tom raced into his house, caught up his rifle, and called for Sharon. She was gone, and he noted that her black mare was gone. She was away, that was the main thing. With Jim, he ran out into the field, where he was joined by Pagones, his wife and daughter, and Dud Kitchen.

The others were coming. It was a flight, and there was no time to prepare or take anything but what lay at hand. Cap Mulholland, his face sullen, went with them, his wife beside him. The Olsens and Greene joined them, and in a compact group they turned away toward the timber along the hillside.

Lamport did not go. He had no idea that Mort Harper was gone. John Kies was in his store, awaiting the uncertain turn of events. Kies had worked with Mort before, and he trusted the younger man's skill and judgment.

It was over. It was finished. Lamport stared cynically at the long buildings of the town. Probably it was just as well, for he would do better in the gold fields. Steady day-to-day work had never appealed to him. Pike Purcell had been an honest but misguided man. Lamport was neither. From the first he had sensed the crooked grain in the timber of Mort Harper, but he didn't care.

Lamport felt that he was self-sufficient. He would stay in as long as the profits looked good, and he would get out when the luck turned against them. He had seen the brilliant conception of theft that had flowered in the brain of Mort Harper. He saw what owning that valley could mean.

It was over now. He had lived and worked with Purcell, but he had no regret for the man. Long ago he had sensed that Harper would kill him someday. Of all the settlers, Lamport was the only one who had read Harper aright, perhaps because they were of the same feeling.

Yet there was a difference. Lamport's hate was a tangible, deadly thing. Harper could hate and he could fight, but Harper was completely involved with himself. He could plot, wait, and strike like a rattler. Lamport had courage with his hate, and that was why he was not running now. He was waiting, waiting in the full knowledge of what he faced.

His hate for Rock Bannon had begun when Bannon rode so much with Sharon. It had persisted, developing from something much deeper than any rivalry over a woman. It developed from the rivalry of two strong men, of two fighting men, each of whom recognizes in the other a worthy and dangerous foe.

Lamport had always understood Harper. Of all those that had surrounded him, Lamport was the only one Mort Harper had feared. Pete Zapata he had always believed he could kill. Lamport was the one man with whom he avoided trouble. He even avoided conversation with him when possible. He knew Lamport was dangerous, and he knew he would face him down if it came to that.

He was a big man, as tall as Rock Bannon, and twenty pounds heavier. When he walked, his head thrust forward somewhat and he stared at the world from pale blue eyes beneath projecting shelves of beetling brows. In his great shoulders there was a massive, slumbering power. Lamport's strength had long since made him contemptuous of other men, and his natural skill with a gun had added to that contempt. He was a man as brutal as his heavy jaw, as fierce as the light in his pale eyes.

Surly and sullen, he made friends with no one. In the biting envy and cantankerousness of Pike Purcell he had found companionship if no more. Lamport was not a loyal man. Purcell's death meant nothing to him. He waited for Rock Bannon now, filled with hatred for the victor in the fight, the man who would win.

Thinking back now, Lamport could see that Rock had always held the winning hand. He had known about Bishop, was a kin to him, had known what awaited here. Also, from the start his assay of Harper's character had been correct.

From the beginning, Lamport had accepted the

partnership with Purcell, rode with the wagon train because it was a way West, and threw in with Harper for profit. In it all, he respected but one man, the man he was now waiting to kill.

When he heard the horses coming, he poured another drink in the deserted bar. Somewhere around, there were three or four more men. The rest had vanished like snow in a desert sun. Hitching his guns into place, he walked to the door and out on the plank porch.

John Kies's white face stared at him from an open window of the store.

"Where's Mort?" Kies said. "That's them coming now."

Lamport chuckled and spat into the dust. He scratched the stubble on his heavy jaw and grinned sardonically at Kies.

"He's around, I reckon, or maybe he blowed out. The rest of 'em have."

Stark fear came into the storekeeper's face. "No! No, they can't have!" he protested. "They'll have an ambush! They'll. . . ."

"You're crazy." Lamport sneered. "This show is busted. You should know that. That's Bannon comin' now, and, when that crowd of his gets through, there won't be one stick on another in this town."

"But the settlers!" Kies wailed. "They'll stop him."

Lamport grinned at him. "The settlers have took

to the hills. They are gone. Me, I'm waitin' to kill Rock Bannon. Then, if I can fight off his boys, I'm goin'."

They came up the street, walking their horses. Rock was in the lead, his rifle across his saddle bows. To his right was Bat Chavez, battle hungry as always. To his left was Red, riding loosely on a paint pony. Behind them, in a mounted skirmishing line, came a dozen hard-bitten Indian-fighting plainsmen, riders for the first big cow spread north of Texas.

A rifle shot rang out suddenly from a cabin in the back of the store, then another. A horse staggered and went down, and Bat Chavez wheeled his horse and with four riders raced toward the cabin. The man who waited there lost his head suddenly and bolted.

A lean blond rider in a Mexican jacket swept down on him, rope twirling. It shot out, and the horse went racing by, and the burly teamster's body was a bounding thing, leaping and tumbling through the cactus after the racing horse. Chavez swung at once, and turned back toward the saloon. The riders fanned out and started going through the town. Where they went, there were gunshots, then smoke.

Rock Bannon saw Lamport standing on the porch. "Don't shoot!" he commanded. He walked the steel-dust within twenty feet. Lamport stood on the edge of the porch, wearing two guns, his dark, dirty red wool shirt open at the neck to display a massive, hairy chest.

"Howdy, Rock!" Lamport said. He spat into the dust. "Come to take your lickin'?"

"To give you yours," Rock said coolly. "How do you want it?"

"Why, I reckon we're both gun handy, Rock," Lamport said, "so I expect it'll be guns. I'd have preferred hand-muckin' you, but that would scarcely give you an even break."

"You reckon not?" Rock slid from the stallion. "Well, Lamport, I always figure to give a man what he wants. If you think you can take me with your hands, shed those guns and get started. You've bought yourself a fight."

Incredulous, Lamport stared at him. "You mean it?" he said, his eyes brightening.

"Stack your duds and grease your skids, coyote," Rock said. "It's knuckle and skull now, and free fighting if you like it."

"Free, he says!" A light of unholy joy gleamed in Lamport's eyes. "Free it is!"

"Watch yourself, boss," Red said, low voiced. "That *hombre* looks like blazin' brimstone on wheels."

"Then we'll take off his wheels and kick the brimstone out," Rock said. He hung his guns over the saddle horn as Bat Chavez rode around the corner.

Lamport faced him in the dust before the

saloon, a huge grizzly of a man with big iron-knuckled hands and a skin that looked like a stretched rawhide.

"Come and get it!" he sneered, and rushed.

As he rushed, he swung a powerful right. Rock Bannon met him halfway and lashed out with his own right. His punch was faster, and it caught the big man flushly, but Lamport took it on the mouth, spat blood, and rushed in, swinging with both fists. Suddenly he caught Bannon and hurled him into the dust with such force that a cloud of dust arose. Rock rolled over like a cat, gasping for breath, and just made it from under Lamport's driving boots as the big man tried to leap on him to stamp his life out.

Rock scrambled to his feet and lunged as he picked his hands out of the dust, butting Lamport in the chest. The big renegade jerked up a stiff thumb, trying for Rock's eye, but Bannon rolled his head away and swung a left to the wind, and then a driving right that ripped Lamport's ear, starting a shower of blood.

Lamport now charged again and caught Bannon with two long swings on the head. His skull roaring with pain and dizziness, Rock braced himself and started to swing in a blind fury, both hands going with every ounce of power he could muster.

Lamport met him, and, spraddle-legged, the two started to slug. Lamport was the bigger, and his punches packed terrific power, but were a trifle slower. It was nip and tuck, dog eat dog, and the two battled until the breath gasped in their lungs and whistled through their teeth. Lamport ducked his battered face and started to walk in, stemming the tide of Bannon's blows by sheer physical power.

Rock shifted his attack with lightning speed. He missed a right, and, following it in with the weight of his body, he slid his arm around Lamport's thick neck. Grabbing the wrist with his left hand, he jerked up his feet and sat down hard, trying to break Lamport's neck.

But the big renegade knew all the tricks, and, as Rock's feet flew up, Lamport hurled his weight forward and to the left, falling with his body half across Bannon. It broke the hold, and they rolled free. Rock came to his feet, and Lamport, cat-like in his speed, lashed out with a wicked kick for his head.

Rock rolled away from it and hurled himself at Lamport's one standing leg in a flying tackle. The big man went down, and, as they scrambled up, Rock hit him with a left and right, splitting his right cheek in a bone-deep gash and pulping his lips.

Lamport was bloody and battered now, yet he kept coming, his breath wheezing. Rock Bannon stabbed a left into his face, set himself, and whipped a right uppercut to the body. Lamport gasped. Bannon circled, and then smashed him in the body with another right, and then another and another. Lamport's jaw was hanging open now, his face battered and bleeding from a dozen cuts and abrasions. Rock walked in, measured him, and then crossed a right to his chin. He followed it up with two thudding, bone-crushing blows. Lamport reeled, tried to steady himself, and then measured his length in the dust.

Rock Bannon weaved on his feet, and then walked to the watering trough and ducked his head into it. He came up spluttering, and then splashed water over his face and body, stripping away the remnants of his torn shirt.

"We got 'em all, boss," Red said. "You want we should go after the settlers?"

"No, and leave their homes alone. Where's Kies?"

"The storekeeper? Inside, I guess."

Rock strapped on his guns and strode up the steps of the store with Red and Chavez at his heels. Kies was waiting behind the counter, his face white.

"Kies," Rock said, "have you got the bills for the goods you sold the settlers?"

"The bills?" Kies's frightened eyes showed doubt and then dismay. "Why, yes."

"Get 'em out."

Fumblingly Kies dug out the bills. Quickly Bannon scanned through them. Then he took a match and set fire to the stack as they lay on the counter.

Kies sprang for them. "What are you doing?" he screamed.

"You're payin' the price of hookin' up with a crooked bunch," Bannon said grimly as Chavez held the angry storekeeper. "You got a horse?"

"Yes, I have a . . . horse, but I. . . ."

"Red," Bannon turned. "Give this man some shells, a rifle, a canteen, and two days' grub, skimpy rations. Then put him on a horse and start him on his way. If he tries to load that rifle or if he doesn't ride right out of the country, hang him."

"But the Indians!" Kies protested. "And my store!"

"You haven't got a store," Bannon told him harshly. "You'll have to look out for the Indians yourself."

"Boss," Chavez touched him on the shoulder, "*hombre* here wants to talk."

Rock Bannon wheeled. Tom Crockett, Pagones, and Dud Kitchen were standing there.

"Bannon," Crockett said, "Harper took my girl. Kitchen saw him tying her to a horse."

Rock's face went white and then stiffened. "I reckon he was the one she wanted," he said. "She had Zapata waitin' for me, and she led that raid to the ranch."

"No, she didn't do that, Rock," Pagones said.

"The raid wasn't even organized when she left. As for Zapata. . . ."

"He forced himself on us," Crockett protested. "And she was tied to the saddle. She didn't want to go with Harper. She was in love with you."

"That's right, Rock," Pagones assured him. "Mary's known that for weeks."

"All right," Rock said. He jerked a shirt from a stack on the counter and began getting into it. "I'll find 'em."

"Who goes along with you?" Bat asked eagerly.

"Nobody," Bannon said. "This is my job."

X

The steel-dust stallion liked the feel of the trail. He always knew when he was going some place that was beyond the place where distance lost itself against the horizon. He knew it now, knew in the sound of Rock Bannon's voice and the easy way he sat in the saddle.

Rock rode through the poplars where the wagon train had spent its last night on the trail, and, as he passed, he glanced down at the ruts, already grown with grass. It seemed such a long time ago, yet it was scarcely more than days since the wagons had waited here. He had observed them from the mountains, looking back for the last time as he rode away from the train.

He turned the stallion up the long, grassy cañon

where Freeman had been killed. The trail Mort Harper had left was plain enough. So far, he had been running; later, he would try to cover it. Yet Bannon was already looking ahead, planning, trying to foresee what plan, if any, could be in the man's mind.

The Day's River region was one of the most rugged in all America. No man knew it well; few knew it even passingly well. Unless a man chose carefully of the trails that offered, he would run into a blind cañon or end in a jump-off or at some blind tangle of boulders.

There were trails through. The Indians had used them. Other Indians, ages before, had left picture writing on the cañon walls, some of them in places almost impossible to reach. No man knew the history of this region.

There were places here with a history stranger than any written—an old weapon washed from the sands of a creek, a strange date on a cañon wall. There was one place miles from here where the date 1642 was carved on a cañon wall among other dates and names, and no man had yet accounted for that date or said who put it there or how he came to be in the country.

From Grass Cañon the trail of the two horses led into a narrow draw with very steep sides over-grown with birch, balsam, and cottonwood. His rifle ready, although anticipating no trouble at this stage, Rock pushed on.

The draw now opened on a vast region of jagged mountain ridges, gorges, cliffs, and mesas. The stallion followed the trail along the edge of a meadow watered by a brawling mountain stream. Some teal flew from the pool of water backed up by a beaver dam, and Rock heard the sharp, warning *slap* of the beaver's tail on the water.

The trail dipped now down a narrow passage between great rock formations that towered heavenward. On one side was an enormous mass of rock like veined marble, and on the other a rock of brightest orange fading to rust red, shot through with streaks of purple.

Boulders scattered the space between the walls, and at times passage became difficult. At one place great slabs of granite had sloughed off from high above and come crashing down upon the rocks below. Far ahead he could see the trail leaving the lowlands and climbing, thread-like, across the precipitous wall of the mountain.

Studying the trail and the speed of the horses he was following, Rock could see that Mort was trying for distance, and fast. Rock knew, too, that unless Harper was far ahead, he would, if watching his back trail, soon know he was followed. From the incredible heights ahead, the whole series of cañons and gorges would be plainly visible except when shoulders of rock or boulders intervened.

The trail up the face of the cliff had been hewn

by Nature from the solid rock itself, cutting across the face of an almost vertical cliff and only emerging at times in bare rock ledges or dipping around some corner of rock into a cool, shadowed gorge.

"He's headin' for Big Track," Rock told himself suddenly. "He sure is. He's headin' for Big Track Hollow."

He knew the place, and certainly, if Harper was following a known or planned route, he could choose no better. Big Track Hollow was a basin over 6,000 feet above sea level where there was a wealth of grass, plenty of water, and sheltering woods.

It would be the best place in this region to hole up for any length of time. Long ago, somebody had built a cabin there, and there were caves in the basin walls. It took its name from gigantic dinosaur tracks that appeared in the rock all along one side.

For Harper the place had the distinct advantage of offering four separate avenues of escape. Each one would take him over a trail widely divergent from the others, so once a follower was committed to one trail, he would have to retrace his steps and start over again to find his quarry. The time consumed would leave him so far behind that it would be impossible to catch up.

Rock Bannon stared thoughtfully at the tracks. It would soon be night, and the two must stop. Yet they had sufficient lead on him to make it difficult to overtake them soon, and at night he could easily get off the trail and lose himself in the spider web of cañons.

Reluctantly he realized he must camp soon. The landscape everywhere now was rock, red rock cliffs towering against the sky, cathedral-shaped buttes, and lofty pinnacles. He rode down the steep trail, dipping into shadowy depths and riding along a cañon that echoed with the stallion's steps. It was like riding down a long hallway carved from solid rock, lonely and empty.

There was no sound but the walking of the horse and the *creak* of the saddle leather. Dwarfed by the lofty walls, he moved as a ghost in a vast, unreal world. Yet he rode warily, for at any point Harper might elect to stop and waylay him.

Now the trail down the long avenue between the walls began to rise, and suddenly he emerged upon a plateau that seemed to hang upon the rim of the world.

Far away and below him stretched miles upon miles of the same broken country, but there were trees and grass in the valleys below, and he turned the horse at right angles and then reined in. Here for a space were gravel and rock. He studied the ground carefully, and then moved on.

The trail was difficult now, and in the fading light he was compelled to slip from the saddle, rifle in hand, and walk along over the ground. They wound around and around, steadily dropping. Then ahead of him he saw a pool and beside it a place where someone had lain to drink.

Sliding to the ground, he stripped the saddle from the stallion and tethered him on a grassy plot. Then he gathered dry sticks for a fire, which he made, keeping it very small and in the shadow of some boulders. When the fire was going, he made coffee and then slipped back from the fire and carefully scouted the surrounding darkness.

Every step of the way was a danger. Mort Harper was on the run now, and he would fight like a cornered rat, where and when and how he could find the means.

Before daylight, Rock rolled out, packed his gear, and saddled the stallion. Yet, when it was light enough to see, there was no trail. The water of the stream offered the best possibility, so he rode into it himself, scanning the narrow banks with attention.

Finally, after being considerably slowed down by the painstaking search, he found where they had left the stream. A short distance farther, after seeing no marks, he found a bruised clump of grass where a horse had stepped and slipped.

He had gone no more than four miles when he found where they had camped. There had been two beds, one back in a corner of rocks away from the other, and cut off from the trail by it.

Mort Harper was taking no chances. Yet when Rock looked around, he glimpsed something under a bush in the damp earth.

Kneeling, he put his head under the bush. Scratched in the earth with a stick were the words BE CAREFUL and then BIG TRACK.

He had been right then. Harper was headed for Big Track. If that was so, they were a good day's ride from there. Bannon thought that over while climbing the next ridge. Then he made a sudden decision. From the ridge, he examined the terrain before him, and then wheeled his horse. As he did so, a shot rang out. Leaping from the horse to a cleft in the rock, he lifted his rifle and waited.

The country on the other side of the ridge was fairly open, but with clumps of brush and boulders. To ride down there after a rifleman, and Harper was an excellent shot, would be suicide. Only his wheeling of the stallion had saved his life at that moment.

Sliding back from the cleft, he retreated down the hillside to the steel-dust. He swung into the saddle, and, keeping the ridge between him and the unseen marksman, he started riding east. He had made his decision, and he was going to gamble on it.

If he continued to follow, as he was following now, he would fall farther and farther behind, compelled to caution by Harper's rifle and the difficulty of following the trail. If Harper reached

Big Track Hollow first, it would be simple for him to take a trail out of there, and then it would be up to Bannon to find which trail.

Rock Bannon had never heard of a cut-off to Big Track, but he knew where he was and he knew where Big Track was. Ahead of him a draw opened and he raced the steel-dust into it and started along it, slowing the horse to a canter. Ahead of him and on the skyline, a sharp pinnacle pointed at the sky. That was his landmark.

The country grew rougher, but he shifted from draw to draw, cut across a flat, barren plateau of scattered rocks and rabbit grass, and traversed a lava flow, black and ugly, to skirt a towering rust-red cliff. A notch in the cliff ahead seemed to indicate a point of entry, so he guided the stallion among the boulders. A lizard darted from under the stallion's hoofs, and overhead a buzzard wheeled in wide, lonely circles.

The sun was blazing hot now, and the rocks caught and multiplied the heat. He skirted the gray, dirty mud shore of a small alkaline lake and rode into a narrow cleft in the mountain.

At one point it was so narrow that for thirty yards he had to pull one foot from the stirrup and drag the stirrup up into the saddle. Then the cleft opened into a spacious green valley, its sides lined with a thick growth of quaking aspen. There was water here, and he stopped to give the stallion a brief rest and to drink.

They had been moving at a rapid clip for the distance and the heat. Yet the horse looked good. Again he checked his guns. It was nip and tuck now. If he were to make Big Track before they reached it, or by the same time, he must hurry. If he failed, then there was not one chance in a dozen that he would ever see Sharon again.

Now every movement, every thought, and every inflection of her voice returned to him, filling him with desperation. She was his. He knew it in every fiber of his being. She was his and had always been his, not only, he understood now, in his own heart, but in hers. He had always known what Mort Harper was. He should never have doubted the girl. It was amazing to him now that he had doubted her even for an instant.

So on he went, although the sun blazed down on the flaming rocks in a torment and the earth turned to hot brass beneath the stallion's hoofs. The mountains grew rougher. There was more and more lava, and then, when it seemed it could get no worse, he rode out upon a glaring white alkali desert that lasted for eight miles at midday, stifling dust and blazing sun.

Rock Bannon seemed to have been going for hours now, yet it was only because of his early start. It was past one in the afternoon, and he had been riding, with but one break, since four in the morning.

On the far side of the desert, there was a spring

of water that tasted like rotten eggs—mineral water. He drank a little, rubbed the horse down with a handful of rabbit grass, and let him graze briefly. Then he mounted again, and went on, climbing into the hills.

Big Track was nearer. Somewhere not far from the great sky-stabbing pinnacle he had seen. Sweat streamed down his face and down his body under the new shirt. He squinted his eyes against the sun and the smart of the sweat. He had to skirt a towering peak to get to the vicinity of Big Track.

He was riding now with all thought lost, only his goal in mind, and a burning, driving lust to come face to face with Mort Harper. Somewhere ahead he would be waiting; somewhere ahead they would meet.

The sun brought something like delirium, and he thought again of the long days of riding over the plains, of Sharon's low voice and her cool hands as he wrestled with pain and fever, recovering from the wounds of a lone battle against Indians. He seemed to feel again the rocking roll of the wagon over the rutted, dusty trail, tramped by the thousands heading for the new lands in the West.

Why had he waited so long to speak? Why hadn't he been able to find words to tell the girl he loved her? Words had always left him powerless; to act was easy, but somehow to shape into words the things he felt was beyond him, and women put so much emphasis on words, on the saying of things, and the way they were said.

He swung down from the saddle after a long time and walked on, knowing even the great stallion's strength was not without limit. The wild, strange country through which he was going now was covered with blasted boulders, the rough, slag-like lava, and scattered pines, dwarfish and wind-bedraggled, whipped into agonized shapes by the awful contortions of the wind.

Then he saw the stark pinnacle almost ahead, and he saw, beyond it, the green of Big Track. He climbed back into the saddle again, and mopped the sweat from his face. The big horse walked wearily now, but the goal was reached. Rock Bannon loosened the guns in their holsters, and, grim-faced, he turned down a natural trail that no man had ridden before him, and into the green lush splendor of Big Track Hollow.

The smell of the grass was rich and almost unbelievable, and he heard a bird singing and the sudden *whir* of wings as some game bird took off in sudden flight. Water sounded, and the gray stallion quickened his pace. He skirted a wide-boled aspen and rode through a grass scattered with purple and pink asters, white sego lilies, and red baneberry. Then he saw the water and rode rapidly toward it.

He dropped from the saddle, taking a quick

look around. No human sound disturbed the calm, utter serenity of Big Track. He dropped to his chest on the ground and drank, and beside him, the steel-dust drank and drank deeply.

Suddenly the stallion's head came up sharply. Warned, Rock felt his every muscle tense. Then he forced himself to relax. The horse was looking at something, and the calling of birds was stilled. He got slowly to his feet, striving to avoid any sudden movement, knowing in every muscle and fiber of his being that he was being watched. He turned slowly, striving for a casual, careless manner.

Mort Harper was standing a short distance away, a pistol in his hand. He was thinner, wolfish now, his face darkened by sun and wind, his eyes hard and cruel. Backed in a corner, all the latent evil of the man had come to the fore. Quick fear touched Rock.

"Howdy," he said calmly. "I see you're not takin' any chances, Mort. Got that gun right where it'll do the most good."

Harper smiled, and with his teeth bared he looked even more vulpine, even more cruel. "We both know what it means to get the drop," Harper said. "We both know it means you're a dead man."

"I ain't so sure," Bannon said, shrugging. "I've heard of men who beat it. Maybe I'm one of the lucky ones."

"You don't beat this one," Mort said grimly. "I've come to kill you, man." Suddenly his eyes darkened with fury. "I'd like to know how in blazes you got here!" he snapped.

"Figured you'd head for this place if you knew the country at all," Bannon replied with a shrug. "So I cut across country."

"There's no other trail," Harper said. "It can't be done."

Rock Bannon stared at him coldly. "Where I want to go, there's always a trail," Bannon said. "I make my trails, Mort Harper, I don't try to follow and steal the work of other men."

Harper laughed. "That doesn't bother me, Rock. I've still got the edge. Maybe I lost on that steal, but I've got your woman. I've got her and I'll keep her! Oh, she's yours, all right . . . I know that now. She's yours, and a hellcat with it, but it'll be fun breaking her, and before I take her out of these hills she'll be broken or dead.

"I've got her, and she's fixed so, if anything happens to me, you'll never find her and she'll die there alone. It'll serve both of you right. Only I'm not going to die . . . you are."

"All rat," Rock said coldly. "A rat, all the way through. I don't imagine you ever had a square, decent thought in your life. Always out to get something cheap, to beat somebody, to steal somebody else's work and fancying yourself a smart boy because of it." Rock Bannon smiled suddenly. "All right, you're going to kill me. Mind if I smoke first?"

"Sure!" Mort sneered. "You can smoke, but keep your hands high, or you'll die quick. Go ahead, have your smoke. I like standing here watching you. I like remembering that you're Rock Bannon and I'm Mort Harper and this is the last hand of the game and I'm holding all winning cards. I've got the girl and I've got the drop."

Carefully Rock dug papers and tobacco from his breast pocket. Keeping his hands high and away from his guns, he rolled a cigarette.

"Like thinking about it, don't you, Harper? Killing me quick would have spoiled that. If you'd shot me while I was on the ground, it wouldn't have been good. I'd never have known what hit me. Now I do know. Tastes good, doesn't it, Mort?"

He dug for his matches and got them out. He struck one, and it flared up with a big burst. Rock smiled, and, holding the match in his fingers, the cigarette between his lips, he grinned at Mort.

"Yes," he said, "it tastes good, doesn't it? And you've got the girl somewhere? Got her hid where I can't find her? Why, Mort, I'll have no trouble. I can read your mind. I can trail you any-where. I could trail a buzzard flying over a snow field, Mort, so trailing you would be. . . ."

The match burned down to his fingers and he gestured with it, then, as the flame touched his fingers, he let out a startled yelp and dropped the match. Jerking his hand from the pain—the hand swept down and up, blasting fire!

Mort Harper, distracted by the gesture and the sudden yelp of pain, was just too late. The two guns boomed together, but Mort twisted with sudden shock, and he took a full step back, his face stricken.

Rock Bannon stepped carefully to one side for a better frontal target, and they both fired again. He felt something slug him, and a leg buckled, but he fired again, and then again. He shifted guns and fired a fifth shot. Harper was on his knees, his face white and twisted. Rock walked up to him and kicked the smoking gun from his hand.

"Where is she?" he demanded. "Tell me!"

Mort's hate-filled face twisted. "Go to the devil!" he gasped hoarsely. "You go . . . plumb to the devil!" He coughed, spitting blood. "Go to the devil!" he said again. Suddenly his mouth opened wide and he seemed to gasp wildly for breath that he couldn't get. Then he fell forward on his face, his fingers digging into the grass, as blood stained the mossy earth beneath him.

Rock walked back to the horse, and stood there, gripping the saddle horn. He felt weak and sick, yet he didn't believe he had been hit hard. There was a dampness on his side, but, when he pulled off the new shirt, he saw that only the skin was cut in a shallow groove along his side above the hip bone.

Digging stuff from his saddlebags, he patched the wound as best he could. It was only then he thought of his leg.

There was nothing wrong with it, and then he saw the wrenched spur. The bullet had struck his spur, twisting and jerking his leg but doing no harm.

Carefully he reloaded his gun. Then he called loudly. There was no response. He called again, and there was no answering sound. Slowly Rock began to circle, studying the ground. Harper had moved carefully through the grass and had left little trail. Rock returned for his horse, and, mounting, he began to ride in slow circles.

Somewhere Mort would have his horses, and the girl would not be far from them. From time to time he called. Two slow hours passed. At times, he swung down and walked, leading the stallion. He worked his way through every grove, examined every boulder patch and clump of brush.

Bees *hummed* in the still, warm air. He walked on, his side smarting viciously, his feet heavy with walking in the high-heeled boots. Suddenly, sharply the stallion's head came up and he whinnied. Almost instantly, there was an answering call. Then Rock Bannon saw a horse, and, swinging into the saddle, he loped across a narrow glade toward the boulders.

The horse was there, and almost at once he saw Sharon. She was tied to the top of a boulder, out of sight from below except for a toe of her boot. He scrambled up and released her, and then unfastened the handkerchief with which she had been gagged.

"Oh, Rock!" Her arms went about him, and for a long moment they sat there, and he held her close.

After a long time she looked up. "When I heard your horse, I tried so hard to cry out that I almost strangled. Then, when my mare whinnied, I knew you'd find us."

She came to with a start as he helped her down. "Rock! Where's Mort? He meant to kill you."

"He was born to fail," Rock said simply. "He was just a man who had big plans, but couldn't win out with anything. At the wrong time he was too filled with hate to even accomplish a satisfactory killin'."

Briefly, as she bathed her face and hands, he told her of what had happened at Poplar. "Your folks will all be back in their homes by now," he said. "You know, in some ways, Lamport was one of the best of the lot. He was a fighter . . . a regular bull. I hit him once with everything I had, every bit of strength an' power and drive in me, and he only grunted."

They sat there in the grass, liking the shade of the white-trunked aspens.

"Dud and Mary are getting married, Rock," Sharon said suddenly.

He reddened slowly under his tan and tugged at a handful of grass. "Reckon," he said slowly, "that'll be two of us."

Sharon laughed gaily and turned. "Why, Rock, are you asking me to marry you?"

"Nope," he said, grinning broadly. "I'm tellin' you. This here's one marriage that's goin' to start off right."

The steel-dust stamped his hoofs restlessly. Things were being altogether too quiet. He wasn't used to it.

The Sixth Shotgun

They were hanging Leo Carver on Tuesday after-noon, and the loafers were watching the gallows go up. This was the first official hanging in the history of Cañon Gap, and the first gallows ever built in the territory. But then, the citizens at the Gap were always the kind to go in for style.

The boys from the ranches were coming in, and the hard-booted men from the mines, and the nine saloons were closing up, but only for the hour of the hanging. On the Street behind the Palace where the cottonwoods lined the creek, Fat Marie had given three hours off to the girls—one for the hanging and one for mourning and the third for drinking their tears away.

For Leo had been a spending man who would be missed along the street, and Leo had been a singing man with a voice as clear as a mountain echo and fresh as a long wind through the sage. And Leo was a handsome man, with a gun too quick to his hand. So they were hanging Leo Carver on the gallows in Cañon Gap, and the folks were coming in from the forks of every creek.

From behind the barred window Leo watched them working. "Build it high!!" he yelled at them. "And build it strong, for you're hanging the best man in Cañon Gap when tomorrow comes!"

Old Pap, who had prospected in the Broken Hills before the first foundation was laid at the Gap, took his pipe from his mouth and spat into the dust. "He's right at that," he said, "and no lie. If the 'Paches were coming over that hill right now, it's Leo Carver I'd rather have beside me than any man Jack in this town."

Editor Chafee nodded his head. "Nobody will deny that he's a fighting man," he agreed. "Leo was all right until civilization caught up with him."

And there it was said, a fit epitaph for him, if epitaph he'd have, and in their hearts not a man who heard it but agreed that what Chafee said was right.

"There'll be some," Old Pap added, "who'll feel a sigh of relief when they spring that trap. When Leo's neck is stretched and the sawbones says the dead word over him, many a man will stop sweating, you can bet on that."

"Better be careful what you say." Jase Ford shifted uneasily. "It ain't healthy to be hintin'."

"Not since they put Leo away, it ain't," Old Pap agreed, "but truth's a luxury the old can afford. There's nothing they can take from me but my life, and that's no use to me. And to do that they'd have to shoot me down from behind, and that's the sort of thing they'd do unless they could hang me legal, like Leo Carver's to be hung."

Nobody said anything, but Chafee looked

gloomy as he stared at the gallows. There was no living doubt that Leo Carver was an outlaw. No doubt that he had rustled a few head here and there, no doubt that he had offended the nice people of the town by carousing at the Palace and down the Street of the cottonwoods. There was no doubt, either, that he'd stuck up the stage that night on the Rousensock—but from there on there was doubt aplenty.

Mitch Williams was dead, buried out there on boot hill with the others gone before him, Mitch Williams, the shotgun messenger who never lost a payload until that night on the Rousensock, the night that Leo Carver stuck up the stage. It was a strange story no matter how you looked at it, but Leo was a strange man, a strange man of dark moods and happy ones, but a man with a queer streak of gallantry in him, and something of a manner all his own.

Mitch had been up on the box that night when Leo Carver stepped from the brush. Oh, he was wearing a mask, all right, wearing a mask that covered his face. But who did not know it was Leo?

He stepped from the brush with a brace of six guns in his hands and said: "Hold those horses, Pete! You can. . . ." He broke off sharp there, for he saw Mitch.

Now Mitch Williams was a hand. He had that shotgun over his knees but the muzzle was away from Leo. Mitch could never have swung that shotgun around under Leo's gun, and he knew it. So did Doc Spender, who was stage driver. Leo Carver had that stage dead to rights and he had Mitch Williams helpless.

"Sorry, Mitch!" He said it loud and clear, so they all heard him. "I thought this was your night off. I'd never rob a stage you were on, and I'd never shoot you or force you to shoot me." He swung his horse. "So long!" And he was gone.

That was Leo for you. That was why they liked him along the Gila, and why as far away as the Nueces they told stories about him. But what happened after that was different.

The stage went on south. It went over the range through Six-Shooter Gap and there was another hold-up. There was a sudden blast of fire from the rocks and Mitch Williams toppled dead from the box, and then another blast—it was a shotgun—and Doc took a header into the brush and coughed out his life there in the mesquite.

Inside, they were sitting still and frightened. They heard somebody crawl up to the box and throw down the strongbox. They heard it hit, and then they heard somebody riding off. One horse, one rider.

The next morning they arrested Leo.

He was washing up at the time, and they'd waited for just that. He had his guns off and they took him without a fight. Not that he tried to make one. He didn't. He just looked surprised.

"Aw, fellers" he protested, "I never done nothing! What's the matter?"

"You call that nothing? You robbed the stage last night."

"Oh, that?" He just grinned. "Put down those guns, boys, I'll come along. Sure, you know by this time I didn't rob it. I just stuck it up for a lark, and, when I seen Mitch, I knowed it was no lark. That *hombre* would have sat still while I robbed it and drilled me when I left. He was a trusty man, that one."

"You said *was*, so I guess you know you killed him."

Leo's face changed then. "Killed who? Say, what is this?"

And then they told him, and his face turned gray and sick. He looked around at their faces and none of them was friendly. Mitch had been a family man, and so had Doc. Both of them well liked.

"I didn't do it," Leo said, "that was somebody else. I left 'em be."

"Until you could get a shotgun!" That was Mort Lewand, who shipped the money for the bank. "Like you said, Mitch would shoot. You knew that, and he had the gun on you, so you backed out. Then you came back later with a shotgun and shot him from ambush."

"That's not true." Leo was dead serious. "And he didn't have me covered. Mitch had that shotgun pointed the other way. I had the drop, and, if I'd been planning to kill him, I'd've shot him then."

Oh, they had a trial! Judge come over from Tucson to hold court. They had a trial and a big one. Folks came from all over, and they made a big thing of it. Not that there was much anybody could say for Leo.

Funny thing, that is. Most of us, right down inside, we knew the kind of man Leo Carver was, but most of what we knew wasn't evidence. Ever stop to think how hard it is to know a man isn't a murderer and yet know that your feeling he isn't ain't evidence?

They made it sound bad. Leo admitted he had killed seven men. Fair, stand-up fights, but still the men were dead by his gun. He admitted to rustling a few cows. Leo could have denied it, and maybe they couldn't have proved it in a court of law, but Leo wasn't used to the ways of courts and he knew darned well we all knew he had rustled them cows. Fact is, I don't think he ever thought of denying it.

He had stuck up a few stages, too. He admitted to that. But he denied killing Mitch Williams and he denied getting that strongbox. $20,000 it held. $20,000 in gold.

Everybody thought Webb Pascal would defend

Leo, but he refused, said he wanted no part of it. Webb had played poker with Leo and they'd been friends, but Webb refused him. Leo took that mighty hard. Lane Moore refused him, too, so all he could do was get that drunken old Bob Keyes to handle his case.

Convicted? You know he was. That's why they are hanging him. Keyes couldn't defend a sick cat from a bath. When they got through asking questions of Leo Carver, he was a dead Injun, believe me.

He had tried to stick up the stage once. He was a known killer. He had rustled cows. He traveled with a bad element in Cañon Gap. He had no alibi. All he had, really, was his own statement that he hadn't done it—that and the thing we knew in our hearts that isn't admissible as evidence.

"Shame for you fellers to go to all that trouble," Leo said now. That was Leo. There was no stopping him. "Why don't we just call the whole thing off?"

Mort Lewand stood in his doorway, chewing his cigar and watching that gallows go up, and it made me sore, seeing it like that, for if ever a man had hated another, Mort Lewand had hated Leo.

Why? No particular reason. Personality, I'd guess you'd say. It was simply that they never tied up right. Mort, he pinched every dime he made. Leo spent his or gave it away. Mort went to church regular and was a rising young businessman. He was the town's banker and he owned the express company, and he had just bought one of the finest ranches in the country.

Leo never kept any money. He was a cattleman when he wanted to be, and as steady a hand as you'd find when he worked. One time he saved the CY herd almost single-handed when they got caught in a norther. He took on the job of ramrodding the Widow Ferguson's ranch after her old man was killed, and he tinkered and slaved and worked, doing the job of a half dozen hands until she had something she could sell for money enough to keep her.

Leo never kept a dime. He ate it up, drank it up, gave it away. The rest of the time he sat under the cottonwoods and played that old guitar of his and sang songs, old songs like my mother used to sing, old Scotch, Irish, and English songs, and some he made up as he went along.

He got into fights, too. He whipped the three Taylor boys single-handed one day. I remember that most particular because I was there. That was the day he got the blood on Ruth Hadlin's handkerchief.

The Hadlins were the town's society. Every town's got some society, and Judge Emory Hadlin was the big man of this town. He had money, all right, but he had name, too. Even in the West some folks set store by a name, and, whenever the judge said his name, it was like ringing a big gong. It had a sound. Maybe that was all some names had, but this one had more. Honor, reputation, square dealing, and no breath of scandal ever to touch any of them. Fine folks, and everybody knew it. Mort Lewand, he set his cap for Ruth but she never seemed to see him. That made him some angered, but tickled most of us. Mort figured he was mighty high-toned and it pleased us when Ruth turned him down flat.

Don't get the idea she was uppity. There was the time Old Pap came down with pneumonia. He was in a bad way and nobody to look after him but little Mary Ryan from down the street. Mary cared for him night and day almost until Ruth Hadlin heard about it.

She came down there and knocked on the door, and, when Mary opened it and saw Ruth, she turned seven colors. There she was, a mighty pert little girl, but she was from the Street, and here was Ruth Hadlin—well, they don't come any further apart.

Mary flushed and stammered and she didn't know what to say, but Ruth came right on in. She turned around and said: "How is he, Mary? I didn't even know he was ill."

Ill, that's what she said. We folks mostly said sick, instead of ill. Mary was shocked, too, never guessing that anybody like Ruth would know her name, or speak to her like that.

"He's bad off, Miss Ruth, but you shouldn't be here. This is the . . . it's the Street."

Ruth just looked at her and smiled, and she said: "I know it is, Mary, but Old Pap is ill and he can be just as ill on the Street as anywhere. I just heard about it, Mary, and how you've been caring for him. Now you go get some rest. I'll stay with him."

Mary hesitated, looking at that beautiful blue gown Ruth was wearing and at the shabby little cabin. "There ain't . . . isn't much to do," she protested.

"I know." Ruth was already bending over Old Pap and she just looked around and said: "By the way, Mary. Tell somebody to go tell Doctor Luther to come down here."

"We tried, Miss Ruth. He won't come. He said all his business was the other side of town, that he'd no time for down here."

She straightened up then. "You go tell him that Ruth Hadlin wants him down here!" Her voice was crisp. "He'll come."

He did, too.

But that was Miss Ruth. She was a thoroughbred, that one. And that was where she first met Leo Carver.

It was the third day she had been sharing and nursing with Mary Ryan, and she was in the shack alone when she heard that horse. He was coming hell-bent for election and she heard him pull up in front of the house, and then the door opened and in stepped Leo Carver.

She knew him right off. How could you miss him? He was two inches over six feet with shoulders wider than two of most men, and he was dark and clean-built with a fine line to his jaw, and he had cold gray eyes. He wore two guns and his range clothes, and right then he had a two-day growth of beard. It must have startled her. Here was a man known as an outlaw, a rustler, and a killer, and she was there alone with a sick man.

He burst in that door, and then drew up short, looking from Ruth to the sick old man. If he was surprised to find her there, he didn't let on. He just swept off his hat and asked: "How is he, Miss Hadlin?"

For some reason she was excited. Frightened, maybe. "He's better," she said. "Miss Ryan and I have been nursing him."

Mary had come into the room behind him, and now she stepped around quickly. "He's a lot better, Leo," she said.

"Maybe I can help nurse him, then," Carver said. He was looking at Ruth and she was white-faced and large-eyed.

Old Pap opened one eye. "Like hell!" he said expressively. "You think I want a relapse? You get on out of here! Seems like," he protested plaintively, "every time I git to talk to a good-looking gal, somebody comes hornin' in!"

Leo grinned then and looked from Ruth to Mary. "He's in his right mind, anyway," he said, and left.

Mary stood there, looking at Ruth, and Ruth looked after Leo, and then at Mary.

"He's . . . he's an outlaw," Ruth said.

Mary Ryan turned very sharply toward Ruth and I reckon it was the only time she ever spoke up to Ruth. "He's the finest man I ever knew!"

And the two of them just stood there looking at each other and then they went to fussing over Old Pap. That was the longest convalescence on record.

But there was that matter of the blood on her handkerchief. Ruth Hadlin was coming down the street and she was wearing a new bonnet, a beautiful gray dress, and a hat with a veil—very uptown and big city. She was coming down the boardwalk and everybody was turning to look— she was a fine figure of a woman and she carried herself well—and just then the doors of the Palace burst open and out comes a brawling mass of men swinging with all their fists. They spilled past Ruth Hadlin into the street and it turns out to be the three Taylors and Leo Carver.

They hit dirt and came up swinging. Leo smashed a big fist into the face of Scot Taylor and he went over into the street. Bob rushed him, and Leo ducked and took him around the knees, dumping him so hard the ground shook.

Bully Taylor was the tough one, and he and Leo stood there a full half minute, slugging it out with both hands, and then Leo stepped inside and whipped one to Bully's chin and the pride of the Taylors hit dirt, out so cold he's probably sleeping yet.

Ruth Hadlin had stopped in her tracks, and now Leo stepped back and wiped the blood from his face with a jerk, and some of it splattered on Ruth's handkerchief. She cried out. He turned around, and then he turned colors.

"Miss Hadlin," he said with a grin on his face, "I'm right sorry. I'd no intention getting blood on you, but . . . it's good red blood, even if it isn't blue."

She looked at him without turning a hair, and then she said coolly: "Don't stand there with your face all blood. Go wash it." And then she added just as coolly: "And next time don't lead with your right. If he hadn't been so all in, he'd have knocked you out." With that she walks off up the street and we all stood there staring.

Leo, he stared most of all. "Well, I'm a skinned skunk!" he said. "Where do you reckon she ever heard about leading with a right?"

Mary Ryan, she heard about it, but she said nothing, just nothing at all, and that wasn't Mary's way. Of course, we all knew about Mary. She was plumb crazy about Leo but he paid no particular attention to any one of the girls. Or all of them, for that matter.

There was talk around town, but there always is. Some folks said this was as good a time as any to get shut of Leo Carver and his like. That it was time Cañon Gap changed its ways and spruced up a bit. Mort Lewand was always for changing things. He even wanted to change the name of Cañon Gap to Hadlin. It was the judge himself who stopped that.

So we sat around now and listened to the hammers and thought of how big an occasion it was to be. Some of the folks from the creek were already in town, camped out ready for the big doings tomorrow.

Ruth Hadlin was not around and none of us gave it much thought. All of this was so far away from the Hadlins. Ruth bought a horse, I remember, about that time. It was a fine big black. The 'breed done sold it to her. Funny thing, come to think of it, because I'd heard him turn down $500 for that horse—and that in a country where you get a good horse for $20—but Ruth had ways and nobody refused her very much. What she wanted with a horse that big I never could see.

Editor Chafee, he hoisted his britches and was starting back toward the shop when Ruth Hadlin came down the street. She stopped nearby and she looked at that gallows. Maybe her face was a little pale, but the fact that all those roughnecks were around never seemed to bother her.

"Tom," she said right off, "what do you believe Leo Carver did with that money?"

Chafee rubbed his jaw. "You know"—he scowled—"I've studied about that. I can't rightly say."

"What has he always done with it before?"

"Why, he spent it. Just as fast as he could."

"I wonder why he didn't use it to hire a better lawyer? He could have had a man from El Paso for that. Or for much less. A good lawyer might have freed him."

"I wondered about that." Chafee looked a little anxiously at Mort Lewand. Mort was a power in town and he disliked Carver and made no secret of it. Lewand was looking that way, and now he started over. "It doesn't really matter now, does it?" Chafee added.

Lewand came up and looked from one to the other, then he smiled at Ruth. "Rather noisy, isn't it, Ruth? Would you like me to escort you home?"

"Why, thank you," she said sweetly, "but I think I'll stay. I've never seen a gallows before. Have you, Mister Lewand?"

"Me?" He looked startled. "Oh, yes. In several places."

She stood there a few minutes, watching the carpenters work. "Well," Ruth said slowly, "it's too bad, but I'm glad no local people lost anything in that hold-up."

We all looked at her, but she was watching the gallows, an innocent smile on her lips.

Editor Chafee cleared his throat. "I guess you weren't told, Miss Hadlin. The fact is, that money belonged to Mort, here."

She smiled brightly. Women are strange folk. "Oh, no, Tom. You've been misinformed! As a matter of fact, that money was a payment on Mister Lewand's ranch, and, when he consigned it for carriage, it became the property of the former owner of the ranch. That was the agreement, wasn't it, Mister Lewand?"

For some reason it made Mort mad, but he nodded. "That's right."

Ruth nodded, too. "Yes, Mister Lewand was telling me about it. He's very far-sighted, I think. Isn't that wonderful, Tom? Just think how awful it would have been if he had paid that whole twenty thousand dollars and then lost it and had to pay it over! My, it would take a wealthy man to do that, wouldn't it, now?"

Editor Chafee was looking thoughtful all of a sudden, and Old Pap had taken the pipe from his lips and was staring at Ruth. Mort, he looked mad as a horny toad, though for the life of me, I couldn't see why. After all, it had been a smart stunt.

"Those awful shotguns!" From the way she was talking, you wouldn't have believed that girl had a brain in her head. "I don't believe people should be allowed to own them. I wonder where Leo got the one he used?"

"Claimed he never owned one," Chafee commented slowly.

"He probably borrowed one from a friend," Mort said carelessly. "I suppose they are easy to find."

"That's just it!" Ruth exclaimed. "The man who loaned him that shotgun is just as guilty as he is. I think something should be done about it."

"I doubt if anybody loaned him one," Mort said, off hand. "He probably stole it."

"Oh, no! Because," she added hastily, "if he did, he returned it. Everybody in town who owns a shotgun still has it. There are only six of them in Cañon Gap. Daddy has two, Editor Chafee has one, Pap here has an old broken one, and Mitch always carried one."

"That's only five," Old Pap said softly.

"Oh!" Ruth put her fingers to her mouth. "How silly of me. I'd forgotten yours, Mister Lewand."

There was the silliest silence I ever did hear with nobody looking at anybody else. Suddenly Ruth looked at a little watch she had, gasped something about being late, and started off.

Editor Chafee began to fill his pipe, and Old Pap scratched his knee, and all of us just sat there looking a lot dumber than we were. Mort Lewand didn't seem to know what to say, and what he finally said didn't help much.

"If a man wanted to find a shotgun," he said, "I don't suppose he'd have much trouble." With that he turned and walked off.

You know something? The sound of those hammers wasn't a good sound. Editor Tom Chafee scratched his chin with the stem of his pipe. "Pete," he says to me, "you were supposed to ride shotgun that night. Whose shotgun would you have used?"

"Mitch always lent me his. I was feeling poorly and Mitch took over for me. Leo, he called my name when he first rode up, if you recall."

That shotgun business was bothering all of us. Where *did* Leo get a shotgun? This was a rifle and pistol country, and shotguns just weren't plentiful. Ruth Hadlin could have narrowed it down even more because everybody knew that Judge Hadlin wouldn't let anybody touch one of his guns but himself. They were expensive, engraved guns, and he kept them locked up in a case.

Where had Leo picked up a shotgun? What had he done with the money?

Editor Chafee looked down at Old Pap all of a sudden. "Pap," he said, "let's walk over to my place. You, too, Pete. I want you to look at my shotgun."

We looked at that gun and she was all covered with grease and dust. That shotgun hadn't been fired in six months, anyway. Or for a long time. It certainly hadn't been the gun that killed Mitch and Doc.

"Just for luck," Chafee said seriously, "we'd better have a look at the judge's guns."

Behind us we could hear those hammers a-pounding, and we could hear O'Brien rehearsing his German band. From where we walked, we could see six or seven wagons coming down the road, all headed into Cañon Gap, for the hanging.

Certain things happened that I didn't hear until later. I didn't hear about Ruth Hadlin, all pretty as ever a picture could be, walking into that jail to see Leo Carver. When she got into the office, the sheriff was standing there looking down at a cake on his desk. That cake had been cut and it was some broken up because he had taken two files from it. Mary Ryan was standing by his side.

Sheriff Jones looked mighty serious. "Mary," he was saying, "this here's a criminal offense, helping a man to break jail. Now where's those other two files? No use you stalling. I know you bought four of 'em."

"You're so smart," she said, "you find 'em!" She tossed her head at him and gave him a flash of those saucy eyes of hers.

Sheriff Jones leaned over the table. "Now, look, Mary," he protested, "I don't want to make trouble for you, but we just can't have no prison break. Why, think of all those folks coming for miles to see a hanging! They'd be mad enough to string *me* up."

"Why not?" she said, short-like. "He's no more guilty than you are."

Jones started to protest again, and then he looked up and saw Ruth Hadlin standing in the door. Her face was cold as she could make it, and, mister, that was cold! In one hand she held Leo's guitar.

The sheriff straightened up mighty flustered. Here he was, talking confidential-like with a girl from the Street! Suppose that got around among the good folks of the town. Be as much as his job was worth, and election coming up, too.

He flushed and stammered. "This here . . . this young woman," he spluttered, "she was trying to smuggle files to the prisoner. She. . . ."

Ruth Hadlin interrupted, her eyes cold and queen-like on the sheriff. "I can assure you, Sheriff Jones, that I am not at all interested in your relations with this young lady, nor in the subject of your conversation. I have brought this guitar to the prisoner," she continued. "I understand he enjoys singing, and we think it cruel and inhuman that he be forced to listen to that banging and hammering while they build a gallows on which to hang him. It is cruel torture."

Jones was embarrassed. "He don't mind, miss," he protested. "Leo, he's. . . ."

"May I take this instrument to him, Sheriff

Jones?" Her voice was cold. "Or do you want to examine me? Do you think I might be smuggling files, too?"

Sheriff Jones was embarrassed. The very idea of laying a hand on Ruth Hadlin, the daughter of old Judge Emory Hadlin, gave him cold shivers.

"No, no, miss! Of course not." He gestured toward the cells. "Just you give it to him, miss! I'm sorry. I. . . ."

"Thank you, Sheriff." Ruth swept by him and up to the cell.

"Young man"—her voice was clear—"I understand that you play a guitar so I have brought you this one. I hope the music that you get out of it will make your heart free."

Leo looked startled, and he took the guitar through the bars. "I wish . . . ," he broke off, his face a little flushed. "I wish you didn't have to see me in here. You see, I didn't . . . I never killed those men. I'd like you to believe that."

"What I believe," Ruth said sweetly, "is of no importance. The music from the guitar will be pleasant for you, if played in private." She turned abruptly and walked out, and she went by Sheriff Jones like a pay-car past a tramp.

Mary told it afterwards, and Mary said that Leo plunked a string on that guitar and then he looked at it, funny-like. It sure didn't sound right, Mary said. I shouldn't wonder.

That was late Monday afternoon. By sundown

there was maybe 200 people camped around town, waiting for the big hanging next afternoon. Old Pap, he wasn't around, nor was Editor Chafee. Some said that, when they left the judge's house, the judge himself was riding with them.

When next I came across Old Pap, he was standing on the corner, looking at that gallows. That was near the jail, and from the window Leo could see us.

"Folks would be mighty upset if they missed their hanging, Pap," Leo said.

"They won't!" Pap was mighty short and gruff. "They'll git their hanging, and don't you forget it."

That gallows looked mighty ghostly, standing there in the twilight, and it didn't make me feel no better. Leo, well, he always seemed a right nice feller. Of course, he had rustled a few head, but I wouldn't want to take no oath I hadn't, nor Old Pap, nor most of us. Leo, he was just a young hellion, that was all.

Even when he stuck up those stages, he just done it for drinking money. Not that I'm saying it's right, because I know it ain't, but them days and times folks excused a lot of a young man who was full of ginger, long as he didn't hurt nobody and was man enough. Especially of Leo's sort. If you was in trouble you just let him know. Come prairie fire, flood, stampede, or whatever, Leo was your man. No hour was too late, no job too miserable for him to lend a hand. And never take a dime for it.

So we all went to bed, and the last thing Leo said was: "I never did cotton to no rope necktie. I don't figure it's becoming."

"Wait'll tomorry," Old Pap said.

The sun was no more than up before the lid blew off the town. Somebody yelled and folks came a-running. I slid into my pants and scrambled outside. The crowd was streaming toward the Plaza and I run down there with 'em. The bars was out of the jail window, filed off clean as you'd wish, then bent back out of the way. Tied to one of them was a sheet of paper. It was a note.

Sorry I couldn't wait, but I don't think you folks want me hanging around here anyway.

Mary Ryan was there by the jail. She had tears in her eyes, but she looked pleased as a polecat in a hen house, too. Sheriff Jones, he took on something fierce.

"Figured she was talking poetry," he said angrily. "She told him the music he'd get out of the guitar would make his heart free. No wonder Mary wouldn't tell me what became of the other two files."

One big-bearded man with hard eyes stared at the sheriff with a speculative eye. "What about the hanging?" he demanded. "We drove fifty mile to see a hanging."

Editor Tom Chafee, Judge Emory Hadlin, and Old Pap came up around them. They looked across the little circle at Jones.

"Ruth figured it right," the judge said. "Only six shotguns in town. My shotguns, and by the dust on the cases you can see they'd not been cleaned in months. Same with Tom's. Old Pap's was broke, and Mitch had his with him. That leaves just one more shotgun."

Everybody just stood there, taking it all in and doing some figuring. Suppose that $20,000 never left the bank? Or suppose it did leave and it was recovered by the man sending it? His debt would be paid and he would still have the money, and a young scamp like Leo Carver'd be blamed for it all.

Of course, Leo was gone. Some folks said he rode that big black Ruth Hadlin bought. What happened to that horse we never did know because Ruth was gone, too, and her gray mare.

The trail headed west, the trail they left, and somebody living on the edge of town swore he heard two voices singing something about being bound for Californy.

We figured the judge would about burst a gasket, but he was a most surprising man. Something was said about it by somebody, and all he did was smile a little.

"Many a thoroughbred," he said, "was a frisky colt. Once they get the bridle on 'em, they straighten out. As far as that goes," he added, "every blue-blooded family can use a little red blood!"

So everybody was happy. We celebrated mighty big. I reckon the biggest in the history of Cañon Gap. O'Brien's German band played, and everybody had plenty to eat and drink.

The folks that came for the hanging wasn't disappointed, either. They got what they wanted. They got their hanging, all right. Maybe it wasn't a legal hanging, but it was sure satisfactory.

We hung Mort Lewand.

West of the Tularosa

I

The dead man had gone out fighting. Scarcely more than a boy, and a dandy in dress, he had been man enough when the showdown came.

Propped against the fireplace stones, legs stretched before him, loose fingers still touching the butt of his .45 Colt, he had smoked it out to a bloody, battle-stained finish. Evidence of it lay all about him. Whoever killed him had spent time, effort, and blood to do it.

As they closed in for the pay-off at least one man had died on the threshold.

The fight that ended here had begun elsewhere. From the looks of it this cabin had been long deserted, and the dead man's spurs were blood-stained. At least one of his wounds showed evidence of being much older than the others. A crude attempt had been made to stop the bleeding.

Baldy Jackson, one of the Tumbling K riders who found the body, dropped to his knees and picked up the dead man's Colt.

"Empty," he said. "He fought 'em until his guns were empty, an' then they killed him."

"Is he still warm?" McQueen asked. "I think I can smell powder smoke."

He ain't been an hour dead, I'd guess. Wonder what the fuss was about?"

"It worries me"—McQueen looked around—"considering our situation." He glanced at Bud Fox and Kim Sartain, who appeared in the doorway. "What's out there?"

"At least one of their boys rode away still losing blood. By the look of things this lad didn't go out alone. He took somebody with him." Sartain was rolling a smoke. "No feed in the shed, but that horse out there carries a mighty fine saddle."

"Isn't this the place we're headed for?" Fox asked. "It looks like the place described."

Sartain's head came up. "Somebody comin'," he said. "Riders, an' quite a passel of them."

Sartain flattened against the end of the fireplace and Fox knelt behind a windowsill. Ward McQueen planted his stalwart frame in the doorway, waiting. "This isn't so good. We're going to be found with a dead man, just killed."

There were a half dozen riders in the approaching group, led by a stocky man on a gray horse and a tall, oldish man wearing a badge.

They drew up sharply on seeing the horses and McQueen. The short man stared at McQueen, visibly upset by his presence. "Who're you? And what are you doin' here?"

"I'll ask the same question," McQueen spoke casually. "This is Firebox range, isn't it?"

"I know that." The stocky man's tone was testy. "I ought to. I own the Firebox."

"Do you now?" Ward McQueen's reply was gentle, inquiring. "Might be a question about that. Ever hear of Tom McCracken?"

"Of course. He used to own the Firebox."

"That's right, and he sold it to Ruth Kermitt of the Tumbling K. I'm Ward McQueen, her foreman. I've come to take possession."

His reply was totally unexpected, and the stocky man was obviously astonished. His surprise held him momentarily speechless, and then he burst out angrily.

"That's impossible! I'm holdin' notes against young Jimmy McCracken. He was the old man's heir, an' Jimmy signed the place over to me to pay up."

"As of when?" Ward asked.

His thoughts were already leaping ahead, reading sign along the trail they must follow. Obviously something was very wrong, but he was sure that Ruth's deed, a copy of which he carried with him, would be dated earlier than whatever this man had. Moreover, he knew that the dead man lying behind him was that same Jimmy McCracken.

"That's neither here nor there. Get off my land or be drove off."

"Take it easy, Webb." The sheriff spoke for the first time. "This man may have a just claim. If Tom McCracken sold out before he died, your paper isn't worth two hoots."

That this had occurred to Webb was obvious, and that he did not like it was apparent. Had the sheriff not been present, Ward was sure, there would have been a shooting. As yet, they did not know he was not alone, as none of the Tumbling K men had shown themselves.

"Sheriff," McQueen said, "my outfit rode in here about fifteen minutes ago, and we found a dead man in this cabin. Looks like he lost a running fight with several men, and, when his ammunition gave out, they killed him."

"Or you shot him," Webb said.

Ward did not move from the door. He was a big man, brown from sun and wind, lean and muscular. He wore two guns.

"I shot nobody." His tone was level, even. "Sheriff, I'm Ward McQueen. My boss bought this place from McCracken for cash money. The deed was delivered to her, and the whole transaction was recorded in the courts. All that remained was for us to take possession, which we have done."

He paused. "The man who is dead inside is unknown to me, but I'm making a guess he's Jimmy McCracken. Whoever killed him wanted him dead mighty bad. There were quite a few of them, and Jimmy did some good shooting. One thing you might look for is a couple of wounded men, or somebody else who turns up dead."

The sheriff dismounted. "I'll look around,

212

McQueen. My name's Foster, Bill Foster." He waved a hand to the stocky cattleman. "This is Neal Webb, owner of the Runnin' W."

Ward McQueen stepped aside to admit the sheriff, and, as he did so, Kim Sartain showed up at the corner of the house, having stepped through a window to the outside. Kim Sartain was said to be as good with his guns as McQueen.

Foster squatted beside the body. "Yeah, this is young Jimmy, all right. Looks like he put up quite a scrap."

"He was game," McQueen said. He indicated the older wound. "He'd been shot somewhere and rode in here, riding for his life. Look at the spurs. He tried to get where there was help but didn't make it."

Foster studied the several wounds and the empty cartridge cases. McQueen told him of the hard-ridden mustang, but the sheriff wanted to see for himself. Watching the old man, McQueen felt renewed confidence. The lawman was careful and shrewd, taking nothing for granted, accepting no man's unsupported word. That McQueen and his men were in a bad position was obvious.

Neal Webb was obviously a cattleman of some local importance. The Tumbling K riders were not only strangers but they had been found with the body.

Webb was alert and aware. He had swiftly catalogued the Tumbling K riders as a tough lot, if pushed. McQueen he did not know, but their foreman wore his guns with the ease of long practice. Few men carried two guns, most of them from the Texas border country. Nobody he knew of used both at once; the second gun was insurance, but it spoke of a man prepared for trouble.

Webb scowled irritably. The set-up had been so perfect. The old man dead, the gambling debts, and the bill of sale. All that remained was to . . . and then this outfit appeared with what was apparently a legitimate claim. Who would ever dream the old man would sell out. But how had the sale been arranged? There might still be a way, short of violence.

What would Silas Hutch say? And Ren Oliver? It angered Webb to realize he had failed, after all his promises. Yet who could have foreseen this? It had all appeared so simple, but who could have believed that youngster would put up a fight like he did? He had been a laughing, friendly youngster, showing no sense of responsibility, no steadiness of purpose. He had been inclined to side-step trouble rather than face it, so the whole affair had looked simple enough.

One thing after another had gone wrong. First, the ambush failed. The kid got through it alive and then had made a running fight of it. Why he had headed for this place Webb could not guess, unless he had known the Tumbling K outfit was to be here.

Two of Webb's best men were dead and three wounded, and he would have to keep them out of sight until they were well again. Quickly he decided the line cabin on Dry Legget would be the best hide-out.

Foster came from the woods, his face serious.

"McQueen, you'd better ride along to town with me. I found sign that six or seven men were in this fight, and several were killed or hurt. This requires investigation."

"You mean I'm under arrest?"

"No such thing. Only you'll be asked questions. We'll check your deed an' prob'ly have to get your boss up here. We're goin' to get to the bottom of this."

"One thing, Foster, before we go. I'd like you to check our guns. Nobody among us has fired a shot for days. I'd like you to know that."

You could have switched guns," Webb suggested.

McQueen ignored him. "Kim, why don't you fork your bronc' and ride along with us? Baldy, you and Bud stay here and let nobody come around unless it's the sheriff or one of us. Got it?"

"You bet." Jackson spat a stream of tobacco juice at an ant. "Nobody'll come around, believe me."

Neal Webb kept his mouth shut but he watched irritably. McQueen was thinking of everything, but, as Webb watched the body of young

McCracken being tied over a saddle, he had an idea. Jimmy had been well liked around town, so if the story got around that McQueen was his killer, there might be no need for a trial or even a preliminary hearing. It was too bad Foster was so stiff-necked.

Kim Sartain did not ride with the group. With his Winchester across his saddle bow he kept off to the flank or well back in the rear where the whole group could be watched. Sheriff Foster noted this, and his frosty old eyes glinted with amused appreciation.

"What's he doin' back there?" Webb demanded. "Make him ride up front, Sheriff."

Foster smiled. "He can ride where he wants. He don't make me nervous, Webb. What's eatin' you?"

The town of Pelona for which they were riding faced the wide plains from the mouth of Cottonwood Cañon, and faced them without pretensions. The settlement, dwarfed by the bulk of the mountain behind it, was a supply point for cattlemen, a stage stop, and a source of attraction for cowhands to whom Santa Fe and El Paso were faraway dream cities.

In Pelona, with its four saloons, livery stable, and five stores, Si Hutch, who owned Hutch's Emporium, was king.

He was a little old man, grizzled, with a stubble of beard and a continually cranky mood. Beneath that superficial aspect he was utterly vicious, without an iota of mercy for anything human or animal.

Gifted in squeezing the last drop of money or labor from those who owed him, he thirsted for wealth with the same lust that others reserved for whiskey or women. Moreover, although few realized it, he was cruel as an Apache and completely depraved. One of the few who realized the depth of his depravity was his strong right-hand man, Ren Oliver.

Oliver was an educated man and for the first twenty-five years of his life had lived in the East. Twice, once in New York and again in Philadelphia, he had been guilty of killing. In neither case had it been proved, and in only one case had he been questioned. In both cases he had killed to cover his thieving, but finally he got in too deep and, realizing his guilt could be proved, he skipped town.

In St. Louis he shot a man over a card game. Two months later he knifed a man in New Orleans, then drifted West, acquiring gun skills as he traveled. Since boyhood his career had been a combination of cruelty and dishonesty, but not until he met Si Hutch had he made it pay. Behind his cool, somewhat cynical expression few people saw the killer.

He was not liked in Pelona. Neither was he disliked. He had killed two men in gun battles since arriving in town, but both seemed to have been fair, stand-up matches. He was rarely seen with Si Hutch, for despite the small population they had been able to keep their co-operation a secret. Only Neal Webb, another string to Hutch's bow, understood the connection. One of the factors that aided Hutch in ruling the Pelona area was that his control was exercised without being obvious. Certain of his enemies had died, by means unknown to either Ren Oliver or Neal Webb.

The instrument of these deaths was unknown, and for that reason Si Hutch was doubly feared.

When Sheriff Foster rode into town with Webb and McQueen, Si Hutch was among the first to know. His eyes tightened with vindictive fury. That damned Webb! Couldn't he do anything right? His own connection with the crimes well covered, he could afford to sit back and await developments.

Ward McQueen had been doing some serious thinking on the ride into town. The negotiations between Ruth Kermitt and old Tom McCracken had been completed almost four months ago. McCracken had stayed on at the Firebox even after the title was transferred and was to have managed it for another six months. His sudden death ended all that.

Webb had said he owned the ranch by virtue of young Jimmy's signing it over to pay a gambling debt. This was impossible, for Jimmy had known

of the sale and had been present during the negotiations. That, then, was an obvious falsehood.
Neal Webb had made an effort to obtain control
of the ranch, and Jimmy McCracken had been
killed to prevent his doing anything about it.

The attempt to seize control of the ranch argued
a sure and careful mind, and a ruthless one.
Somehow he did not see Webb in that rôle,
although Webb was undoubtedly a part of the
operation. Still, what did he know? Pelona was a
strange town and he was a stranger. Such towns
were apt to be loyal to their own against any out-
sider. He must walk on cat feet, careful to see
where he stepped. Whoever was in charge did not
hesitate to kill, or hesitate to lose his own men in
the process.

Sheriff Foster seemed like an honest man, but
how independent was he? In such towns there
were always factions who controlled, and elected
officials were often only tools to be used.

Faced with trickery and double-dealing as well
as such violence, what could he do? When Ruth
arrived from the Tumbling K in Nevada, there
would be no doubt that she owned the Firebox
and that Jimmy had known of it. That would
place the killing of young Jimmy McCracken at
Neal Webb's door.

Ren Oliver was on the walk in front of the Bat
Cave Saloon when they tied up before the
sheriff's office. He had never seen either

McQueen or Sartain before but knew them instantly for what they were, gunfighters, and probably good.

McQueen saw the tall man in the gray suit standing on the boardwalk. Something in the way he carried himself seemed to speak of what he was. As he watched, Oliver turned in at the Emporium. Ward finished tying his roan and went into the sheriff's office.

Nothing new developed from the talk in the office of the sheriff, nor in the hearing that followed. Young Jimmy McCracken had been slain by persons unknown after a considerable chase. The evidence seemed to establish that several men had been involved in the chase, some of whom had been killed or wounded by McCracken.

Ward McQueen gave his own evidence and listened as the others told what they knew or what the tracks seemed to indicate. As he listened, he heard whispering behind him, and he was well aware that talk was going around. After all, he and the Tumbling K riders were strangers. What talk he could overhear was suspicion of his whole outfit.

Neal Webb had a bunch of tough men around him and he was belligerent. When telling what he knew, he did all he could to throw suspicion on the Tumbling K. However, from what McQueen could gather, all of Webb's riders were present and accounted for. If Webb had been one of those involved in the killing of McCracken, it must have been with other men than his own.

After the inquest McQueen found himself standing beside the sheriff. "What kind of a country is this, Sheriff? Do you have much trouble?"

"Less than you'd expect. Webb's outfit is the biggest, but his boys don't come in often. When they want to have a blowout, they ride down to Alma. They do some drinkin' now an' again, but they don't r'ar up lookin' for trouble."

"Many small outfits?"

"Dozen or so. The Firebox will be the largest if you run cows on all of it." Foster studied him. "Do you know the range limits of the Firebox?"

"We figure to run stock from the Apache to Rip-Roaring Mesa and Crosby Creek, south to Dillon Mountain, and up to a line due east from there to the Apache."

"That's a big piece of country but it is all Firebox range. There are a few nesters squatted in Bear Cañon, and they look like a tough outfit, but they've given me no trouble."

"Miss Kermitt holds deeds on twelve pieces of land," Ward explained. "Those twelve pieces control most of the water on that range, and most of the easy passes. We want no trouble, but we'll run cattle on range we're entitled to."

"That's fair enough. Watch your step around Bear Cañon. Those boys are a mean lot."

II

Kim Sartain was somewhere around town but McQueen was not worried. The gunslinging *segundo* of the Tumbling K was perfectly capable of taking care of himself, and in the meanwhile Ward had business of his own to take care of. He glanced up and down the street, studying the stores. Two of them appeared better stocked than the others. One was Hutch's Emporium, a large store apparently stocked to the doors with everything a rancher could want. The other stores were smaller but were freshly painted and looked neat.

McQueen walked along to the Emporium. A small man with a graying beard looked up at him as he came to the counter. It was an old-fashioned counter, curved inward on the front to accommodate women shoppers who wore hoopskirts.

"Howdy there! Stranger in town?"

"Tumbling K. We've taken over the Firebox, and we'll need supplies."

Hutch nodded agreeably. "Glad to help. The Firebox, hey? Had a ruckus out there, I hear."

"Nothing much." Ward walked along, studying the goods on the shelves and stacked on tables. He was also curious about the man behind the counter. He seemed genial enough, but his eyes were steel-bright and glassy. He was quick-moving and obviously energetic.

"Troublin' place, the Firebox. Old McCracken seemed to make it pay but nobody else ever done it. You reckon you'll stay?"

"We'll stay."

McQueen ordered swiftly and surely, but not all they would need. There were other stores in town, and he preferred to test the water before he got in too deep. The Firebox would need to spend a lot of money locally and he wanted to scatter it around. Hutch made no comment until he ordered a quantity of .44-caliber ammunition.

"That's a lot of shootin'. You expectin' a war?"

"War? Nothing like that, but we're used to wars. Jimmy McCracken was killed for some reason by some right vicious folks. If they come back, we wouldn't want them to feel unwelcome."

The door opened and Neal Webb walked in. He strode swiftly to the counter and was about to speak when he recognized McQueen. He gulped back his words, whatever they might have been.

"Howdy. Reckon you got off pretty easy."

McQueen took his time about replying. "Webb, the Tumbling K is in this country to stay. You might as well get used to us and accept the situation. Then we can have peace between us and get on with raising and marketing cattle. We want no trouble, but we're ready if it comes. We did business with McCracken and I couldn't have found a finer man. His son seemed cut from the same pattern.

"They didn't belong to my outfit, so I'm dropping this right here. If it had been one of my men, I'd back-trail the killers until I found where they came from. Then I'd hunt their boss and I'd stay with him until he was hanged, which is what he deserves."

Behind McQueen's back Hutch gestured, and the hot remarks Webb might have made were stifled. Puzzled, McQueen noticed the change and the sudden shift of Webb's eyes. Finishing his order, he stepped into the street.

As he left, a gray-haired, impatient-seeming man brushed by him. "Neal," he burst out, "where's that no-account Bemis? He was due over to my place with that horse he borried. I need that paint the worst way."

"Forget it," Webb said. "I'll see he gets back to you."

"But I want to see Bemis. He owes me money."

Ward McQueen let the door close behind him and glanced across the street. A girl with red-gold hair was sweeping the boardwalk there. She made a pretty picture and he crossed the street.

As he stepped up on the walk, she glanced up. Her expression changed as she saw him. Her glance was the swiftly measuring one of a pretty girl who sees a stranger, attractive and possibly unmarried. She smiled.

"You must be one of that new outfit the town's talking about. The Tumbling K, isn't it?"

"It is." He shoved his hat back on his head. *Kim should see this girl,* he thought. *She's lovely.* "I'm the foreman."

She glanced across the street toward Hutch's store. "Started buying from Hutch? Like him?"

"I don't know him. Do you run this store?"

"I do, and I like it. What's more I almost make money with it. Of course Hutch gets most of the business. I've had no trouble with him, so far."

He glanced at her. Did that mean she expected trouble? Or that Hutch was inclined to cause trouble for competitors?

"I'm new here so I thought I'd scatter my business until I find out where I get the best service." He smiled. "I want to order a few things."

A big man was coming up the walk, a very big man, and Ward McQueen sensed trouble in the man's purposeful stride. He was taking in the whole walk, and he was bareheaded. His worn boots were run down at the heels and his faded shirt was open halfway down his chest for lack of buttons. His ponderous fists swung at the ends of powerfully muscled arms, and his eyes darkened savagely as he saw Ward McQueen.

"Watch yourself," the girl warned. "That's Flagg Warneke."

The big man towered above McQueen. When he came to a stop in front of Ward, his chin was on a level with Ward's eyebrows and he seemed as wide as a barn door.

"Are you McQueen? Well, I'm Flagg Warneke, from Bear Cañon. I hear you aim to run us nesters off your range. Is that right?"

"I haven't made up my mind yet," Ward replied. "When I do, I'll come to see you."

"Oh, you haven't made up your mind yet? Well, see that you don't. And stay away from Bear Cañon! That place belongs to us, an', if you come huntin' trouble, you'll get it."

Coolly Ward McQueen turned his back on the giant. "Why not show me what stock you have?" he suggested to the girl. "I. . . ."

A huge hand clamped on his shoulder and spun him around. "When I talk to you, face me!" Warneke roared.

As the big hand spun him around, Ward McQueen threw a roundhouse right to the chin that knocked the big man floundering against the post of the overhang. Instantly Ward moved in, driving a wicked right to the body, and then swinging both hands to the head.

The man went to his knees and McQueen stepped back. Then, as if realizing for the first time that he had been struck, Warneke came off the walk with a lunge. He swung his right but Ward went inside, punching with both hands. The big man soaked up punishment like a sponge takes water, and he came back, punching with remarkable speed for such a big man.

A blow caught McQueen on the jaw and he crashed against the side of the store, his head ringing. Warneke followed up on the punch, but he was too eager for the kill and missed.

Ward stepped in, smashing his head against the big man's chin, and then punching with both hands to the body. His head buzzed and his mouth had a taste of blood. The big man clubbed at his kidneys and tried to knee him, but Ward slid away and looped a punch that split Warneke's ear and showered Ward with blood.

Warneke staggered but, recovering, came back, his eyes blazing with fury. When Warneke threw a punch, Ward went under it and grabbed the big man by the knees, upending him. The big man hit the walk on his shoulder blades with a crash that raised dust, but he came up fast, landing a staggering right to Ward's head. Ward countered with a left, and then crossed a right to the jaw. The big man went to his haunches.

A crowd had gathered and the air was filled with shouted encouragement to one or the other. Ward's shirt was torn, and, when he stepped back to let Warneke get up again, his breath was coming in great gasps. The sheer power and strength of the big man was amazing. He had never hit a man so hard and had him still coming.

McQueen, no stranger to rough-and-tumble

fighting, moved in, circling a little. Warneke, cautious now, was aware he was in a fight. Before, his battles had always ended quickly; this was different. McQueen stabbed a left to the mouth, feinted, and did it again. He feinted again, but this time he whipped a looping uppercut to the body that made Warneke's mouth fall open. The big man swung a ponderous blow that fell short and McQueen circled him warily. The speed was gone from the Bear Cañon man now, and McQueen only sought a quick way to end it.

McQueen, oblivious of the crowd, moved in warily. Warneke, hurt though he was, was as dangerous as a cornered grizzly. McQueen's greatest advantage had been that Warneke had been used to quick victories and had not expected anything like what had happened. Also, McQueen had landed the first blow and followed it up before the bigger man could get set. He stalked him now, and then feinted suddenly and threw a high hard one to the chin. Warneke was coming in when the blow landed.

For an instant he stiffened, and then fell forward to the walk and lay still.

McQueen stepped back to the wall and let his eyes sweep the faces of the crowd. For the first time he saw Sartain standing in front of the store, his thumbs hooked in his belt, watching the people gathered about.

Nearest the porch was a tall man in a gray suit,

a man he had observed before when he first rode into town.

"That was quite a scrap," said the man in gray. "My congratulations. If there is ever anything I can do, just come to me. My name is Ren Oliver."

"Thanks."

Ward McQueen picked up his fallen hat, and then tentatively he worked his fingers. Nothing was broken but his hands were stiff and sore from the pounding. He gave Sartain a half smile. "Looks like we've picked a tough job. That was a Bear Cañon nester."

"Yeah." Kim gave him a wry look. "Wonder who put him up to it?"

"You think it was planned?"

"Think about it. You've made no decision on Bear Cañon. You ain't even seen the place or its people, but he had the idea you were going to run them off. And how did he know where you were and who you were? I think somebody pointed you out."

"That's only if somebody has it in for him, or for us."

Sartain's smile was cynical. "You don't think they have? You should have seen how green Webb turned when you said you had title to the Firebox. If the sheriff hadn't been there, he'd have tried to kill you. And why was the sheriff there? That's another thing we'd better find out."

McQueen nodded. "You're right, Kim. "While you're around, keep your eyes and ears open for a man named Bemis. You won't see him, I think, but find out what you can about him."

"Bemis? What do you know about him?"

"Darned little." McQueen touched his cheek with gentle fingers where a large red, raw spot had resulted from Warneke's fist. "Only he ain't around, and he should be."

Sartain walked off down the street and the crowd drifted slowly away, reluctant to leave the scene. McQueen hitched his guns into place and straightened his clothes. He glanced around and saw a sign: CLARITY'S STORE.

The girl had come back into her doorway, and he glanced at her. "Are you Clarity?"

"I am. The first name is Sharon and I'm Irish. Did they call you McQueen?"

"They did. And the first name is Ward."

He stepped into the store, anxious to get away from the curious eyes. The store was more sparsely stocked than Hutch's much larger store, but the stock gave evidence of careful selection and a discriminating taste. There were many things a Western store did not normally stock.

"I have a wash basin," she suggested. "I think you'd better take a look at yourself in a mirror."

"I will," he said, grinning a little, "but I'd rather not." He glanced around again. "Do you stock shirts by any chance? Man-size shirts?"

She looked at him critically. "I do, and I believe I have one that would fit you."

She indicated the door to the wash basin, and then went among the stacks of goods on the shelves behind the counter.

A glance in the mirror and he saw what she meant. His face was battered and bloody, his hair mussed. He could do little about the battering, but the blood he could wash away, and he did so. The back door opened on a small area surrounded by a high fence. It was shaded by several old elms and a cottonwood or two, and in the less shaded part there were flowers. He washed his face, holding compresses on his swollen cheek bones and lip. Then he combed his hair.

Sharon Clarity came with a shirt. It was a dark blue shirt with two pockets. He stripped off the rags of his other shirt and donned the new one and dusted off his hat.

She gave him a quick look and a smile when he emerged, saying: "It's an improvement, anyway." She folded some other shirts and returned them to the shelves.

He paid for the shirt she had provided, and she said: "You know what you've done, don't you? You've whipped the toughest man in Bear Cañon. Whipped him in a stand-up fight. Nobody has ever done that, and nobody has even come close. Nobody has even tried for a long time."

She paused, frowning a little. "It puzzles me a

little. Warneke isn't usually quarrelsome. That's the first time I ever saw him start a fight."

"Somebody may have given him an idea. I hadn't had time to even think about Bear Cañon. I haven't even ridden over the ranch, and yet he had the idea we were about to run the nesters off."

She looked at him appraisingly, at the wide shoulders, the narrow hips. There was power in every line of him, a power she had just seen unleashed with utter savagery. Having grown up with four brawling brothers, she knew something about men. This one had fought coolly, skillfully. "You've started something, you know. That Bear Cañon outfit is tough. Even Neal Webb's boys fight shy of them."

"Webb has a tough outfit?"

"You've seen some of them. There are two or three known killers in the bunch. Why he keeps them, I couldn't say."

"Like Bemis, for example?"

"You know Harve Bemis? He's one of them, but not the worst by a long shot. The worst ones are Overlin and Bine."

These were names he knew. Bine he had never seen, but he knew a good deal about him, as did any cattleman along the border country of Texas. An occasional outlaw and suspected rustler, he had run with the Youngers in Missouri before riding south to Texas.

Overlin was a Montana gun hand known around

Bannock and Alder Gulch, but he had ridden the cattle trails from Texas several times and was a skilled cowhand, as well. McQueen had seen him in Abilene and at Doan's Crossing. On that occasion he himself had killed an outlaw who was trying to cut the herd with which McQueen was riding. The fact that such men rode with Webb made the situation serious.

He purchased several items, and then hired a man with a wagon to freight the stuff to the Firebox. Kim Sartain was loitering in front of the saloon when McQueen came down to get his horse.

"Bemis ain't around," he confided, "an' it's got folks wonderin' because he usually plays poker at the Bat Cave Saloon. Nobody's seen him around for several days." He paused. "I didn't ask. I just listened."

III

For three days the Firebox was unmolested, and in those three days much was accomplished. The shake roof needed fixing, and some fences had to be repaired. Baldy had that job, and, when he finished, he stood back and looked it over with satisfaction. "Bud, that there's an elephant-proof fence."

"Elephant-proof? You mean an elephant couldn't get past that fence? You're off your trail."

"Of course it's elephant-proof. You don't see any elephants in there, do you?"

Bud Fox just looked at him and rode away.

All hands were in the saddle from ten to twelve hours a day. The cattle were more numerous than expected, especially the younger stuff. Several times McQueen cut trails made by groups of riders, most of them several days old. Late on the afternoon of the third day he rode down the steep slope to the bottom of a small cañon near the eastern end of the Dillons and found blood on the grass.

The stain was old and dark but unmistakably blood. He walked his horse around, looking for sign. He found a leaf with blood on it, then another. The blood had come from someone riding a horse, a horse that toed in slightly. Following the trail he came to where several other horsemen had joined the wounded man. One of the other horses was obviously a led horse.

Men had been wounded in the fight with McCracken. Could these be the same? If so, where were they going? He rode on over the Dillons and off what was accepted as Firebox range. He had crossed a saddle to get into this narrow cañon, but farther along it seemed to open into a wider one. He pushed on, his Winchester in his hands.

The buckskin he rode was a mountain horse

accustomed to rough travel. Moreover, it was fast and had stamina, the sort of horse a man needed when riding into trouble. The country into which he now ventured was unknown to him, wild and rough. The cañon down which he rode opened into a wider valley that tightened up into another deep, narrow cañon. Before him was a small stream. The riders had turned downcañon.

It was dusk and shadows gathered in the cañons, only a faint red glow from the setting sun crested the rim of the cañon. Towering black walls lifted about him, and on the rocky edge across the way a dead, lightning-blasted pine pointed a warning finger from the cliff. The narrow valley was deep in the mystery of darkness, and the only sound that came from the stream was a faint rustling. Then wind sighed in the junipers and the buckskin stopped, head up, ears pricked.

"*Ssh*," he whispered, putting a warning hand on the buckskin's neck. "Take it easy, boy. Take it easy now."

The horse stepped forward, seeming almost to walk on tiptoe. This was the Box, one of the deepest cañons in the area. McCracken had spoken of it during their discussions that led to his sale of the ranch.

Suddenly he glimpsed a faint light on the rock wall. Speaking softly to the buckskin, he slid from the saddle, leaving his rifle in the scabbard.

Careful to allow no jingle of spurs, he felt his way along the sandy bottom. Rounding a shoulder of rock, he saw a small campfire and the moving shadow of a man in a wide hat. Crouching near a bush, he saw that shadow replaced by another, a man with a baldhead.

In the silence of the cañon, where sounds were magnified, he heard a voice. "Feelin' better, Bemis? We'll make it to Dry Leggett tomorrow."

The reply was huskier, the tone complaining. "What's the boss keepin' us so far away for? Why didn't he have us to the Runnin' W? This hole I got in me is no joke."

"You got to stay under cover. Were not even suspected, an' we won't be if we play it smart."

His eyes picked out three men lying near the fire, covered with blankets, one with a bandaged head. One of those who was on his feet was preparing a meal. From the distance he could just make out their faces, the shape of their shoulders, and of the two on their feet the way they moved. Soon he might be fighting these men, and he wanted to know them on sight. The man in the wide hat turned suddenly toward him.

Hansen Bine!

Never before had he seen the man but the grapevine of the trails carried accurate descriptions of such men and of places as well. Gunfighters were much discussed, more than prize fighters or baseball players, even more than racehorses or buckers.

Bine was known for his lean, wiry body, the white scar on his chin, and his unnaturally long, thin fingers. "What's the matter, Bine?" Bemis asked.

"Somethin' around. I can feel it."

"Cat, maybe. Lots of big ones in these cañons. I saw one fightin' a bear one time. A black bear. No lion in his right mind would tackle a grizzly."

Bine looked again into the night, and then crossed to the fire and seated himself. "Who d'you reckon those riders were who went to the cabin after we left? I saw them headed right for it."

"The boss, maybe. He was supposed to show up with the sheriff."

There was silence except for the crackling of the fire, only barely discernible at the distance. The flames played shadow games on the rock wall. Then Bemis spoke: "I don't like it, Hans. I don't like it at all. I been shot before, but this one's bad. I need some care. I need a doctor.

"Take it easy, Bemis. You'll get there, all in good time."

"I don't like it. Sure, he doesn't want nobody to know, but I don't want to die, either."

Talk died down as the men sat up to eat, and Ward drew carefully back and walked across the sand to his horse. He swung into the saddle and turned the animal, but, as the buckskin lined out to go back along the cañon, its hoof clicked on stone.

He had believed himself far enough away not to be heard, but from behind him he heard a startled exclamation, and Ward put the horse into a lope in the darkness. From behind him there was a challenge, and then a rifle shot, but he was not worried. The shot would have been fired on chance, as Ward knew he could not be seen and there was no straight shot possible in the cañon.

He rode swiftly, so swiftly that he realized he had missed his turn and was following a route up a cañon strange to him. The bulk of the Dillons arose on his right instead of ahead or on his left as they should be. By the stars he could see that the cañon up which he now rode was running east and west and he was headed west. Behind him he heard sounds of pursuit but doubted they would follow far.

The riding was dangerous, as the cañon was a litter of boulders and the trunks of dead trees. A branch cañon opened and he rode into it, his face into a light wind. He heard no further sounds of pursuit and was pleased, wanting no gun battle in these narrow, rock-filled cañons where a ricochet could so easily kill or wound a man. He saw the vague gleam of water and rode his horse into a small mountain stream. Following the stream for what he guessed was close to a mile, he found his way out of the stream to a rocky shelf. A long time later he came upon a trail and the shape of some mountains he recognized.

As he rode, he considered what he had heard. Harve Bemis, as he suspected, had been one of those who attacked Jimmy McCracken. More than likely Bine had been there as well. That, even without what else he knew of Neal Webb, placed the attack squarely on Webb's shoulders.

With Jimmy McCracken slain and a forged bill of sale, Webb would have been sure nothing could block his claim to the Firebox range.

So what would he do now? Relinquish his attempt to seize the Firebox and let the killing go for nothing? All McQueen's experience told him otherwise. Webb would seek some other way to advance his claim, and he would seek every opportunity to blacken the reputation of the Tumbling K riders.

The men he had seen in the cañon were headed for Dry Leggett. Where was that? What was it? That he must find out; also he must have a talk with Sheriff Bill Foster. Ruth Kermitt would not like this. She did not like trouble, and yet those who worked for her always seemed to be fighting to protect her interests. Of late she had refused to admit there might be occasions when fighting could not be avoided. She had yet to learn that in order to have peace both sides must want it equally. One side cannot make peace; they can only surrender. Ward McQueen knew of a dozen cases where one side had agreed to lay down their arms if allowed to leave peacefully. In every case of which he knew, the ones who surrendered their arms were promptly massacred.

He had been in love with Ruth since their first meeting, and they had talked of marriage. Several times they had been on the verge of it but something always intervened. Was it altogether accident? Or was one or both of them hesitating? Marriage would be new for each, yet he had always been a freely roving man, going where he willed, living as he wished.

He shook such thoughts from his head. This was no time for personal considerations. He was a ranch foreman with a job to do, a job that might prove both difficult and dangerous. He must put the Firebox on a paying basis.

Their Nevada ranch was still the home ranch, but Ruth had bought land in other states, in Arizona and New Mexico as well as Utah, and she had traded profitably in cattle. One of the reasons for his hesitation, if he was hesitating, was because Ruth Kermitt was so wealthy. He himself had done much to create that wealth and to keep what she had gained. From the time when he had saved her herd in Nevada he had worked untiringly. He knew cattle, horses, and men. He also knew range conditions. The Tumbling K range fattened hundreds of white-faced cattle. The

Firebox, farther south and subject to different weather conditions, could provide a cushion against disaster on the northern range. She had bought, on his advice, for a bargain price. Old Tom and young Jimmy had planned to return to a property they owned in Wyoming. As Tom had known Ruth's father, he offered her a first chance.

On Ward's advice she had purchased land around water holes, insuring her of water so they would control much more land than they owned.

It was almost daybreak when McQueen rolled into his bunk in the Firebox bunkhouse. Sartain opened an eye and glanced at him curiously. Then he went back to sleep. Kim asked no questions and offered no comments but missed little.

IV

Baldy Jackson was putting breakfast together when McQueen awakened. He sat up on his bunk and called out to Baldy in the next room. "Better get busy and muck this place out," Ward suggested. "Ruth . . . Miss Kermitt . . . may be down before long."

"Ain't I got enough to do? Cookin' for you hungry coyotes, buildin' fence, an' mixin' 'dobe? This place is good enough for a bunch of thistle-chinned cowhands."

"You heard me," McQueen said cheerfully. "And while you're at it, pick out a cabin site for the boss. One with a view. She will want a place of her own."

"Better set up an' eat. You missed your supper."

"Where's the boys? Aren't they eating?"

"They et an' cleared out hours ago." Baldy glanced at him. "What happened last night? Run into somethin'?"

"Yes, I did." He splashed water on his face and hands. "I came upon a camp of five men, three of them wounded. They were headed for a place called Dry Leggett."

"Cañon west of Plaza."

"Plaza?"

"Kind of settlement, mostly Mexicans. Good people. A few 'dobes, a couple of stores, and a saloon or two."

"How well do you know this country, Baldy?"

Jackson gave him a wry look. "Pretty well. I punched cows for the SU south of here, and rode into Plaza more times than I can recall. Been over around Socorro. Back in the old days I used to hole up back in the hills from time to time."

Baldy was a good cowhand and a good cook, but in his younger years he had ridden the outlaw trail until time brought wisdom. Too many of his old pals had wound up at the end of a rope.

"Maybe you can tell me where I was last night. I think I was over around that cañon they used to call the Box." He described the country and

Baldy listened, sipping coffee. "Uhn-huh," he said finally, "that cañon you hit after crossing the Dillons must have been Devil. You probably found them holed up in the Box or right below it. Leavin', you must have missed Devil Cañon and wound up on the south fork of the Frisco. Then you come up the trail along the Centerfire and home."

Racing hoofs interrupted. McQueen put down his cup as Bud Fox came through the door.

"Ward, that herd we gathered in Turkey Park is gone! Sartain trailed 'em toward Apache Mountain."

"Wait'll I get my horse." Baldy jerked off his apron.

"You stay here," McQueen told him. "Get down that Sharps and be ready. Somebody may have done this just to get us away from the cabin. Anyway, I've a good idea who is responsible."

Riding swiftly, Fox led him to the tracks. Kim Sartain had followed after the herd. The trail skirted a deep cañon, following an intermittent stream into the bed of the Apache, and then crossed the creek into the rough country beyond.

Suddenly McQueen drew up, listening. Ahead of them they heard cattle lowing. Kim came down from the rocks.

"Right up ahead. Four of the wildest, roughest-lookin' hands I've seen in years."

"Let's go," McQueen said. Touching spurs to

his horse as he plunged through the brush and hit the flat land at a dead run with the other two riders spreading widely behind him. The movements of the cattle killed the sound of their charge until they were almost up to the herd. Then one of the rustlers turned and slapped a hand for his six-shooter. McQueen's gun leaped to his hand and he chopped it down, firing as it came level. The rush of his horse was too fast for accurate shooting and his bullet clipped the outlaw's horse across the back of the neck. It dropped in its tracks, spilling its rider. Ward charged into the rustler, knocking him sprawling, almost under the hoofs of the buckskin.

Swinging wide, McQueen saw that Sartain had downed his man, but the other two were converging on Bud Fox. Both swung away when they saw Kim and McQueen closing in. One of them swung a gun on Kim and Kim's gun roared. The man toppled from the saddle and the last man quickly lifted his hands.

He was a thin, hard-featured man with narrow, cruel eyes. His hair was uncut, his jaws unshaved. His clothing was ragged. There was nothing wrong with his gun; it was new and well-kept.

Now his face, despite its hardness, wore a look of shock. His eyes went from McQueen to Sartain to Fox. "You boys shoot mighty straight but you'll wish you never seen the day!"

Fox took his rope from the saddle tree. "He's a rustler, Ward, caught in the act, an' there's plenty of good trees."

"Now, look . . . !" the man protested, suddenly frightened.

"What gave you the idea you could run off our stock?" Ward asked.

"Nothin'. The stock was in good shape." He looked suddenly at McQueen who still wore the marks of battle. "You're the gent who whipped Flagg. He'll kill you for that, if not for this. You won't live a week."

"Bud, tie this man to his saddle and tie him tight. We'll take him into town for the law to handle. Then we'll visit Bear Cañon."

"You'll do what?" their prisoner sneered. "Why, you fool! Flagg will kill you! The whole bunch will!"

"No," Ward assured him, "they will not. If they'd left my stock alone, they could have stayed. Now they will get out or be burned out. That's the message I'm taking to them."

"Wait a minute." The man's eyes were restless. Suddenly his arrogance was gone and he was almost pleading. "Lay off Bear Cañon. This was none o' their doin', anyway."

"You're talking," Ward said, and waited.

"Neal Webb put us up to it. Promised us fifteen bucks a head for every bit of your stock we throwed into the Sand Flats beyond Apache."

"Will you say that to a judge?"

His face paled. "If you'll protect me. That Webb outfit, they kill too easy to suit me."

When they rode down the street of Pelona to the sheriff's office, the town sprawled lazily in the sunshine. By the time they reached the sheriff's office, nearly fifty men had crowded around. Foster met them at the door, his shrewd old eyes going from McQueen to the rustler.

"Well, Chalk"—he spat.—"looks like you run into the wrong crowd." His eyes shifted to McQueen. "What's he done?"

"Rustled a herd of Firebox stock."

"Him alone?"

"There were four of them. The other three were in no shape to bring back. They won't be talking. This one will."

A man at the edge of the crowd turned swiftly and hurried away. McQueen's eyes followed him. He went up the walk to the Emporium. A moment later Ren Oliver emerged and started toward them.

"Who were the others, Chalk? Were they from Bear Cañon?"

"Only me." Chalk's eyes were haunted. "Let's get inside."

"Hang him!" somebody yelled. "Hang the rustler!"

The voice was loud. Another took it up, then

still another. McQueen turned to see who was shouting. Somebody else shouted: "Why waste time? Shoot him!"

The shot came simultaneously with the words, and Ward McQueen saw the prisoner fall, a hole between his eyes.

"Who did that?" Ward's contempt and anger were obvious. "Anybody who would shoot an unarmed man with his hands tied is too low-down to live."

The crowd stirred but nobody even looked around. Those who might know were too frightened to speak. On the edge of the crowd Ren Oliver stood with several others who had drawn together. "I didn't see anybody fire, McQueen, but wasn't the man a rustler? Hasn't the state been saved a trial?"

"He was also a witness who was ready to testify that Neal Webb put him up to the rustling and was paying for the cattle."

Startled, people in the crowd began to back away, and from the fringes of the crowd they began to disappear into stores or up and down the street. There seemed to be no Webb riders present, but Kim Sartain, sitting his horse back from the crowd, a hand on his gun butt, was watching. He had come up too late to see the shooting.

"Webb won't like that, McQueen," Ren Oliver said. "I speak only from friendship."

"Webb knows where to find me. And tell him this time it won't be a kid he's killing."

Sheriff Foster chewed on the stub of his cigar. His blue eyes had been watchful. "That's some charge you've made, McQueen. Can you back it up?"

Ward indicated the dead man. "There's my witness. He told me Webb put him up to it, and that Bear Cañon wasn't involved. As for the rest of it. . . ."

He repeated the story of the tracks he had followed, of the men holed up in the Box.

"You think they went on to Dry Leggett?" Foster asked.

"That was what I heard them say, but they might have changed their minds. Bemis was among the wounded and he was worried. He had a wound and wanted care." Then he added: "Bine did most of the talking."

Ward McQueen tied his horse in front of Sharon Clarity's store, where there was shade. With Sartain at his side he crossed to the Bat Cave.

The saloon was a long, rather narrow room with a potbellied stove at either end and a bar that extended two-thirds the room's length. There were a roulette table and several card tables.

A hard-eyed, baldheaded bartender leaned thick forearms on the bar, and three men loafed there, each with a drink. At the tables several men played cards. They glanced up as the Tumbling K men entered, then resumed their game.

McQueen ordered two beers and glanced at Ren Oliver, who sat in one of the card games. Had Oliver been only a bystander? Or had he fired the shot that killed Chalk?

Oliver glanced up and smiled. "Care to join our game?" McQueen shook his head. He would have enjoyed playing cards with Oliver, for there are few better ways to study a man than to play cards with him. Yet he was in no mood for cards, and he hadn't the time. He had started something with his comments about Webb. Now he had to prove his case.

He finished his beer, and then, followed by Sartain, he returned to the street. Ren Oliver watched them go, then cashed in, and left the game. When he entered the Emporium, Hutch glared at him.

"Get rid of him!" Hutch said. "Get rid of him now!"

Oliver nodded. "Got any ideas?"

Hutch's eyes were mean. "You'd botch the job. Leave it to me!"

"You?" Oliver was incredulous.

Hutch looked at him over his steel-rimmed glasses. Ren Oliver, who had known many hard men, remembered only one such pair of eyes.

They were the eyes of a big swamp rattler he had killed as a boy. He remembered how those eyes had stared into his. He felt a chill.

"To me," Hutch repeated.

V

It was dark when Ward McQueen, trailed by Kim and Bud Fox, reached the scattered, makeshift cabins in Bear Cañon. It was a small settlement, and he had heard much about it in the short time he had been around. The few women were hard-eyed slatterns as tough as their men. Rumor had it they lived by rustling and horse thieving or worse.

"Bud," McQueen said, "stay with the horses. When we leave, we may have to leave fast. Be ready, and, when you hear me yell, come a-running."

Followed by Kim, he walked toward the long bunkhouse that housed most of the men. Peering through a window, he saw but two men, one playing solitaire, the other mending a belt. The room was lighted by lanterns. Nearby was another house, and, peering in, they saw a short bar and a half dozen men sitting around. One of them was Flagg Warneke.

Ward McQueen stepped to the door and opened it. He stepped in, Kim following, moving quickly left against the log wall.

Flagg saw them first. He was tipped back in his

chair and he let the legs down carefully, poised for trouble.

"What d' you want?" he demanded. "What're you doin' here?"

All eyes were on them. Two men, four guns, against six men and eight guns. There were others around town.

"This morning Chalk and some other riders ran off some of our cows. We had trouble and three men got killed. I told Chalk, if he told me who was involved, I'd not ride down here. He didn't much want me to come to Bear Cañon, and to tell you the truth I hadn't been planning on coming down here. Chalk started to talk, and somebody killed him."

"Killed him? Killed Chalk? Who did it?"

"You make your own guess. Who was afraid of what he might say? Who stood to lose if he did talk?"

They absorbed this in silence, and then a fat-faced man at the end of the table asked: "Those fellers with Chalk? You say you killed them?"

"They chose to fight."

"How many did you lose?"

"We lost nobody. There were three of us, four of them. They just didn't make out so good."

"What're you here for?" Flagg demanded.

"Two things. To see if you have any idea about who killed Chalk and to give you some advice. Stay away from Firebox cattle."

Silence hung heavily in the room. Flagg's face was still swollen from the beating he had taken and the cuts had only begun to heal. His eyes were hard as he stared at McQueen.

"We'll figure out our own answers to the first question. As to the second, we've no use for Firebox cows. As for you and that feller with you . . . get out."

McQueen made no move. "Remember, friend, Bear Cañon is on Firebox range. What you may not know is that Firebox owns that land, every inch of it. You stay if Firebox lets you, and right now the Firebox is me. Behave yourselves and you'll not be bothered, but next time there will be no warning. We'll come with guns and fire."

He reached for the latch with his left hand, and, as the door opened, Flagg said: "I put my mark on you, anyway."

McQueen laughed. "And you're wearing some of mine. Regardless of how things work out, Flagg, it was a good fight and you're a tough man to whip."

He opened the door, and Kim Sartain stepped out and quickly away. He followed. Yet they had taken no more than three steps when the door burst open and the fat-faced man lunged out, holding a shotgun in both hands. He threw the shotgun to his shoulder. As one man, Ward and Kim drew and fired. The fat-faced man's shotgun sagged in his hands and he backed up slowly and sat down.

Men rushed from the bunkhouse and Kim shot a man with a buffalo gun. Ward shot through the open door at the hanging lantern. It fell, spewing oil and flame. In an instant the room was afire.

Men and women rushed from the other buildings and the two backed to their horses, where Bud awaited them on the rim of the firelight.

Several men grabbed a heavy wagon by the tongue and wheeled it away from the fire. Others got behind to shove. Of Flagg, McQueen saw nothing.

As the three rode away, they glanced back at the mounting flames. The saloon was on fire, as well as the bunkhouse.

"Think this will move them out?" Kim asked.

"I've no idea. I'm no hand for the sort of thing. Not burning folks out. They'd no right there, and that's deeded land, as I told them. They may have believed it to be government land. If they'd acted halfway decent, I'd have paid them no mind."

"There's no good in that crowd," Kim said.

"Maybe not, but Flagg fought a good fight. He had me worried there, for a spell."

"He didn't get into this fight."

"No, and I think he'd have acted all right. I think he has judgment, which I can't say for that fat-faced gent. He just went hog wild."

Baldy Jackson was pacing the yard and muttering when they rode in. "Durn it all! You fellers ride away with your shootin' irons on. Then we hear nothin' of you! Where've you been?"

"What do you mean *we?*" Kim said. "Since when have you become more than one?"

"He was including me, I think." Sharon Clarity got up from the chair where she had been sitting, "but I've only been here a few minutes. I came to warn you."

"To warn us?"

"To warn you, Mister McQueen. Sheriff Foster is coming for you. He will arrest you for killing Neal Webb."

"For what?" Ward swung down from his horse and trailed the reins. "What happened to Webb?"

"He was found dead on the trail not fifteen minutes after you left town. He had been shot in the back."

Neal Webb killed. Ward McQueen sat down in one of the porch chairs. By whom, and for what? Ward McQueen knew what Western men thought of a back-shooter. That was a hanging offense before any jury one could get, but more often a lynch mob would handle such cases before the law got around to it.

Kim Sartain had been with him, but he would be considered a prejudiced witness.

"Pour me some coffee, Baldy," he suggested.

He glanced over at Sharon Clarity. "And thanks." He hesitated. "I hope your riding to warn me won't make enemies for you."

"Nobody knew," she replied cheerfully. "Anyway, I think you and the Tumbling K are good for this country. Things were getting kind of one-sided around here."

"Neal Webb killed?" Ward mused. "I wonder what that means? I'd sort of thought he was behind all the trouble, but this makes me wonder."

"It does, doesn't it?" Sharon said. "Almost as if he was killed purely to implicate you."

He glanced at her. "That's a shrewd observation. Any idea who would want to do a thing like that? After all, my trouble was with Webb."

She did not reply. She got to her feet. "My father used to box," she said. "Back in the old country he was considered quite good. They had a rule in boxing. I've heard him quote it. It was 'protect yourself at all times.' I am going back to town, but I think you should be very, very careful. And you'd better go. Foster will have about thirty riders in that posse. You'd better start moving."

"I've done nothing. I'll wait for them to come.

She went to her horse. "When you get thirty men together," Sharon said, "you get all kinds. You have to consider their motives, Mister McQueen."

"Kim, ride along with Miss Clarity, will you? See that she gets safely home."

"Yes, sir." Kim had been tired. Suddenly he was no longer so. "But what about that posse?"

"There'll be no trouble. Take good care of Miss Clarity. She is a very bright young woman."

In Pelona, Oliver went to the Bat Cave and seated himself at the card table. The saloon was empty save for himself and the bartender, a man with whom he was not particularly friendly, but the cards were there and he gathered them up and began to shuffle. He always thought better with cards in his hands. He carefully laid out a game of solitaire, but his mind was not on the cards.

He was both puzzled and worried. For some years now he had considered himself both an astute and a wise young man. He made his living with his adept fingers and his skill at outguessing men with cards. He knew all the methods of cheating and was a skilled card mechanic, but he rarely used such methods. He had a great memory for cards and the odds against filling any hand. He won consistently without resorting to questionable methods. He rarely won big. The show-off sort of thing that attracted attention he did not want. He played every day, and, when he lost, it was only small amounts. The sums he won were slightly larger. Sometimes he merely broke even, but over the months he was a clear and distinct winner. At a time when a cowhand was pulling down \$30 to \$40 a month, and a clerk in a store might work for as little as half that, Ren Oliver could pull down \$200 to \$250 without attracting undue attention. When a professional gambler starts winning big pots, he becomes suspect.

Even Hutch did not realize how well he was doing, and Hutch was providing him with a small income for rendering various services not to be discussed. Over the past year Ren Oliver had built up a nice road stake, something to take with him when he left, for he was well aware that few things last, and many difficulties could be avoided by forming no lasting attachments and keeping a fast horse.

Now Ren Oliver was disturbed. Neal Webb had been killed. By whom was a question, but an even larger question was why.

It disturbed him that he did not know. The obvious answer was that he had been killed by Ward McQueen, but Oliver did not buy that, not for a minute. McQueen might kill Webb in a gun battle, but he would not shoot him in the back.

Moreover, there had been no confrontation between them. The other answer was that Neal had outlived his usefulness and was killed to implicate McQueen.

But who had actually killed him?

It disturbed Oliver that he did not know. Obviously Hutch was behind it, but who had done the killing? One by one he considered the various men available and could place none of them in the right position. This worried him for another reason. He had considered himself close to Hutch, yet he now realized that, like Webb when he ceased to be useful, he might be killed. He was merely a pawn in another man's game.

For a man of Oliver's disposition and inclinations it was not a pleasant thought. He did not mind others believing he was a pawn, but he wished to be in control so he could use those who believed they were using him. Now he had the uncomfortable sensation that too much was happening of which he was not aware and that any moment he might be sacrificed.

He had no illusions about himself. He was without scruples. It was his attitude that human life was cheap, and like most men engaged in crime he regarded people as sheep to be sheared. He was cold and callous and had always been so.

Outwardly he was friendly and ingratiating. He went out of his way to do favors for people even while holding them in contempt. You never knew when such people might appear on a jury. For the same reason he had allied himself with Hutch.

It was unsettling to realize there was someone more cunning than he himself. He knew Hutch was hunching over his community like a huge spider of insatiable appetite. Within that community he was considered to be something of a skinflint but nothing more. Men came and went from his store because, after all, it was the town's leading emporium, as its name implied. That all those people might not be buying was not considered. Oliver believed Hutch hired his killing done, but who did he hire?

Bine, of course, but who else? When Oliver looked over his shoulder, he wanted to know who he was looking for. The fact that there was an unsuspected actor in the play worried him.

He had the uncomfortable feeling that Neal Webb had been killed not only to implicate McQueen but to serve as a warning to him and perhaps to others. A warning that nobody was indispensable.

Oliver shuffled the cards again, ran up a couple of hands with swiftness and skill, then dealt them, taking several off the bottom with smoothness and ease, yet his mind was roving and alert.

Would Hutch manage it? He had never yet, so far as Oliver knew, encountered such a man as McQueen. Not that Oliver had any great opinion of McQueen. He was typically a cowman, honest, tough, and hard-working. That he was good with a gun was obvious, and that *segundo* of his, Kim Sartain, was probably almost as good.

Did McQueen have brains? How would he fare against Hutch, particularly when, as Oliver believed, McQueen did not know who his enemy was.

Hutch had planted the Webb killing squarely on McQueen. The timing had been good and there would be witnesses, Oliver was sure. Trust the old man for that.

He watched Sheriff Foster leave town with his posse, and knew that several of the men in that posse were owned by Hutch. If the slightest excuse was offered, they were to shoot to kill. He knew their instructions as if he had heard them himself.

The door opened and a squat, powerful man entered, his hair shaggy and untrimmed. His square, granite-like face was clean-shaved. He had gimlet eyes that flickered with a steely glint. He wore two guns, one in a holster, the other thrust into his waistband. This was Overlin, the Montana gunman.

"Where's Foster goin'?"

"After McQueen, for the Webb killing."

"Webb? Is he dead?"

Oliver nodded. "Out on the trail." Overlin could have done it. So could Hansen Bine, but, so far as anyone knew, Bine was with the wounded men at Dry Leggett. "There's a witness to swear he did it."

"He might have," Overlin commented, "only don't believe it. I've heard of McQueen. Made quite a reputation along the cattle trails and in the mining camps. He's no bargain."

"He's only one man. Maybe he'll be your dish one day."

"Or yours," Overlin agreed. "Only I'd like him, myself."

Ren Oliver remembered McQueen and said: "You can have him." He could not understand such men as Overlin. The man was good with a gun, but why would he go out of his way to match skills with a man he believed might be just as good? Overlin had to be the best. He had to know he was best.

Oliver believed he was faster with a gun than either Bine or Overlin but he was a sure-thing man. He had pride in his skill but preferred to take no chances. He would enjoy killing Ward McQueen if he could do so at no risk to himself.

A horse loped into the street, the rider waving at someone out of sight. It was Sharon Clarity. Now where had she been at this hour of the night?

"See you around," he said to Overlin, and went into the night.

He dug a cigar from his pocket and lighted it. Sharon Clarity's horse had been hard-ridden.

VI

Ward McQueen was working beside Baldy Jackson, building a pole corral, when the sheriff and the posse rode into the ranch yard. McQueen continued to place a pole in position and lash it there with rawhide. Then he glanced around at the posse.

"Howdy, Foster. Looks like you're here on business."

"I've come for you, McQueen. There's witnesses says you shot Neal Webb, shot him in the back."

McQueen kept his hands in sight, moving carefully not to give any false impressions. His eyes caught the slight lift to the muzzle of a Winchester and he eyed the man behind it, staring at him until the man's eyes shifted and he swallowed.

"All you had to do was send for me, Sheriff. I'd have come right in. No need for all this crowd." He paused. "And you know, Sheriff, I'd never shoot any man in the back. What would be the point? Webb was never supposed to be good with a gun, and, if I wanted him killed that bad, all I'd have to do would be to pick a fight with him in town. Webb's temper had a short fuse, and killing him would have been no trick."

"That may be so, but you've got to come in with me and answer charges. There will have to be a trial."

"We'll see. Maybe I can prove I was elsewhere."

"By one of your own men?" The man who spoke had a sallow face and buckteeth. "We'd not be likely to believe them."

"By others, then? Kim Sartain was with me, however, and, if you believe he's a liar, why don't you tell him so?"

"We want no trouble, McQueen. Saddle a horse and come along." Foster's eyes went to the cabin. Was there somebody inside the window?

"I'll come on one condition. That I keep my guns. If I can't keep 'em, you'll have to take me and you'll have some empty saddles on your way back to town.

Foster was angry. "Don't give me any trouble, McQueen! I said, saddle your horse!"

"Sheriff, I've no quarrel with you. You're just doing your duty and I want to co-operate, but you've some men riding with you who would like to make a target of my back. Let me keep my guns and I'll go quiet. In case you'd like to know there are two men behind you with Winchesters. They will be riding along behind us."

Sheriff Foster studied McQueen. Inwardly he was pleased. This McQueen was a hardcase but a good man. Shoot a man in the back? It was preposterous. Especially Neal Webb.

"All right," he said, "saddle up."

"My horse is ready, Foster. A little bird told me you were coming, and my horse has been ready."

It was a black he was riding this day, a good mountain horse with bottom and speed. As he mounted and settled into the saddle, he glanced at the man who had lifted his rifle.

"Just so everybody will understand. Two of my boys are going to follow us into town. Either one of them could empty a Winchester into the palm of your hand at three hundred yards."

He sat solidly and well in the saddle, his black Frisco jeans tight over his thighs, his broad chest and shoulders filling the dark gray shirt. His gun belts were studded with silver, the walnut grips worn from use. "All right, Sheriff, let's go to town."

He rode alongside of Foster, but his thoughts were riding ahead, trying to foresee what would happen in town, and asking himself the question again: why kill Neal Webb? Who wanted him dead?

He had believed Webb the ringleader, the cause of his troubles. Most ranchers wanted more range, most of them wanted water, so the attempt to seize the Firebox came as no surprise. In fact, he would have been surprised had it not been claimed. Good grass was precious, and, whenever anybody moved or died, there was always someone ready to move in. The difference here was that McCracken had been a shrewd man and he had purchased the land around the various water holes, as well as the trails into and out of the range he used. The claim on Firebox range by McCracken was well established.

Webb, he was beginning to suspect, had been a mere pawn in the game, and had been disposed of when his usefulness ceased to be. But Webb's dying had implicated Ward McQueen and apparently somebody had decided to have him killed, either in capturing him or in the ride to town. A posse member could shoot him, claiming McQueen had made a move to escape.

Behind this there had to be a shrewd and careful brain. If there were witnesses to something that had not happened, his supposed murder of Neal Webb, then somebody had provided them.

Who? Why?

The Firebox was valuable range. The only other large ranch was Webb's Running W, and who was Webb's heir? Or did he himself own that ranch?

The Bear Cañon crowd? It wasn't their sort of thing. They might drygulch him, steal his horses or cattle, or even burn him out, but the Webb killing was more involved. Anyway, Webb had left the Bear Cañon crowd alone.

Would Sharon Clarity know? She was a handsome, self-reliant girl, yet something about her disturbed him. Why had she ridden out to warn him the sheriff was coming? Had she believed he would run?

Liking for him? Dislike of somebody else? Women's thinking was not part of his expertise. He had trouble reading their brands. Did she know who plotted against him? Did she herself hope to seize the Firebox when the shooting was over?

Who now owned the Running W? This he must

discover. If that unknown owner also owned th
Firebox, he would control all the range aroun
Pelona and the town as well. It made a neat, com
pact package and a base from which one migh
move in any direction.

Ruth Kermitt owned the Firebox now, and Rut
had no heirs. Ward McQueen was suddenly gla
his boss was not among those present.

Pelona's main street was crowded with rigs an
saddle horses when they rode in. Word had sprea
swiftly, and the people of the range country—th
few scattered small ranchers, farmers, and gar
deners—had come in, eager for any kind of
show. All had known Neal Webb, at least b
sight. Many had not liked him, but he was one c
their own. This Ward McQueen was a strange
and, some said, a killer. The general attitude wa
that he was a bad man.

A few, as always, had misgivings. Their doubt
increased when they saw him ride into town si
ting his horse beside the sheriff. He was not i
irons. He still wore his guns. Evidently Foste
trusted him. Western people, accustomed t
sizing up a man by his looks, decided he didn
look like somebody who needed to drygulch any
body. It was more likely Webb would try t
drygulch him!

Some of those who came to see drifted u
between the buildings into the street. Amon
these was Bud Fox, with his narrow-brimme

266

gray hat and his long, lean body, looking like an overgrown schoolboy. The pistol on his belt was man-size, however, and so was the Winchester he carried.

Kim Sartain, young, handsome, and full of deviltry, they recognized at once. They had seen his sort before. There was something about him that always drew a smile, not of amusement but of liking. They knew the guns on his belt were not there for show, but the West had many a young man like him, good cowhands, great riders, always filled with humor. They knew his type. The guns added another dimension, but they understood that, too.

The pattern was quickly made plain. The preliminary hearing was already set and the court was waiting. McQueen glanced at the sheriff. "Looks like a railroading, Foster. Are you in this?"

"No, but I've nothing against the law movin' fast. It usually does around here."

"When who is to get the brunt of it? Who's the boss around town, Foster? Especially when they move so fast I have no time to find witnesses."

"You know as much as I do." Foster was testy. "Move ahead!"

"If I'd been around as long as you have, I'd know plenty."

The judge was a sour-faced old man who McQueen had seen about town. Legal procedures on the frontier were inclined to be haphazard, although often they moved not only swiftly but efficiently as well. The old Spanish courts had often functioned very well indeed, but the Anglos were inclined to follow their own procedures. McQueen was surprised to find that the prosecuting attorney, or the man acting as such, was Ren Oliver, said to have practiced law back in Missouri.

Sartain sat down beside McQueen. "They've got you cornered, Ward. Want me to take us out of here?"

"It's a kangaroo court, but let's see what happens. I don't want to appeal to Judge Colt unless we have to."

The first witness was a cowhand Ward had seen riding with Webb's men. He swore he had dropped behind Webb to shoot a wild turkey. He lost the turkey in the brush and was riding to catch up when he heard a shot and saw McQueen duck into the brush. He declared McQueen had fired from behind Webb.

McQueen asked: "You sure it was me?"

"I was sworn in, wasn't I?"

"What time was it?"

"About five o'clock of the evenin'."

"Webb comes from over east of town when he comes to Pelona, doesn't he? From the Running W? And you say you saw me between you and Webb?"

"I sure did." The cowboy was emphatic, but he glanced at Oliver, uncertainly.

"Then"—McQueen was smiling—"you were lookin' right into the setting sun when you saw somebody take a shot at Webb? And you were able to recognize me?" As the crowd in the court-room stirred, McQueen turned to the judge. "Your Honor, I doubt if this man could recognize his own sister under those circumstances. I think he should be given a chance to do it this evening. It's nice and clear like it was the other night and the sun will be setting before long. I think his evidence should be accepted if he can distinguish four out of five men he knows under the conditions he's talking about."

The judge hesitated and Oliver objected.

"Seems fair enough!" A voice spoke from the crowd, and there was a murmured assent.

The judge rapped for silence. "Motion denied! Proceed!"

Behind him McQueen was aware of changing sentiment. Western courtrooms, with some exceptions, were notoriously lax in their proce-dure, and there were those who had an interest in keeping them so. Crowds, however, were partisan and resentful of authority. The frontier bred freedom, but with it a strong sense of fair play and an impatience with formalities. Most Western men wanted to get the matter settled and get back to their work. Most of the men and women

present had ridden over that road at that time c
the evening, and they saw immediately the poir
of his argument.

There was a stir behind them, and, turning, the
saw Flagg Warneke shoving his way through th
crowd and then down the aisle.

"Judge, I'm a witness. I want to be sworn in."

The judge's eyes flickered to Oliver, wh
nodded quickly. Warneke still bore the marks c
McQueen's fists, and his evidence could only b
damning.

Warneke was sworn in and took the stand. Kir
muttered irritably but Ward waited, watching th
big man.

"You have evidence to offer?" the judge askec

"You bet I have," Warneke stated violently. "
don't know who killed Neal Webb, but I kno
Ward McQueen didn't do it."

Ren Oliver's face tightened with anger. H
glanced swiftly toward a far corner of the room,
glance that held appeal and something mor
McQueen caught the glance and sat a litt
straighter. The room behind him was seethin;
and the judge was rapping for order.

"What do you mean by that statement?" Oliv
demanded. He advanced threateningly towar
Warneke. "Be careful what you say an
remember, you are under oath."

"I remember. McQueen whipped me th
evenin', like you all know. He whipped me goc

but he whipped me fair. Nobody else ever done it or could do it. I was mad as a steer with a busted horn. I figured, all right, he whipped me with his hands but I'd be durned if he could do it with a six-shooter, so I follered him, watchin' my chance. I was goin' to face him, right there in the trail, an' kill him.

"'Bout the head of Squirrel Springs Cañon I was closin' in on him when a turkey flew up. That there McQueen, he slaps leather and downs that turkey with one shot! You hear me? One shot on the wing, an' he drawed so fast I never seen his hand move."

Flagg Warneke wiped the sweat from his brow with the back of his hand. "My ma, she never raised any foolish children. Anybody who could draw that fast and shoot that straight was too good for anybody around here, and I wanted no part of him.

"Important thing is, McQueen was never out of my sight from the time he left town headin' west an' away from where Webb was killed until he reached Squirrel Springs Cañon, and that's a rough fifteen miles, the way he rode. It was right at dusk when he shot that turkey, so he never even seen Webb, let alone killed him."

Ren Oliver swore under his breath. The crowd was shifting; many were getting up to leave. He glanced again toward the corner of the room and waited while the judge pounded for order.

Oliver attacked Warneke's testimony but could not shake the man. Finally, angered, he demanded: "Did McQueen pay you to tell this story?"

Warneke's face turned ugly. "Pay me? Nobody lives who could pay me for my oath. I've rustled a few head of stock, and so has every man of you in this courtroom if the truth be known. I'd shoot a man if he crossed me, but by the eternal my oath ain't for sale to no man.

"I got no use for McQueen. He burned us out over in Bear Cañon. He shot friends of mine, but he shot 'em face to face when they were shootin' at him. The man I'd like to find is the one who killed Chalk. Shot him off his horse to keep him from tellin' that Webb put them up to rustlin' Firebox stock."

Ward McQueen got to his feet. "Judge, I'd like this case to be dismissed. You've no case against me."

The judge looked at Ren Oliver, who shrugged and turned away.

"Dismissed!"

The judge arose from his bench and stepped down off the platform. Ward McQueen turned swiftly and looked toward the corner of the room where Oliver's eyes had been constantly turning. The chair was empty.

People were crowding toward the door. McQueen's eyes searched their faces. Only one turned to look back. It was Silas Hutch.

McQueen pushed his way through the crowd to Flagg Warneke. The big man saw him coming and faced him, eyes hard.

"Warneke," McQueen said, "I'd be proud to shake the hand of an honest man!"

The giant's brow puckered and he hesitated, his eyes searching McQueen's features for some hint of a smirk or a smile. There was none. Slowly the big man put his hand out and they shook.

"What are your plans? I could use a hand on the Firebox."

"I'm a rustler, McQueen. You've heard me admit it. You'd still hire me?"

"You had every reason to lie a few minutes ago, and I think a man who values his word that much would ride for the brand if he took a job. You just tell me you'll play it straight and rustle no more cattle while you're working for me and you've got a job."

"You've hired a man, McQueen. And you have my word."

As the big man walked away, Sartain asked: "You think he'll stand hitched?"

"He will. Warneke has one thing on which he prides himself. One thing out of his whole shabby, busted-up life that means anything, and that's his word. He'll stick, and we can trust him."

VII

Tough as Ward McQueen felt himself to be, when he rode back to the ranch, he was sagging in the saddle. For days he had little sleep and had been eating only occasionally. Now, suddenly, it was hitting him. He was tired, and he was half asleep in the saddle when they rode into the yard at the Tumbling K's Firebox.

Lights in the cabin were ablaze and a buckboard stood near the barn. Stepping down from the saddle, he handed the reins to Kim. No words were necessary.

He stepped up on the low porch and opened the door.

Ruth Kermitt stood with her back to the fireplace, where a small fire blazed. Even at this time of the year, at that altitude, a fire was needed.

She was tall, with a beautifully slim but rounded body that clothes could only accentuate. Her eyes were large and dark, her hair almost black. She was completely lovely.

"Ward." She came to him quickly. "You're back."

"And you're here." He was pleased but worried also. "You drove all the way from the ranch?"

"McGowan drove. Shorty rode along, too. He said it was to protect me, but I think he had a idea you were in trouble. Naturally, if that were the case, Shorty would have to be here."

"Ruth," he told her, "I'm glad to have you here. Glad for me, but I don't think you should have come. There is trouble, and I'm not sure what we've gotten into."

He explained, adding: "You know as well as I do that where there's good grass, there will always be somebody who wants it, and what some of them haven't grasped is that we are not moving in on range. We own the water holes and the sources of water."

He put his hands on her shoulders. "All that can wait." He drew her to him. His lips stopped hers and he felt her body strain toward him and her lips melt softly against his. He held her there, his lips finding their way to her cheek, her ears, and her throat. After a few minutes she drew back, breathless.

"Ward! Wait!"

He stepped back and she looked up at him.

"Ward? Tell me. Has there been trouble? Baldy said you were in court, that you might have to go on trial."

"That part is settled, but there's more to come, I'm afraid."

"Who is it, Ward? What's been happening?"

"That's just the trouble." He was worried. "Ruth, I don't know who it is, and there may be a joker in the deck that I'm not even aware of."

She went to the stove for the coffee pot. "Sit down and tell me about it."

"The ranch is a good one. Excellent grass, good water supply, and, if we don't try to graze too heavy, we should have good grass for years. McCracken handled it well and he developed some springs, put in a few spreader dams to keep the run-off on the land, but he wanted to sell, and I am beginning to understand why."

"What about the trouble? Has it been shooting trouble?"

"It has, but it started before we got here." He told her about the killing of McCracken, then his own brush with rustlers, and the fight with Flagg Warneke and the killing of Chalk, Flagg Warneke's brother, before he could talk. And then the killing of Neal Webb.

"Then he wasn't the one?"

"Ruth, I believe Webb had played out his usefulness for whoever is behind this, who deliberately had Webb killed, with the hope of implicating me. He'd have done it, too, but for Warneke."

"He must be a strange man."

"Warneke's a big man. You'll see him. He's also a violent man, but at heart he's a decent fellow. His word is his pride. I think he's going to shape up into quite a man. Some men get off on the wrong foot simply because there doesn't seem any other way to go. Without him, I think that

Bear Cañon outfit will drift out and move away. I doubt if they will try to rebuild what was destroyed."

"Ward, we've been over this before. I hate all this violence. The fighting, the killing. It's awful. My own brother was killed. But you know all that. It was you who pulled us out of that."

"I don't like it, either, but it is growing less, Ruth, less with each year. The old days are almost gone. What we have here is somebody who is utterly ruthless, someone who has no respect for human life at all. You're inclined to find good in everybody, but in some people there just isn't any. Whoever is behind this, and I've a hunch who it is, is someone who is prepared to kill and kill until he has all he wants. He's undoubtedly been successful in the past, which makes it worse. No honest man would have such men as Hansen Bine and Overlin around. They did not ride for Webb . . . we know that now. They ride for whomever it was Webb was fronting. I've got to ride down to Dry Leggett and roust out those wounded men, but you must be careful Ruth . . . this man will stop at nothing."

"But I'm a woman!"

"I don't believe that would matter with this man. He's not like a Western man."

"Be careful, Ward. I just couldn't stand it if anything happened to you."

"You could. You've got the heart as well as the

stamina. You've come a long way, Ruth, but you're pioneer stock. There's a rough time in any country, any new, raw country like this, before it can settle down."

As they talked, they wandered out under the trees, and, when they returned to the house, only Baldy was awake.

"Wonder folks wouldn't eat their supper 'stead of standin' around in the dark. A body would think you two wasn't more'n sixteen."

"Shut up, you old squawman," Ward said cheerfully, "and set up the grub. I'm hungry enough to eat even your food."

"Why, Ward," Ruth protested. "How can you talk like that? You know there isn't a better cook west of the Brazos."

Baldy perked up. "See? See there? The boss knows a good cook when she sees one. Why you an' these cowhands around here never knowed what good grub was until I came along. You et sowbelly an' half-baked beans so long you wouldn't recognize real vittles when you see 'em."

A yell interrupted Ward's reply. "Oh, Ward? Ward McQueen!"

Baldy Jackson turned impatiently and opened the door.

"What the . . . !"

A bullet struck him as a gun bellowed in the night, and Baldy spun half around, dropping the coffee pot. Three more shots, fast as a man could lever a rifle, punctured the stillness. The light went out as Ward extinguished it with a quick puff and dropped to the floor, pulling Ruth down with him.

As suddenly as it had begun, it ended. In the stillness that followed they heard a hoarse gasping from Baldy. Outside, all was dark and silent except for the pound of hoofs receding in the distance.

As he turned to relight the lamp, there was another shot, this from down the trail where the rider had gone. Glancing out, Ward saw a flare of fire against the woods.

"Take care of Baldy!" he said, and went out fast.

He grabbed a horse from the corral, slipped on a halter, and went down the trail riding bareback. As he drew near the fire, he heard pounding hoofs behind him and slowed up, lifting a hand.

Suddenly he saw a huge man standing in the center of the trail, both hands uplifted so there would be no mistakes.

"McQueen! It's me! I got him!" the man shouted. It was Flagg Warneke.

McQueen swung down, as did Kim Sartain, who had ridden up behind him. A huge pile of grass, dry as tinder, lay in the center of the road, going up in flames. Nearby lay a rider. He was breathing, but there was blood on his shirt front and blood on the ground.

Warneke said: "I was ridin' to begin work tomorrow and I heard this *hombre* yell, heard the shot, so I throwed off my bronc', grabbed an armful of this hay McCracken had cut, and throwed it into the road. As this gent came ridin', I dropped a match into the hay. He tried to shoot me, but this here ol' Spencer is quick. He took a Fifty-Six right in the chest."

It was the sallow-faced rider Ward had seen before, one of those who had ridden in the posse. "Want to talk?" he asked.

"Go to the devil! Wouldn't if I could!"

"What's that mean? Why couldn't you talk?"

The man raised himself to one elbow, coughing. "Paid me from a holler tree," he said. "I seen nobody. Webb, he told me where I'd get paid an' how I'd . . . how I'd get word."

The man coughed again and blood trickled over his unshaved chin.

"Maybe it was a woman," he spoke clearly, suddenly. Then his supporting arm seemed to go slack and he fell back, his head striking the ground with a thump. The man was dead.

"A woman?" Ward muttered. "Impossible."

Warneke shook his head. "Maybe . . . I ain't so sure. Could be anybody."

VIII

When the sun was high over the meadows, Ward McQueen was riding beside Ruth Kermitt near a *ciénaga*, following a creek toward Spur Lake. They had left the ranch after daybreak and had skirted some of the finest grazing land in that part of the country. Some areas that to the uninitiated might have seemed too dry she knew would support and fatten cattle. Much seemingly dry brush was good fodder.

"By the way," Ruth inquired, "have you ever heard of a young man, a very handsome young man named Strahan? He spells it with an H but they call him Strann. When I was in Holbrook, there was a Pinkerton man there who was inquiring about this man. He is badly wanted, quite a large reward offered. He held up a Santa Fe train, killing a messenger and a passenger. That was about four months ago. Before that he had been seen around this part of the country, as well as in Santa Fe. Apparently he wrecked another train, killing and injuring passengers. Each time he got away he seemed headed for this part of the country."

"Never heard of him," Ward admitted, "but we're newcomers."

"The Pinkerton man said he was a dead shot with either rifle or pistol, and dangerous. They trailed him to Alma once, and lost him again on the Gila, southeast of here."

They rode on, Ward pointing out landmarks that bordered the ranch. "The Firebox has the best range around," he explained. "The Spur Lake country, all the valley of Centerfire, and over east past the Dry Lakes to Apache Creek. There's timber, with plenty of shade for the hot months. and most of our range has natural boundaries that prevent stock from straying."

"What about this trouble you're having, Ward? Will it be over soon or hanging over our heads for months?"

"It won't hang on. We're going to have a showdown. I'm taking some of the boys, and we're going to round up some of the troublemakers. I'm just sorry that Baldy is laid up. He knows this country better than any of us."

"You'll have trouble leaving him behind, Ward. That was only a flesh wound, even though he lost blood. It was more shock than anything else."

They turned their horses homeward. Ward looked at the wide, beautiful country beyond Centerfire as they topped the ridge. "All this is yours, Ruth. You're no wife for a cowhand now."

"Don't start that. We've been over it before. Who made it all possible for me? If you had not come along when you did, I'd have nothing. Just nothing at all. And if my brother had not been killed, he could not have handled this. Not as you have. He was a fine boy, and no girl ever had a better brother, but he wasn't the cattleman you are.

"And it isn't only that, Ward. You've worked long and you've built my ranch into something worthwhile. At least twice you've protected me when I was about to do something foolish. By rights half of it should belong to you, anyway."

"Maybe what I should do is leave and start a brand of my own. Then I could come back with something behind me."

"How long would that take, Ward?" She put her hand over his on the pommel. "Please, darling, don't even think about it. The thought of you leaving makes me turn cold all over. I have depended on you, Ward, and you've never failed me."

They rode on in silence. A wild turkey flew up, and then vanished in the brush. Ahead of them two deer, feeding early, jumped off into the tall grass and disappeared along the stream.

"Don't you understand? I'm trying to see this your way. You've told me what has to be done and I'm leaving it up to you. I'm not going to interfere. I'm a woman, Ward, and I can't bear to think of you being hurt. Or any of the other boys, for that matter. I'm even more afraid of how all this killing will affect you. I couldn't stand it if you became hard and callous."

"I know what you mean but there's no need to

worry about that now. Once, long ago, maybe. Every time I ride into trouble I hate it, but a man must live, and there are those who will ride roughshod over everybody, given a chance. Unfortunately force is the only way some people understand."

When they dismounted at the cabin, she said: "Then you're riding out tomorrow?"

"Yes."

"Then good luck." She turned quickly and went into the house.

Ward stared after her, feeling suddenly alone and lost. Yet he knew there was no need for it. This was his woman, and they both understood that. She had come with a considerable investment, but with too little practical knowledge of range or cattle. With his hands, his savvy, and his gun he had built most of what she now possessed.

Under his guidance she had bought cattle in Texas, fattened them on the trail north, sold enough in Kansas to pay back her investment, and driven the remainder farther west. Now she controlled extensive range in several states. Alone she never could have done it, nor could Kim, one of the best men with a gun who ever walked, have had the judgment to handle a ranch, and he would have been the first to side-step the responsibility.

Kim came down now. "Tomorrow, Ward?"

"Bring plenty of ammunition, both rifle and pistol. I'll want you, Bud Fox, Shorty Jones, and. . . ."

"Baldy? Boss, if you don't take him, it'll kill him. Or you'll have to hog-tie him to his bunk, and I'm damned if I'd help you. That ol' catamount's a-rarin' to go, an' he's already scared you're plannin' to leave him behind."

"Think he can stand the ride?"

Kim snorted. "Why, that ol' devil will be sittin' a saddle when you an' me are pushin' up daisies. He's tougher'n rawhide an' whalebone."

Daylight came again as the sun chinned itself on the Continental Divide, peering over the heights of the Frisco Mountains and across the Frisco River. In the bottom of the Box, still deep in shadow, rode a small cavalcade of horsemen. In the lead, his battered old hat tugged down to cover his bald spot from the sun, rode Baldy Jackson.

Behind him, with no talking, rode McQueen, Sartain, Fox, and Jones. They rode with awareness, knowing trouble might explode at any moment. Each man knew what he faced on this day, and, once begun, there'd be no stopping. It was war now, a war without flags or drums, a grim war to the death.

For some reason Ward found his thoughts returning time and again to Ruth's account of the Pinkerton who was trailing the handsome killer named Strahan. It was a name he could not remember having heard.

He questioned Baldy. "Strahan? Never heard of a youngster by that name, but there was some folks lived hereabouts some years back named that. A bloody mean outfit, too. Four brothers of them. One was a shorty, a slim, little man but mean as pizen. The others were big men. The oldest one got hisself shot by one o' them Lincoln County gunfighters. Jesse Evans it was, or some friend of his.

"Two of the others, or maybe it was only one of them, got themselves hung by a posse somewhere in Colorado. If this here Strahan is one o' them, watch yourselves because he'd be a bad one."

Their route kept the ridge of the Friscos on their left, and, when they stopped at Baldy's uplifted hand, they were on the edge of a pine-covered basin in the hills.

Ward turned in his saddle and said: "This here's Heifer Basin. It's two miles straight ahead to Dry Leggett. I figure we should take a rest, check our guns, and get set for trouble. If Hansen Bine is down there, this will be war."

Dismounting, they led their horses into the trees. Baldy located a spring he knew, and they sat down beside it. McQueen checked his guns, and then slid them back into their holsters. He rarely had to think of reloading, for it was something he did automatically whenever he used a gun.

"Mighty nice up here," Kim commented. "I always did like high country."

"That's what I like about cowboyin'," Shorty Jones commented. "It's the country you do it in."

"You ever rode in west Texas when the dust was blowin'?" Bud wanted to know.

"I have, an' I liked it. I've rid nearly every kind of country you can call to mind."

"*Ssh!*" Ward McQueen came to his feet in one easy movement. "On your toes. Here they come."

Into the other end of the basin rode a small group of riders. There were six men, and the last one McQueen recognized as Hansen Bine himself.

Kim Sartain moved off to the right. Baldy rolled over behind a tree trunk and slid his Spencer forward. Jones and Fox scattered in the trees to the left of the spring.

McQueen stepped out into the open. "Bine! We're takin' you in! Drop your gun belts!"

Hansen Bine spurred his horse to the front and dropped from the saddle when no more than fifty paces away. "McQueen, is it? If you're takin' me, you got to do it the hard way!"

He went for his gun.

McQueen had expected it, and the flat hard bark of his pistol was a full beat before Bine's. The bullet struck Bine as his gun was coming up and he twisted sharply with the impact. Ward walked closer, his gun poised. Around him and behind him he heard the roar of guns, and, as Bine fought to bring his gun level, McQueen shot again.

Bine fell, dug his fingers into the turf, heaved himself, trying to rise, and then fell and lay quietly.

Ward looked around to find only empty saddles and one man standing, his left hand high, his right in a sling. "Your name?"

"Bemis." The man's face was pale with shock, but he was not afraid. "I did no shooting. Never was no good with my left hand."

"All right, Bemis. You've been trailing with a pack of coyotes, but, if you talk, you can beat a rope. Who pays you?"

"Bine paid me. Where he got it, I don't know." His eyes sought McQueen's. "You won't believe me but I been wantin' out of this ever since the McCracken shootin'. That was a game kid."

"You helped kill him," McQueen replied coldly. "Who else was in it? Who ran that show?"

"Somebody I'd not seen around before. Young, slight build, but a ring-tailed terror with a gun. He came in with Overlin. Sort of blondish. I never did see him close up. None of us did, 'cept Overlin." Bemis paused again. "Said his name was Strahan."

That name again. The Pinkerton man had been right. Such a man was in this country, hiding out or whatever. Could it be he who was behind this? That did not seem logical. Strahan by all accounts was a hold-up man, gunfighter, whatever, not a cattleman or a cautious planner.

"You goin' to hang me?" Bemis demanded. "If you are, get on with it. I don't like waitin' around."

McQueen turned his eyes on Bemis, and the young cowhand stared back boldly. He was a tough young man, but old in the hard ways of Western life.

"You'll hang, all right. If not now, eventually. That's the road you've taken. But as far as I'm concerned, that's up to the law. Get on your horse."

The others were mounted, and Bine was lying across a saddle. Kim looked apologetic. "He's the only one, boss. The rest of them lit out like who flung the chuck. I think we winged a couple here or there, but they left like their tails was afire."

Kim Sartain looked at Bemis. "Dead or gone, all but this one. Maybe on the way in . . . you know, boss, it's easier to pack a dead man than a live one."

Bemis looked from Sartain to McQueen and back. "Now, see here," he said nervously. "I said I didn't know who did the payin', but I ain't blind. Bine an' Overlin, they used to see somebody, or meet somebody, in the Emporium. There or the Bat Cave. They used to go to both places."

"So do half the men in the county," McQueen said. "I've been in both places myself." He paused. "How about Strahan?"

"Never seen him before . . . or since."

"Put him on a horse and tie him," McQueen said. "Well give him to Foster."

Ward led the way toward Pelona. There trouble awaited, he knew, and secretly he hoped Foster would be out of town. He wanted no trouble with the old lawman. Foster was a good man in his own way, trying to steer a difficult course in a county where too many men were ready to shoot. Foster was a typical Western sheriff, more successful in rounding up rustlers, horse thieves, and casual outlaws than in dealing with an enemy cunning as a prairie wolf and heartless as a lynx.

They rode swiftly down the cañon to the Tularosa, and then across Polk Mesa to Squirrel Springs Cañon. It was hard riding, and the day was drawing to a close when they reached the plains and cut across toward Pelona. They had ridden far and fast, and both men and horses were done in when they walked their horses up the dusty street to the jail.

Foster came to the door to greet them, glancing from McQueen to Bemis.

"What's the matter with him?"

"He rode with the crowd that killed Jimmy McCracken. Jimmy gave him the bad arm. I've brought him in for trial."

"Who led 'em?" Foster demanded of Bemis.

Bemis hesitated, obviously worried. He glanced around to see who might overhear. "Strahan," he said then. "Bine was in it, too."

Foster's features seemed to age as they watched. For the first time he looked his years.

"Bring him in," Foster said. "Then I'll go after Bine."

"No need to." McQueen jerked his head. "His body's right back there. Look," he added, "we've started a clean-up. We'll finish it."

"You're forgettin' something, McQueen! I'm the law. It's my job."

"Hold your horses, Sheriff. You are the law, but Bine is dead. The boys who were with him are on the run, except for Bemis, and we're turning him over to you. Anybody else who will come willing, we'll bring to you."

"You ain't the law," Foster replied.

"Then make us the law. Deputize us. You can't do it alone, so let us help."

"Makes me look like a quitter."

"Nothing of the kind. Every lawman I know uses deputies, time to time, and I'm asking for the job."

"All right," Foster replied reluctantly. "You brought Bemis in when you could have hung him. I guess you aim to do right."

Outside the sheriff's office, Baldy waited for McQueen. "You name it," he said, as McQueen emerged. "What's next?"

"Fox, you, and Shorty get down to the Emporium. If Hutch comes out, one of you follow him. Let anybody go in who wants to, but watch him." He turned to Jackson. "Baldy, you get across the street. Just loaf around, but watch that other store.

"Watch that female? What d'you take me for? You tryin' to sidetrack me out of this scrap?"

"Get going and do what you're told. Kim, you come with me. We're going to the Bat Cave."

Foster stared after them, and then walked back into his office. Bemis stood inside the bars of his cell door. "I'm gettin' old, Bemis," Foster said. "Lettin' another man do my job."

He sat down in his swivel chair. He was scared—he admitted it to himself. Scared not of guns or violence but of what he might find. Slowly the fog had been clearing, and the things he had been avoiding could no longer be avoided. It was better to let McQueen handle it, much better.

"Leave it to McQueen," Bemis was saying. "McQueen was right, and he's square." He clutched the bars. "Believe me, Sheriff, I never thought I'd be glad to be in jail, but I am. Before this day is over men will die. Foster, you should have seen McQueen when he killed Bine. I never would have believed anybody could beat Bine so bad. Bine slapped leather and died, just like that."

"But there's Overlin," Foster said.

292

"Yeah, that will be somethin' to see. McQueen an' Overlin." Suddenly Bemis exclaimed: "Foster! I forgot to tell them about Ren Oliver!"

"Oliver? Don't tell me he's involved?"

"Involved? He might be the ringleader, the boss man. And he packs a sneak gun. A stingy gun. Whilst you're expecting him to move for the gun you can see, he kills you with the other one."

Foster was on his feet. "Thanks, Bemis. We'll remember that when you're up for trial."

As Foster went out of the door, Bemis said: "Maybe, but maybe it's too late."

IX

The Bat Cave was alive and sinning. It was packed at this hour, and all the tables were busy. Behind one of them, seated where he could face the door, was Ren Oliver. His hair was neatly waved back from his brow, his handsome face composed as he dealt the tricky pasteboards with easy, casual skill. Only his eyes seemed alive, missing nothing. In the stable back of the house where he lived was a saddled horse. It was just a little bit of insurance.

At the bar, drinking heavily, was Overlin. Like a huge grizzly he hulked against the bar. The more he drank, the colder and deadlier he became. Someday that might change, and he was aware of it. He thought he would know when that time came, but for the present he was a man to be left strictly alone when drinking. He had been known to go berserk. Left alone, he usually drank the evening away, speaking to no one, bothering no one until finally he went home to sleep it off.

Around him men might push and shove for places at the bar, but they avoided Overlin.

The smoke-laden atmosphere was thick, redolent of cheap perfume, alcohol, and sweaty, unwashed bodies. The night was chill, so the two stoves glowed cherry-red. Two bartenders, working swiftly, tried to keep up with the demands of the customers.

Tonight was different, and the bartenders had been the first to sense it. Overlin only occasionally came in, and they were always uncomfortable until he left. It was like serving an old grizzly with a sore tooth. But Overlin was only part of the trouble. The air was tense. They could feel trouble.

The burning of Bear Cañon, the slaying of Chalk Warneke, and the gun battle in Heifer Basin were being talked about, but only in low tones. From time to time, in spite of themselves, their eyes went to Overlin. They were not speculating if he would meet McQueen, but when.

Overlin called for another drink, and the big gunfighter ripped the bottle from the bartender's hand and put it down beside him. The bartender retreated hastily, while somebody started a tear-jerking ballad at the old piano.

The door opened and Ward McQueen stepped in, followed by Kim Sartain.

Kim, lithe as a young panther, moved swiftly to one side, his eyes sweeping the room, picking up Ren Oliver at once, and then Overlin.

Ward McQueen did not stop walking until he was at the bar six feet from Overlin. As the big gunman reached again for the bottle, McQueen knocked it from under his hand.

At the crash of the breaking bottle the room became soundless. Not even the entry of Sheriff Foster was noted, except by Sartain.

"Overlin, I'm acting as deputy sheriff. I want you out of town by noon tomorrow. Ride, keep riding, and don't come back."

"So you're McQueen? And you got Bine? Well, that must have surprised Hans. He always thought he was good. Even thought he was better'n me, but he wasn't. He never saw the day."

McQueen waited. He had not expected the man to leave. This would be a killing for one or the other, but he had to give the man a chance to make it official. Proving that he had had a hand in the murder of Jimmy McCracken would have been difficult at best.

Overlin was different from Bine. It would take a lot of lead to sink that big body.

"Where's Strahan?" McQueen demanded.

Ren Oliver started, and then glanced hastily toward the door. His eyes met those of Kim Sartain, and he knew that to attempt to leave would mean a shoot-out, and he was not ready for that.

"Strahan, is it? Even if you get by me, you'll never get past him. No need to tell you where he is. He'll find you when you least expect it."

Deliberately Overlin turned his eyes away from McQueen, reaching for his glass with his left hand. "Whiskey! Gimme some whiskey!"

"Where is he, Overlin? Where's Strahan?"

The men were ready, McQueen knew. Inside of him, Overlin was poised for the kill. McQueen wanted to startle him, to throw him off balance, to wreck his poise. He took a half step closer. "Tell me, you drunken lobo. Tell me!"

As he spoke, he struck swiftly with his left hand and slapped Overlin across the mouth.

It was a powerful slap and it shocked Overlin. Not since he was a child had anybody dared to strike him, and it shook him as nothing else could have. He uttered a cry of choking rage and went for his gun.

Men dived for cover, falling over splintering chairs, fighting to get out of range or out the door.

McQueen had already stepped back quickly, drawn his gun, and then stepped off to the left as he fired, forcing Overlin to turn toward him.

McQueen's first bullet struck an instant before Overlin could fire, and the impact knocked Overlin against the bar, his shot going off into the floor as McQueen fired again.

Overlin faced around, his shirt bloody, one eye gone, and his gun blazed again. McQueen felt himself stagger, shaken as if by a blow, yet without any realization of where the blow had come from.

He fired again, and, not aware of how many shots he had fired, he drew his left-hand gun and pulled a border shift, tossing the guns from hand to hand to have a fully loaded gun in his right.

Across the room behind him, another brief drama played itself out. Ren Oliver had been watching and thought he saw his chance. Under cover of the action, all attention centered on McQueen and Overlin, he would kill McQueen. His sleeve gun dropped into his hand and cut down on McQueen, but the instant the flash of blue steel appeared in his hand, two guns centered on him and fired. Sartain was at the front door and Sheriff Foster on his left rear. Struck by a triangle of lead, Oliver lunged to his feet, one hand going to his stomach. In amazement, he stared at his bloody hand and his shattered body. Then he screamed.

In that scream was all the coward's fear of the death he had brought to so many others. In shocked amazement he stared from Foster to

Sartain, both holding guns ready for another shot if need be. Then his legs wilted and he fell, one hand clutching at the falling deck of cards, his blood staining them. He fell, and the table tipped, cascading chips and cards over him and into the sawdust around him.

At the bar, Overlin stood, indomitable spirit still blazing from his remaining eye. "You . . . ! You . . . !"

As he started to fall, his big hand caught at the bar's rounded edge and he stared at McQueen, trying to speak. Then the fingers gave way and he fell, striking the brass rail and rolling away.

Ward McQueen turned as if from a bad dream, seeing Kim at the door and Sheriff Foster, gun in hand, inside the rear door.

Running feet pounded the boardwalk, and the door slammed open. Guns lifted expectantly.

It was Baldy Jackson, his face white, torn with emotion. "Ward! Heaven help me! I've killed a woman! I've killed Sharon Clarity!"

The scattered spectators were suddenly a mob. "What?" They started for him.

"Hold it!" McQueen's gun came up. "Hear him out!" Ward McQueen was thumbing shells into his gun. "All right, Baldy. Show us."

"Before my Maker, Ward, I figured her for somebody sneakin' to get a shot at me! I seen the gun, plain as day, an' I fired!"

Muttering and angry, the crowd followed.

Baldy led the way to an alley behind the store, where they stopped. There lay a still figure in a riding habit. For an instant Ward looked down at that still, strangely attractive face.

Then he bent swiftly, and, as several cried out in protest, he seized Sharon Clarity's red gold hair and jerked.

It came free in his hand, and the head flopped back on the earth, the close-cropped head of a man.

Ward stooped, gripped the neckline, and ripped it away. With the padding removed, all could see the chest of a man, lean, muscular, and hairy.

"Not Sharon Clarity," he said, "but Strahan."

Kim Sartain wheeled and walked swiftly away, McQueen following. As they reached the Emporium, Bud Fox appeared.

"Nobody left here but that girl. She was in there a long time. The old man started out, but we warned him back. He's inside."

Ward McQueen led the way, with Sheriff Foster behind him, then Sartain, Jackson, Fox, and Jones.

Silas Hutch sat at his battered roll-top desk. His lean jaws seemed leaner than ever. He peered at them from eyes that were mean and cruel. "Well? What's this mean? Bargin' in like this?"

"You're under arrest, Hutch, for ordering the killing of Jimmy McCracken and Neal Webb."

Hutch chuckled. "Me? Under arrest? You got a

lot to learn, boy. The law here answers to me. I say who is to be arrested and who is prosecuted. You got no proof of anything. You got no evidence. You're talkin' up the wind, sonny."

Baldy Jackson pushed forward. "Ward, this here's the one I told you about. This is the first time I've had a good look at him. He's Shorty Strahan, the mean one. He's an uncle, maybe, of that one out there who made such a fine-lookin' woman."

"Hutch, you had your killings done for you. All but one. You killed Chalk Warneke." He turned to Foster. "Figure it out for yourself, Sheriff. Remember the position Chalk was in, remember the crowd, and Warneke on a horse. There's only one place that shot could come from . . . that window. And only one man who could have fired it. Him."

Silas Hutch shrank back in his chair. When Foster reached for him, he cringed. "Don't let them hang me," he pleaded.

"You take it from here, Foster," McQueen said. "We can measure the angle of that bullet and you've got Bemis. He can testify as to the connection between Neal Webb and Hutch as well as that with Chalk. He knows all about it."

Ward McQueen turned toward the door. He was tired, very tired, and all he wanted was rest. Besides, his hip bone was bothering him. He had been aware of it for some time, but only now was it really hurting. He looked down, remembering something hitting him during the battle with Overlin.

His gun belt was somewhat torn and two cartridges dented. A bullet had evidently struck and glanced off, running two perfectly good cartridges and giving him a bad bruise on the hip bone. "Kim," he said, "let's get back to the ranch."

Acknowledgments

"Showdown Trail" under the byline Jim Mayo first appeared in *Giant Western* (Winter, '48). Copyright © 1948 by Best Publications, Inc. Copyright not renewed.

"The Sixth Shotgun" first appeared in *Ranch Romances* (1st September Number = 8/29/52). Copyright © 1952 by Best Books, Inc. Copyright not renewed.

"West of the Tularosa" under the byline Jim Mayo first appeared in *West Magazine* (3/51). Copyright © 1951 by Better Publications, Inc. Copyright not renewed.

Center Point Publishing
600 Brooks Road ● PO Box 1
Thorndike ME 04986-0001 USA

(207) 568-3717

US & Canada:
1 800 929-9108
www.centerpointlargeprint.com